Love Around the Table

A collection of Short Stories

by

Rachel Jones
Linda Joyce
Constance Gillam
Marilyn Baron
Melissa Klein
Ciara Knight

This is a work of fiction. Names, characters, places, and incidents are either the product of the authors' imagination or are used fictitiously, and any resemblance to actual persons, living or dead, business establishments, events or locales is entirely coincidental.

Love Around the Table

COPYRIGHT © 2017 by Rachel Jones, Linda Joyce Clements, Constance Gillam, Marilyn Baron, Melissa Klein, and Ciara Knight

Thank you for purchasing this book. All rights are reserved. No part of this book may be used or reproduced in any manner whatsoever without written permission from the author of the specific story, except in the case of a brief quotation embodied in critical articles or reviews. This book may not be redistributed to others for commercial or noncommercial purposes.

Contact Information: linda@linda-joyce.com
Cover Art by EJR Digital Art
Edited by Cheryl Walz

Published by Rachel Jones, Linda Joyce, Constance Gillam, Marilyn Baron, Melissa Klein, and Ciara Knight

Publishing History
Digital ISBN-978-0-692-95323-5
Print ISBN-978-0-692-95324-2

Dedication

This book is dedicated to the Atlanta Ronald McDonald House Charities, the leadership, staff, volunteers, and sponsors in honor of the love and support they provide to children and their families who call it
home away from home.

MISSION

The mission of Atlanta Ronald McDonald House Charities is to nurture the health and well-being of children and families.

VISION

By serving more families and enhancing services, we will strive to be one of the children's charities of choice in metro Atlanta.

CORE VALUES
Hospitality • Expectation of Excellence • **Affirmation**
• **Respect** • Teamwork

Table of Contents

A Sister's Quandary	1
Rachel's Summer Squash Casserole	54
Layers of Love	57
Linda's Carrot Cake with Orange Glaze	108
Mississippi Catfish	111
Constance's Southern Fried Catfish	160
No More Lonely Hearts	163
Marilyn's Spaghetti Alla Carbonara	210
Table for Six	215
Melissa's Chicken Squares	266
Turning The Table On Love	269
Ciara's Slow Cooker Pot Roast	318
Keeping Families Close™	321
The Authors	323

A Sister's Quandary

Rachel Jones

Acknowledgments

Love Around The Table is a collaborative effort of six authors. However, it's the brainchild of Linda Joyce. Thank you, Linda, for pursuing the idea and providing direction throughout the entire process. Linda, Melissa Klein, and Marilyn Baron spent many hours editing our stories to make them the best for our readers. Thank you for your time, ladies.

To my critique partners, Melissa and Linda, thank you for cheering me on and nudging my writing back on track when I needed it. I am blessed to call you my friends.

Thanks to my RN co-worker Brandi Shaw, who shared her insight as a kidney donor patient. Your information helped guide the accuracy of my story.

I appreciate the support of talented authors, Ciara Knight and Constance Gillam. Thank you for the stories you've written for this anthology. I've enjoyed the time we've spent sharing and learning together.

And to my husband Randy, who makes all this possible through his love and support of my new creative passion.

I am grateful and proud to be a part of this project.

Rachel Jones

A Sister's Quandary

Chapter One

Sophie Harris hit *end* on her cell phone, her eyes wide with disbelief. "Jim says he's sorry, but can't go through with it. I guess I'm back to square one." Her gaze settled on her grandmother and then passed to her boyfriend.

The gray-haired woman with short, tight curls placed her wrinkled hand on Sophie's arm. "There's always Brooke."

"I'd consider dying before accepting a kidney from my sister!" She jerked away from her grandmother and landed with a plop on the worn leather sofa that had occupied the same space since the day she and her twin had come to live with their grandparents forever ago.

"I can't believe Jim gave in to his wife. You were counting on him."

Her boyfriend joined her on the sofa. He stroked Sophie's hair and kissed her temple. His touch had a calming effect, and her body relaxed.

"We'll figure something out. If it comes down to it, you'll go on the waitlist," Ben said.

"Please, Sophie, don't discount your sister. We know she's a match. She won't let you down."

"I can't believe we're having this conversation. Brooke walked out on us eight years ago—with my fiancé. Besides, what makes you think she'd be a donor for me? She's selfish."

"That's not fair, Sophie," Nana said. "Brooke has matured. She had it rough for a while until she found Kent. And now her life is hard again. Widowed and raising her daughter alone. Doing the best she can to raise Lindsey without family support. Sounds to me like she needs you as much as you need her."

Ben pulled his ringing cell phone from his pocket and checked the caller ID. "Excuse me. It's work." He stood and slipped into the dining room.

Nana moved from her chair to sit beside Sophie. She patted her hand. "Honey, when are you going to forgive Brooke for making a foolish girl's mistake? If karma is a real thing, she's more than paid for hurting you. What's it going to take to get you girls together again? Like the family you should be."

"I don't know, Nana."

"She offered her kidney when we found out you needed a transplant. She'll offer again since your donor backed out. Why won't you let her do this for you?"

"Maybe she's not doing it for the right reason. Maybe she thinks if I take her kidney, we'll be even. And then she can come home to Smyrna."

"Would that be a bad thing, her coming back? Don't you want to know your niece? I'd love to squeeze and hug my great-granddaughter. She's five, and all I've done is talk to her on the phone."

"I'm sorry, Nana. I just don't want her here. Even if I considered giving us a chance, it would start out long distance by phone or text."

"Would I be too far off the mark if I said you don't want her here because of Ben?"

"I *don't* want her around Ben. He and I are serious." Just like she and Dean had been. Engaged serious. "I don't want to lose him to someone that looks just like me. Even though we are entirely different on the inside."

"Sophie, that's a young girl's insecurity talking. You're a woman now."

"Aging doesn't make insecurities magically disappear, Nana."

Ben returned. He bent down and kissed Sophie's head. "Sorry, hon. I've got to go. One of the systems is down, and I'm on call. I'll talk to you tomorrow."

She attempted a smile. "Night, Ben."

"Bye, Ruth."

Nana touched her hand to her lips and blew a kiss in his direction. "Good night, Ben. Drive safely."

The door closed, and Nana continued as though the interruption had never occurred. "Talking on the phone is good. Talking in person is even better."

"What are you saying, Nana?"

"Brooke and Lindsey will be here tomorrow. I convinced her to come home while you recover."

Sophie pulled away from the woman who had raised her and her twin from age thirteen. "I can't believe this. You went behind my back and invited her into our lives again. After what she did—"

"Please, Sophie. They need us. Maybe it's time to allow Brooke to apologize and tell you what Dean was really like. Take this time before they arrive to search your soul. To decide to give her a chance to be happy again."

"What do you mean?"

"It's bad enough Dean left a young girl alone without money in a strange town. Can you imagine how frightened she must have felt?"

"How about me? There's only one reason I was able to move on with my life. I put her out of my mind. Now you want to dredge all that up when I'm facing a major surgery and recovery?"

"Brooke learned from her mistake, met a different kind of man and fell in love. They had five years together before he died. Now she's raising her daughter alone. How can you not feel badly for her? She's your flesh and blood. If you have no compassion for your sister, then maybe you haven't matured. If that's the case, Sophie, I have to say I'm disappointed. So please do a lot of maturing during the night. They'll be here tomorrow around noon. Good night, Granddaughter." Nana rose and left the room.

Sophie drew in a deep breath. How had the dial spun in her direction, labeling her the mean one? She had always been the sweet, smiling granddaughter, always doing the right thing. Sure, she had been upset when Brooke left with Dean, had cried for a week straight. When the crying was out of her system, Nana, along with her best friend, Taylor, had worked hard to help her forget and move on. College classes started. Concentrating hard on her work kept her thoughts away from her twin and the sin she had propagated against her. Eventually, she was okay with not sharing her life with Brooke, but deep down inside, there was a piece of her missing. But she was not about to let the world, especially Nana, know she was hurting over the loss of her twin.

Tomorrow would be a showdown with Brooke and meeting the niece she had wondered about since learning of her existence. Too bad she couldn't see one without the other. Sophie wasn't ready for a reunion. However, the ticking of the grandfather clock in the corner of the room declared the inevitable meeting would happen in a matter of hours. There was no way she'd sleep tonight.

Chapter Two

Brooke kept her eyes on the road. Her nerves tingled throughout her body, making it difficult to relax and admire the beautiful kaleidoscopic scenery of fall colors on parade. She wanted to help her sister, wanted her daughter to meet her family. Living on her own after Kent's death had been hard and tiring. She wanted Lindsey to have more than one adult in her life she could count on. And Brooke would welcome their support. Life had been lonely this past year without the husband she'd loved with her whole heart.

Nana had been asking for two years now to meet her great-granddaughter, but Brooke couldn't bring herself to expose Lindsey to Sophie's indifference. Her little girl was too young to understand the rift between them. Nana had suggested Lindsey wouldn't notice. Maybe that had been true when she was three, but now she was an inquisitive-about-everything five-year-old.

Fate forced this reunion. Nana had called in tears last week, asking her to consider a visit while Sophie recovered from the transplant. She lived every day with guilt since learning of Sophie's disease. They were identical twins. Why had she escaped while her younger sibling had been caught up in a web of medical maliciousness?

It was time to come face-to-face with her twin. She had dreaded this day for eight years, the day of rectification. She had to right things with Sophie. The apology would be the easy part. She could be sincere about it, too. It hadn't been long before Dean had left her alone in a strange town eight years ago that she knew the pain her sister had endured six months earlier after she had run off with Sophie's fiancé.

She checked the rearview mirror. "How are you doing back there, sweetie?"

"I'm tired of riding. I think I have to go to the bathroom."

"Okay, let me find a place that looks like it might have a clean restroom."

Lindsey's vocabulary expressed the wisdom of a seven-year-old, which amazed Brooke but also brought concern. Had her precious girl grown up too fast because of the life they'd been dealt?

Brooke exited the interstate and pulled into a restaurant parking lot. "We'll give this place a try." She helped her curly-haired child out of the booster seat and took her hand.

They finished their bathroom business and returned to the car.

"Mommy, I'm thirsty."

After settling Lindsey in her seat, Brooke reached inside the mini cooler and pulled out a six-ounce bottle. She twisted off the lid and handed it to her daughter. "Do you remember who you're going to meet today?"

Lindsey swallowed some water. "Your nana and your sister."

"She's your nana, too. And my sister is your aunt. Aunt Sophie."

"I never had an aunt or a nana."

"They've always been your family. You just haven't met them. But you will today. Are you excited?"

"I talk to Nana on the phone. Why don't I talk to Aunt Sophie?"

Lord, please help me use the right words.

"One day, a long time ago, I made Sophie mad. Remember when Charlie got mad at you because you caught his ball in the park, and you didn't want to give it back?"

"You made me give it back, but he went home anyway. He said he didn't want to play with me anymore."

"Right. So when Sophie got mad, we stopped talking. But that's going to change because we're going to see her and Nana today. Ready to go?"

Lindsey nodded and handed back the bottle.

"Okay, little girl. Let's hit the road."

And hope Sophie is ready for a reunion.

****

Sophie sat in her room attempting to read. Days spent as a scholarly communications librarian at Vanderbilt University Library reading about data curation, intellectual property rights, and copyright laws made the romance genre an appealing choice for her leisure reading. The novels took her miles and sometimes ages away, providing hours of enjoyment. Today it couldn't hold her focus.

The doorbell rang. Her stomach tensed.

They're here.

It wasn't fair how last minute Nana had thrown their visit on her. But then, Nana was no fool. If she'd given Sophie any notice, she'd have found a way to avoid them.

Knock, knock.

Nana's voice came through the door. "Sophie, Brooke and Lindsey are here."

Looking in the mirror, Sophie wondered if she'd recognize her twin. It was after their parents' deaths, two weeks before their thirteenth birthday, she and her sister had moved in with their grandparents. The changes in Brooke occurred almost immediately. She cut her hair. Sophie continued to wear hers long. Then at fourteen, Brooke defied Nana by wearing makeup, but only at school because Nana had said not until they turned fifteen. Of course, Sophie had waited.

Brooke changed in other ways. She started hanging with girls who were mean and imitating their dressing habits. Sophie couldn't see the appeal and had kept to her small circle of three friends. She worked hard in her classes and had good grades while her sibling gave only enough attention for passing grades. Brooke could have done better if she had just applied herself, as Nana had said more than once. But when it came to the chorus, her twin excelled with her rich, beautiful voice. Funny how they were identical twins, and she couldn't produce the same sound with her voice. Brooke liked the limelight, but Sophie preferred to blend in with the other singers.

At some point, she would have to face her twin and all the baggage between them. Most of it put there by Brooke. Might as well be now.

Sophie walked into the empty living room. Maybe she had dreamed Nana coming to her door and announcing their arrival. Then she heard it. The bright sound of a child's laughter. She followed it to the kitchen, the best place in the house.

Brooke sat with her back to the door, and this gave Sophie a minute to gather her wits before pressing forward. The voice she'd heard belonged to a small blonde-haired doll of a child with bright blue eyes, the shade of robin eggs.

"Are you my aunt Sophie?" the little one asked.

Brooke turned at her question but remained in her seat. "Hello, Sophie. It's so good to see you."

A sliver of the built-up hate melted when her sister smiled. Sophie looked into Brooke's eyes and saw the urgency, the regret, and the pain.

She struggled to make her voice work. "Hi." The unexpected bombardment of emotion made her knees cave. She settled quickly in a chair, her attention diverted from Brooke's face by the tugging on her shirtsleeve. She looked at the source. An angelic face with the sweetest smile stared at her.

"Are you my aunt Sophie?"

"I don't know. I'm supposed to meet a little girl named Lindsey. Do you have any idea where I might find her?"

Lindsey giggled. "Silly, that's me."

She ached to pull the child close in a hug. A sudden urge made her wonder how she could have messed up so many lives because of jealousy and bitterness.

"Well, hello, Lindsey. I'm your aunt Sophie."

"I knew it, I knew it," the little girl chanted as she jumped about.

Sophie smiled as the little, amazing wonder claimed her heart.

****

Brooke pulled out the chair beside her. "All right, wild child, have a seat."

"Okay." She settled in the chair and turned her attention to Sophie. "Do you like *Super Why*?"

"I'm not sure. What is it?"

"It's a TV show. It's one of three shows Mommy lets me watch. Do you watch TV?"

"Lindsey, take your backpack over by the sliding door and pull out your crayons and coloring book. Get a little sunshine on that pretty skin."

"Okay, Mommy."

The little girl hopped from the chair.

With the distraction removed, things were about to get real.

"Hold on. I need to do something," Brooke said. She approached Lindsey and knelt beside her. Pulling bright pink, child-sized headphones from the backpack, she said, "Here, sweetie. Put these on and listen to *Frozen* while you color."

The little girl's response was a glance up from her coloring book and a smile.

Brooke returned to the table. Her heart pounded. She steadied herself to take whatever Sophie wanted to dish out. "Now we can talk. Nana tells me you need a donor."

"We found one before; we'll just look again."

"Why, Sophie? I'm sitting right in front of you. I'm the answer to your medical situation."

"I don't want to owe you. Or worse, let you think you *own* me."

Brooke squeezed back threatening tears. She'd had plenty of practice keeping them at bay around Lindsey after Kent died. "I'd never do that."

"What do you want out of this? Surely you have some angle. Now that your husband's dead, are you looking for a replacement? Did you find out about Ben, and that's why you're here? Take two—let's do it again."

A sharp pain squeezed her heart. She had been wrong. Sophie's words cut deeply. Brooke pushed back her chair and hurried away, only stopping when she found herself in Nana and Gramp's room. She sat on the bed, wrapped her arms against her chest, and let the tears go.

Life was hard without Kent. She had no desire to look for another man. Her life was full taking care of her daughter, the child entrusted to her care. Everything she did or didn't do depended on how it would affect Lindsey. Everything, except her decision to give Sophie a kidney. Both times.

Shortly after their arrival, Nana had told her about Sophie's donor backing out. She hadn't allowed Nana to put herself through the difficulty of asking and had volunteered her kidney again as a replacement.

What if something went wrong during her surgery or recovery? Lindsey had to grow up without a father. She shouldn't have to do without a mother as well. Nana would say she was putting the cart before the horse. Sophie hadn't yet agreed to her offer. Now that things were in motion, she realized she hadn't thought the offer through to the consequences.

Perhaps it was their twin connection that had her making the split-second decision without thinking of her child. She wouldn't take back her offer as the other donor had done. She'd just have to make sure family would have her back and Lindsey's future. And it was that same twin connection that made Brooke realize she wanted and needed her sister back in her life. No matter how difficult it might be to make it happen.

Chapter Three

Sophie wore a path in the carpet between her bed and the window. Brooke had appeared genuinely upset at her accusation.

But I have to guard my future with Ben.

The best way to do that was to send Brooke back to Memphis as quickly as possible. If she accepted her kidney, that wouldn't happen for a least a month, maybe longer.

The muffled ring of her cell phone halted her steps. She scrambled to her bed, flipping her pillows to find her phone as it continued to ring.

"Ms. Harris, Dr. Berger here."

"Hello, Dr. Berger. How are you?"

"Fine, thanks. We need to talk about your situation."

"Okay. I can come to your office this afternoon."

"No need. It's straightforward. Will you be accepting your sister's kidney for the transplantation?"

Sophie bit down on the edge of her thumb. Now was the time to stand her ground. Send Brooke away. But the desire to be finished with this horrid nightmare interfering with her path to her happily-ever-after made her pause. "I'm not sure."

"Time is not a luxury. I need your answer by the end of office hours tomorrow. If you decide to accept, we'll make preparations for the procedure. If you choose against the transplant, I need to release the facility and staff for another case. But I must reiterate you'll risk the level of health you have now if you choose to go on the waitlist."

"I understand."

"So, I'll hear from you by five o'clock tomorrow?"

"Sure. Thank you, Dr. Berger."

She sat on the bed and fell backward. She wanted to blame someone for the upheaval in her life. Jim? For backing out, leaving her with two equally unappealing scenarios. Maybe God, for allowing a disease to invade her body? The stellar part of Sophie wanted to handle this challenge with grace and dignity, but she wasn't convinced she possessed the qualities needed to pull it off.

If Ben weren't in the picture, she might welcome Brooke back home. The urge to hug her twin had taken her by surprise when their eyes met for the first time in eight years. A piece of her heart wanted that kind of homecoming. A renewal of what they had meant to one another. But a bigger, blackened chunk of her heart prompted her to remember Brooke's betrayal. So she had hung back and focused on the precious child that was her flesh and blood, too.

Her phone rang again. "Hey, handsome. How'd you know I could use a little dose of you right about now?" Her voice sobered. "Thanks for checking on me, Ben."

"Not a problem. I love you, babe. How did it go?"

"I have the most adorable niece. I can't wait for you to meet her. Nana is thrilled beyond words that she's here."

"How are things between you and Brooke?"

"Unsettled. I've done a lot of deep breathing this afternoon."

"How about meeting me for an early dinner, and you can tell me as much or as little as you want about the reunion. Roy's Grill at five?"

"Sounds good. I love you, Ben Pritchard."

"See you soon."

How long will he continue to say "I love you" after he meets Brooke?

Sophie dropped her phone on the bed and resumed pacing. "That's my answer. I love him, and I won't allow anything or anyone to come between us. Brooke doesn't need to unpack because she has no reason to stay. I'll make that crystal clear. I'll wait for another kidney."

****

"This trip was a mistake," Brooke said when Nana entered the bedroom carrying her great-granddaughter.

The older woman put her finger to her lips, signaling for silence. With Brooke's help, they settled a drowsy Lindsey for a nap and left the room.

Nana filled the teakettle and set it on the stove. She pulled cups and saucers from the cupboard and placed them on the table alongside a tin box of assorted teas, then took a seat beside Brooke. "This is the first morning I've felt a solid nip in the air. Autumn is here, ready or not."

"We could tell on the drive from Memphis. The leaves have started changing colors. It's a beautiful sight, but I still love summer best."

"Let's save the chitchat for later and get to the serious stuff. You can't expect Sophie to welcome you with open arms. It doesn't work that way. Years of pent-up bitterness won't drop away at the sight of a long-lost sibling."

The kettle whistled, and Brooke moved to the stove. After pouring steaming water in their cups, they each selected a tea bag in silence.

"There's got to be a way to reach Sophie, to make her understand I'm not in some contest with her to win over the man in her life."

"He's the one. I'm sure of it. Ben loves her with his whole heart. I know because I've watched him stand by her from the beginning of this nightmare. He gives her strength."

"I've gotten the impression during our phone calls it's a serious relationship. So, what's the problem?"

"Sophie. The evening she told him about Goodpasture syndrome, he ended their night by offering marriage. He told her he had plans to ask her. Even had bought a ring. He chose to propose then because he wanted her to know how much he loves her and wants to take care of her."

"And that didn't sit well with my baby sister."

"It did not. But she used her head. Instead of running from him, Sophie said she'd give him an answer when she was healthy again. If he didn't want to wait or changed his mind at any time, he was free to leave the relationship."

"You think that was a smart move?"

"She could have turned him down and told him goodbye forever. Sophie needs to deepen her faith in Ben, to realize he's not going to run out on her."

"Oh, Nana. It's my fault for leaving with Dean. I did this to Sophie."

"You surely have a part in her inability to trust entirely, but denying it even happened is not the way to learn and grow. Your homecoming is a way to make Sophie acknowledge and deal. And it doesn't hurt that you've brought the cutest, smartest five-year-old in the state of Tennessee with you."

Nana's words brought a smile to Brooke's face. "She is amazing."

"Lindsey may be the buffer you need while you work things out with Sophie."

"It took less than five minutes for Lindsey to hook her aunt. Even if we can't make it work between us again, my baby will come out a winner because she'll have her amazing aunt doting on her for life."

****

Sophie rushed into the restaurant. Time was not her friend—ever. All her adult life she had struggled with procrastination. Her biggest regret to date had been missing out on Katy Perry concert tickets about a decade ago. She had managed to top that by quieting the little voice urging her to see a doctor. So, procrastination had finally caught up with her in a mighty way; if she hadn't put off seeing a physician, maybe her situation wouldn't be this severe. To the point of upsetting the lives of everyone who cared about her.

Her gaze caught Ben's as he waved. She moved to him and claimed the kiss he placed on her cheek.

"Sorry I'm late."

He took her hand. "I can think of worse character flaws." He winked. "I love everything about you, Sophie."

Choked with emotion, Sophie squeezed his hand. Thoughts of losing him sent chills deep to her bone marrow. Why would he want to stay with someone possessing a severe malady? If he met Brooke, the whole sister, would he want her instead? No, Ben was not like Dean. He was an honorable man. He had never wavered once since this nightmare had begun. The symptoms, diagnosis, and treatments—each obstacle found him at her side. Still, trepidation lingered in her mind.

With an uncertain future, Sophie was determined not to waste their evening together. After receiving their drinks and placing their orders, she spoke up. "I decided not to accept Brooke's kidney." She turned away. Couldn't look the man she loved in the eyes.

He placed his thumb and index finger around her chin, gently guiding it until her gaze met his. "Want to tell me why?"

She dropped her hands into her lap. "Brooke's and my relationship is complicated. Capital C complicated."

"I disagree. How can you label something that you don't have as difficult? You've spent almost a decade of your life shutting out a relationship with your sister. I understand she did a horrible thing, but you're not eighteen anymore. You're a woman who's missing out on a richer life because you refuse to walk through the pain it will take to rebuild a relationship that should be one of the most cherished treasures you have."

"Wow. I didn't see that coming."

"Sophie, I love you. I want to marry you. You've told me you wouldn't accept my proposal until you're healthy again.

If the transplant is your ticket to the health you want, why are you waiting? I can't believe you'd put your life in further jeopardy just because you don't want to be my wife."

She pressed steepled fingers against her nose and shook her head. "No, Ben. That's not it at all. I wanted this, especially after Jim became a donor option. The situation has changed, and so have my choices."

Ben took her hands in his. "The situation is the same—you need a kidney transplant. You have two options. Accept your sister's precious gift or go on the waitlist. I told myself I wouldn't try to influence your decision, but I love you too much not to have my say."

Teary eyes blurred her vision. Tightening in her chest caused a hitch in Sophie's breathing.

"Please have the transplant now."

She shook her head.

"Take the life it offers instead of the delay of waiting. I hate the thought of you becoming sicker if you turn Brooke away." Ben stood. "I'm sorry. I can't talk about this anymore." He pulled out his wallet and threw some bills on the table. "I need some air and time."

As she watched him walk away—something he'd never done—Sophie decided to accept his challenge of leaving the past in the past. And moving on to a better future, though the process would bring emotional as well as physical pain.

Unable to think about food, Sophie left the restaurant. It was best she talk with Brooke before her mixed feelings turned in the opposite direction, causing her to change her mind.

When she arrived home, she found Nana and Brooke in the living room watching the evening news. Whether alone or with companions, Gramps had never missed the nightly broadcast. Nana was usually busy taking care of the house or them, so she rarely joined him in front of the TV. She watched each night faithfully, since Gramps passed away ten years ago. Perhaps Nana felt closer to him for that hour of the day.

Focused on Sophie as she entered the room, Brooke's eyes held the hopeful look of a child on Christmas morning staring at the pile of presents.

"Dr. Berger called today to tell me I have to give my decision about the transplant by five p.m. tomorrow." Both women held their breath, waiting for her announcement. "I've decided to do it." She turned to Brooke. "I'll let you know what I find out."

Brooke sat at attention. "That's wonderful. I—"

Sophie threw up her hand. "Save it. I'm going to work on this, but don't expect it to be like flipping a switch and suddenly everything is good between us." She didn't wait for a reply but moved down the hall toward her room.

I just hope I'm doing the right thing.

After changing into her pajamas and settling in bed, Sophie debated whether to call Ben. He had asked for space and time. Time was a precious commodity, and as Dr. Berger had said earlier in the day, not a luxury. She decided to text him.

I'm sorry not to have recognized your emotional stake in this situation. Our situation, not just mine. Thank you for talking from your heart tonight. I just told Brooke that I'll contact Dr. Berger in the morning to schedule the transplant.

I love you, Ben Pritchard, and I want to accept your marriage proposal sooner rather than later.

Chapter Four

The aroma of Southern-fried fare drifted from the kitchen to the dining room as Nana prepared her mouthwatering recipes. Sophie stopped setting the table and inhaled deeply. Although the menu was off limits to her, it had been her request that Nana make Brooke's favorite dishes tonight. She wanted to keep her twin's attention focused on something other than Ben when they met for the first time.

She returned to the kitchen. "The table is set, though I don't know why we're using the good china."

"Tonight is significant. It calls for using my special dishes." Nana stopped mashing potatoes and looked at Sophie. "Are you sure about this?"

"Not a hundred percent, but Ben and Brooke have to meet sometime."

"I'm talking food, not people."

"Miss your cooking, but a salad is fine. I have plans to treat myself to a serving or two of your Southern cuisine after the transplant. Your cooking made the list of pros for having the procedure *now* rather than later."

Nana smiled. "You just let me know when and what you'd like me to make." She set the potato masher aside. Taking Sophie's hand, she led her to a chair and sat beside her. "So, you're still worried about Ben meeting your sister."

"I don't want to be. I just can't shake the anxiety."

"This is where your faith in Ben has to stand firm. Since you've become serious, has he ever given you a reason to worry about other women?"

Sophie shook her head.

"I didn't think so, or you would have dumped him quicker than a summer afternoon downpour. And it's not fair to put all the blame on Brooke. She was persuaded to leave. She did not concoct some devilish scheme to swipe Dean away from you. I know this because we have discussed it several times over the years. As painful as it may be, you girls have to talk this out."

Lindsey skipped into the room. "Nana, I'm all ready. Mommy even braided my hair. Aunt Sophie, do you like my dress?"

"It's pretty. How did you know purple is my favorite color?"

She shrugged. "It is? I don't know what you like. Mommy talks most about Nana and Gramps. Gramps died, like my Daddy."

Brooke stood silently behind Lindsey, her eyes turning watery.

"I'm sorry about that. I wish you could have met Gramps. He gave the best hugs."

Ding, dong.

Lindsey's hands shot to her cheeks. "He's here."

Sophie stood. "Who?"

"Your boyfriend. Nana said we're going to meet him tonight."

Ding, dong.

Lindsey took Sophie's hand and pulled her toward the living room. "Can I meet him now?"

"Sure. His name is Ben."

Sophie opened the door. Ben sat on the porch railing dressed in the jeans that rocked his physique, paired with a Henley that stretched across his chest and showed the bulges of his biceps. As much as she enjoyed the picture, why couldn't he have chosen something less eye-catching? While holding a bouquet of flowers in one hand, he focused his eyes on her face. He crossed the threshold and reached for her. Their lips almost touched.

"Are you Aunt Sophie's Ben?"

Sophie pulled her lips inward and then smiled. "Honey, this is my niece, Lindsey." She picked her up, so he wouldn't tower over the child. She tapped Lindsey on the nose. "And yes, this is Ben."

My Ben.

Sophie pulled in a deep breath as the trio entered the kitchen. "Ben, this is my sister, Brooke." She planted Lindsey firmly on the floor between the two strangers. "Brooke, this is Ben Pritchard."

"Hello. It's nice to meet you, Ben."

"You, too. Hey, Ruth. Something smells good."

"Fried chicken and mashed potatoes."

"But Sophie can't eat that."

Nana held up her hand and then pointed at Sophie. "She planned the menu."

Brooke picked up the pitcher of iced tea. "I'll just put this on the sideboard." She hurried out of the kitchen.

Sophie followed her sister.

"Why did you do that?" Brooke whispered.

"I wanted Nana to make your favorites because it's been a while since you've had her cooking. I'll be okay with a salad."

"You didn't like salads much before..."

"Sometimes you have to accept what life throws at you. After the transplant, I'll be able to eat some of the things I've had to give up temporarily. How about you?"

"Me? I haven't had to give up any foods."

"I mean, how long have you been without your husband?"

Brooke's hands tightened around the knob at the top of the chair. "Kent has been gone one year, two months, and seventeen days."

"Have you accepted it?"

"In my head, but not my heart."

"Look, Mommy. Nana let me bring the basket of biscuits."

"Thank you, sweetie. I'll take that." She placed it on the table. "Come on, Sophie. Let's help with the food."

"Okay, but we'll get back to this heart business later."

****

After dinner, Nana started to clear the table. Brooke stood. "Let me do that."

"She's right, Nana." Sophie agreed. "You cooked, so Ben and I will clean up. Lindsey, why don't you and your mommy teach Nana how to play that ABC game you brought with you?"

"Come on, Nana. Let's play my game, please. Mommy, you stay with Aunt Sophie. I want Ben to play."

Brooke caught Ben's exchanged glance with Nana.

"Sure, honey. Go ahead." Brooke nodded. Maybe now, she could actually clear the air with her sister.

"Are there rules to this game?" Ben asked, rising from the table.

"Yes. We follow the rules because it's not nice to cheat." Lindsey took Nana's hand as she reached for Ben's.

"Okay, then," Sophie muttered. Gathering glasses from the table, she headed to the kitchen and opened the dishwasher, leaving Brooke to stack plates alone. Sophie didn't speak to her as they made a few trips between the dining room and kitchen.

The chill of silence grew colder by the minute. Brooke set down the last platter. "All clean in the dining room."

Sophie busied herself loading the dishwasher. Trying to be patient, Brooke made a sink of sudsy, hot water. She plunked a pot, a lid, and several cooking utensils into it. Even when suds peppered Sophie's arm, her sister said nothing. They worked side by side until the pressure of the silence nearly choked Brooke.

She dried her hands as she turned and faced her sister. "I agree with Nana. We have to talk this out."

When Sophie didn't respond, Brooke continued. "Dean told me he loved me. I believed his lies and left with him. I'm sorry. If I say it a thousand times, will it ever be enough, Sophie?"

As she turned to face Brooke, her elbow pushed the gravy boat off the counter. It hit the floor with a crash, breaking as the contents sloshed on the tiled surface. Sophie bent and picked up the pieces as Brooke grabbed paper towels and did a quick wipe up.

Nana appeared in the doorway. "Everything all right in here?"

"No, I knocked your gravy boat off the counter. I'm sorry, Nana." Sophie stood, holding the broken china.

Nana took the flower-patterned pieces, looking them over before placing them in the trash. "Accidents happen. Goodness knows my life will go on without that dish."

"But it's the last gift Gramps gave you."

Nana placed her hand on Sophie's shoulder. "It's all right, dear. I'd better get back to the game."

Brooke hadn't missed the sadness in Nana eyes or the guilt in Sophie's. Speaking in a soothing voice, she said, "Nana doesn't blame you."

"But her china pattern is retired. It's not like I can run to Macy's and replace it."

"She's not going to disown you over this." Brooke's tone lost its soothing quality. "Forget about the china. I want an answer to my question. Will anything I do ever be enough?"

Sophie's hands went to her hips. "This isn't about Dean. I've grown up enough to know he was a jerk. It's about you. Why would you do that to me? Will you do it again if I let you back in my life?"

Brooke slid into a chair. Her shoulders slumped.

Sophie kept her distance. "You changed after we moved here. I didn't like a lot of the things you did, but I never thought you would hurt me. Guess I was wrong."

"We can't fix us with just a conversation or two. That's why I agreed to come for a visit while you recover. I'd hoped to have several weeks with you as a captive audience, so we could work through eight plus years of anger, fear, and grief. Now we'll have a level playing field since we'll be recovering together."

"I didn't ask you to come."

"Look, you may not care if things go on the way they have, but I do. And I'm not asking only for me. Let's work this out for Nana and Lindsey."

Sophie walked toward the living room. "I'll think about it."

Brooke raised her voice. "The time for thinking is over. The transplant is in two days."

****

Brooke finished the last page of *Katy No Pocket* and looked over at Lindsey. Her little angel had fallen asleep before the story ended. Brooke stood and placed the book on the bedside table before bending to kiss her daughter's head. "Good night, little one. Sleep well."

She changed into her nightgown and slipped into bed beside Lindsey, but sleep would not come. She was too wound up about the surgery tomorrow. It wasn't the procedure per se, but the niggling thought that something might go wrong that had her getting out of bed and tying her robe around her.

She moved noiselessly down the hallway and knocked lightly on Sophie's door. Brooke didn't want to disturb her if she was asleep, but if she was awake—

Her fist lost contact as the door opened. "Did I wake you?"

"No, I just hung up from talking to Ben. Can't sleep?"

"I'm a little keyed up."

"Come in." She pointed to the bed, giving Brooke an invitation to sit. "Having second thoughts?"

Brooke sat on the bed and drew her long legs into a lotus position. "No, I'm going through with the surgery, but I need something from you." Her heartbeat shifted into high gear.

What if Sophie refused?

"Okay. What is it?"

As the older sister by three minutes, Brooke had felt a duty when they were young to look out for Sophie. Now she sought her twin's support to carry her through her anxiety. "My recovery has more potential for complications than yours. I need to know I can count on you to take care of Lindsey if something unspeakable should happen to me."

"Me? Why not Nana?"

"She raised her children, then us. I can't ask her to raise her great-granddaughter, too."

"You're talking crazy. Nothing's going to happen to you."

"Just like I expected going to the store for ice cream would be uneventful."

"What are you talking about?"

"Kent. He went out to buy ice cream for dessert while I finished dinner on a regular Thursday evening. He never came home."

Sophie touched Brooke's arm. "I'm sorry. But we're talking about a procedure that's performed multiple times a day all around the country. The world."

"Maybe so, but I have to know Lindsey will be all right if something unexpected happens to me. That's what I need."

"All right, but I only agree so you'll relax and sleep. Nothing will happen to you."

Please, God, give us both a good outcome.

Chapter Five

Brooke sat at just the right angle to allow the early afternoon rays of sunshine to fall on her book. Unable to concentrate, she set the book aside on the swing. Pulling in a deep breath, she recalled several weeks back when her anxiety level about the transplant had been high. Worry about potential complications had faded with every passing day she remained stable during her recovery over the last six weeks.

She looked up when the screen door scraped against the floor in protest as it was pushed open. Nana could use some help with the upkeep of the house.

Sophie buttoned her denim jacket and joined Brooke on the porch swing. "How long have you been outside? It's November, you know."

"I'm tired of being indoors. The weatherman declared a high of sixty-two today. The sun's shining, and there's no wind. I decided to read my book out here until Lindsey comes back from Becca's house."

"Who knew that your tattooed, lip-pierced bud from high school would one day be a responsible mother of two?"

"Not nice, Sophie."

"I never understood why you picked the people you did for friends. You seemed drawn to girls with low self-esteem and outrageous behavior."

"Maybe I was just as troubled."

"I was disoriented and sad after Mom and Dad died, but I didn't push aside what they taught us. Your behavior was a nightmare for Gramps and Nana. Most of the time."

"Back then I didn't think I deserved a good life after what I had done."

"You've lost me. What did you do?"

"In my juvenile state, I had convinced myself I was responsible for Dad and Mom dying."

"Where did you get an idea like that? The timing was wrong. If they hadn't been at the mall, they would most likely be alive today."

"True. Do you know why Mom and Dad went to the mall?"

"Just out shopping, I guess."

"I heard them talking the night before. They planned to shop for my birthday present. I was so excited to find out they had decided to buy me an iPod. Instead, it cost us our parents."

"Does Nana know this?"

"I never told anyone about what I'd heard. When we moved in with Gramps and Nana, I acted out. In retrospect, I believe to bury my guilt and grief."

"You don't still believe you're responsible, do you?"

"No, Sophie. Like you, I grew up and realized my guilt was misplaced. After Dean left me, a caring boss encouraged me to seek counseling for my issues. All of them."

The psychologist had suggested a face-to-face with Sophie more than once. There were many times she had wanted to come home but was waiting for some sign to tell her all was forgiven. The sign never came. But instead, the man of her dreams walked into her life, providing a distraction from her estranged relationship with her twin.

Sophie put her arm around her sister. "So all the weird, sometimes bad behavior, the blowing off studying, doing just enough to get by, was because you felt responsible for our loss."

Brooke settled her head on Sophie's shoulder. "Wish I could cry 'do over' and change everything that's happened the last fourteen years."

"You don't mean everything, just the bad stuff. My niece is one of the best things you've ever done."

Brooke smiled. "I wouldn't want to live without my Lindsey."

"And we wouldn't have gotten cooking lessons from Nana."

Brooke straightened and scooted back against the end of the swing. "Do you remember the first thing she taught us to cook?"

"Squash casserole. Remember the summer our garden had enough squash to feed the whole neighborhood?"

"Right, and Gramps told us it tasted better than Nana's. But I saw him wink at her after he said it."

"I miss him."

Brooke anchored her foot to the floor as she pushed the swing, causing a gentle back and forth movement. Their emotional talk had been draining, but good. The tension between them was melting just like Antarctic icebergs. Slow, but real. Brooke closed her eyes, relaxing as the swing continued to move. She opened them at the sound of a car door closing.

Lindsey made her way to the porch, along with her new friends, Zoey and Peyton.

Brooke called out, "Hi, Becca. Thanks for letting Lindsey spend the morning with your girls."

"No problem. They had a great time. I know it's short notice, but Peyton's birthday party is tomorrow. Lindsey is welcome to join us."

"Great. I'll give you a call tonight."

"It's a shame you're going back to Memphis soon. Okay, girls. We have to do a little shopping before dinner. Bye, Lindsey."

Brooke helped her daughter into the swing.

Maybe we don't belong in Memphis anymore.

****

"Good morning, Nana," Brooke said. She pulled out a chair and motioned for her to sit. The aroma of coffee filled the kitchen. Butterflies took flight in Brooke's stomach as she waited for the right moment to make her announcement.

Sophie turned from the stove and presented Nana with a plate of crisp bacon and gourmet French toast. Brooke added a small glass of orange juice beside her coffee cup.

Nana cut into the thick toast and tried a bite. "You girls are spoiling me. Dinner last night and now a delicious breakfast. It's got to stop."

"Why?" Brooke asked.

"Yeah," echoed Sophie. "You deserve a little rest every once in a while."

"I could get used to this. Having all my family around me. Where is my little sweetheart this morning?"

"Lindsey and her accomplice here talked me into one more Disney movie which lasted past her bedtime. I'll wake her in a bit. She's going to Peyton's birthday party, and I don't want her to be cranky from a lack of sleep."

"Come on, Brooke. You need to relax her routine once in a while. When you're a kid, it's more fun to watch a movie when you're supposed to be sleeping."

"If she stays around you, I'm going to have a rebel on my hands."

"No chance of that happening. It's been six weeks since the transplant. You'll be going back to Memphis soon."

"How was your appointment with Dr. Berger yesterday?" Nana asked.

A smile lit up Brooke's face. "No more doctor visits. He released me."

"That's great news," Nana said.

"I'm glad you persuaded me to come home."

Sophie joined them at the table. "We'll have to do something special with Lindsey before you leave. I love that little girl."

Brooke glanced at Nana and saw her misty eyes. She scooted her chair closer and put a comforting arm around her shoulder. "No tears, Nana."

"Can't help it. I'm going to miss you both so much."

"Maybe not. Lindsey loves it here, so we're going back to Memphis to pack our things and come home."

****

Sophie choked on her juice. "What?"

"We're moving back to Smyrna. After Kent died, I promised my friends I wouldn't make any significant changes in our lives for at least a year. That timeline has expired."

"You can stay here until you find your own place."

"Thanks, Nana. Oh, I don't want to tell Lindsey just yet, so please don't say anything."

Brooke's announcement initiated heart palpitations, almost stalling Sophie's breathing. The last few weeks of interaction with Brooke had thawed the frigid feelings she had harbored for so long. Sophie had seen it as a positive step in reuniting their family someday after she married Ben. "It's probably best not to tell Lindsey if you're not one hundred percent sure about the move."

"Oh, I'm sure. I've carried extreme sadness in my heart for years, and now it's time to let it go. I just want to ease Lindsey into the idea, so she's not overwhelmed."

"A wise move, Brooke. We'll keep it quiet," Nana said.

Sophie pushed her plate aside and stood.

"You're not hungry?" Brooke asked.

"Not so much. I've got to answer some work-related emails. Catch up with you later." She had forgiven Brooke, but that had been when she expected her to return to Memphis. As much as Sophie wanted to conquer the apprehension, it wouldn't go away. Especially now that her sister would be living in the same town.

Chapter Six

Sophie stood at the counter, layering the ingredients of homemade lasagna into a baking dish. Deep in thought, she didn't hear Nana enter the kitchen and jumped when her grandmother touched her elbow.

"Mmm, Ben's favorite. Does that mean he'll be here for dinner?"

"No, but we can save him a plate for later."

"You're stewing over something."

"Home early from your quilting club. It's usually the opposite."

"Phyllis is sick. When Jean started coughing, the rest of us decided to call it a day. We didn't want to take a chance and share a bug, especially with Thanksgiving on next week's calendar."

"That's smart. Sick is no fun."

"Changing the subject won't make it go away." Nana pulled a bag of pecan halves from the cupboard. "Since you're cooking dinner, I'll get a start on chopping pecans for holiday cooking and baking." She settled at the table with a knife and wooden board.

Finished with assembling the main course for dinner, Sophie covered the dish and placed it in the refrigerator. She began cleaning up. "I was blown away by Brooke's announcement yesterday."

"Isn't it wonderful? They're coming home."

Sophie didn't respond, just rubbed harder on the spotless countertop.

"Is it wonderful?" She joined Nana at the table. "I don't know."

****

Brooke closed the front door and hurried to the room she shared with Lindsey. How did they manage to leave behind the card Lindsey had labored over when she heard about the party? The homemade gift rested on the desk beside the crayons positioned neatly in their box. Sometimes Brooke wondered if her baby bordered on the edge of OCD. Another advantage to moving back to Smyrna would be having someone to share her thoughts, receiving feedback from a source other than the voice in her head.

Brooke had every intention of saying a quick goodbye. But hearing her name pop up in conversation and the irritation in Sophie's voice caused her to stand quietly by the kitchen doorway.

"Why does every good thing have a downside? The kidney transplant renewed my life, but it brought Brooke back home. And now she's going to stay. Actually, you're the one responsible for bringing her here. Why couldn't you leave things the way they were?"

Nausea pooled in Brooke's gut. Hadn't she learned her lesson about eavesdropping? That it brought nothing but heartache? Heartache over her parents and now over the sister who didn't want her coming home. The idea of raising Lindsey near family lost its appeal as Brooke realized Sophie would never forgive her mistake. She turned and hurried away.

****

Sophie clasped her hands together to still their shaking. "Nana, I don't know what to do."

Nana set the knife on the board and pulled Sophie to her chest. She leaned her head against Nana's shoulder.

"Tell me."

"I was wrong. Having Brooke and Lindsey here has been phenomenal. But at some point, I expected they'd leave. Now everything is chaotic—at least in my mind. Brooke is coming home for good. I thought maybe Ben and I would be married before that happened. And I'd feel less threatened."

Nana grasped Sophie's shoulders and stared into her eyes. "You can't think that way. I once said your faith in Ben needs to be firm, but now you must put that same faith in your future marriage. You and Ben will face plenty of challenges along the way as you grow old together. No sense obsessing about one that isn't real."

It sounded easy enough when Nana explained it. But in her experience, the things that meant the most didn't always come with ease. Sophie squared her shoulders, ready to spend the effort it would take to accept Brooke's decision to return to Smyrna.

****

In the early morning hour, Brooke loaded the car in the dark. The only illumination came from the streetlights, but it was sufficient. She carried her sleeping daughter and positioned her in the booster seat, resting her head on a small pillow. Brooke hurried back to the house. Her hand remained on the handle after she closed the door as if to make the connection she'd achieved with her family last a few seconds longer.

I'm sorry, Lindsey. That we can't stay here because of my past. I hope I can make it up to you someday.

She rejoined her sleeping child and wasted no time driving away. They'd be back in Memphis in time for breakfast. The fog cut Brooke's visibility, causing her to let up on the gas pedal. Yes, she wanted to put distance between herself and Sophie as quickly as possible, but her precious cargo made it imperative to do it safely.

She had been upset after returning from the birthday party, feigned a headache and skipped dinner. Brooke put the time to good use and packed their clothes while Lindsey remained with Nana and Sophie in the kitchen.

Brooke had hoped coming home would bring balance to her life. She was only twenty-seven but at times felt twice her age. From the death of her parents to the death of her husband, her life had been an emotional volcanic eruption spewing havoc, sometimes without warning. Occasionally she managed to repair the damage or at least move on and begin a new chapter. She craved peace and had thought she finally found it, that Sophie had forgiven her.

Stopping at a red light, Brooke glanced back at Lindsey. Her angel remained asleep and appeared comfortable. When the light turned green, she proceeded across the intersection.

The impact caught her by surprise. The sound of metal crunching and glass shattering exploded in her ears. The car stopped abruptly. The front airbag deployed. A blaring car horn broke the morning silence. Brooke found it difficult to breathe. The tight safety cushion made it impossible to exit the car or get to Lindsey.

My baby must be terrified.

After the initial shock, Brooke directed her focus to comforting Lindsey. It took only seconds to realize she wasn't crying or moving.

"Lindsey, talk to Mommy. Lindsey! Please, God, no. Don't take my baby, too."

Chapter Seven

Sophie rushed into the emergency department with Nana following behind, trying her best to keep up. They approached the registration window. "My sister and niece"—a tremor in Sophie's voice revealed her anxiety—"were brought in by ambulance. Brooke and Lindsey Vickers."

Nana gripped her hand as they waited for a response.

"Take a breath," the woman instructed calmly. "They're here. Have a seat in the waiting area, and someone will talk with you soon."

They veered around a corner to an area with lighting so bright it made Sophie blink. A half dozen people sat scattered throughout the large space.

She selected two chairs in direct line of the door where a doctor or nurse would enter. Sophie sat without speaking, knowing Nana was in silent communication with God. Sending prayers to ask Him to watch over her loves.

I can't lose Brooke—or Lindsey. My animosity, it's done. I just need the chance to tell her that.

While Nana prayed, Sophie focused on the nondescript barrier keeping her separated from family, all the while knowing the intensity of her stare wouldn't speed up the process of waiting.

The door opened. Sophie's heart pounded.

Please, God, let them be all right.

"Vickers family?"

Sophie stood. "We're here."

The man approached. His kind smile caught her gaze. His graying hair gave away his years, but his eyes told her he understood.

"I'm Dr. Dixon. How are you related?"

"Brooke is my twin sister, and Lindsey is my niece." Sophie touched Nana's shoulder. "This is Ruth Nelson, our grandmother."

He took the seat next to Nana. "We're taking care of Lindsey in our pediatric emergency department, and Mrs. Vickers is in a nearby cubicle. Has her husband been contacted?"

"My granddaughter is widowed."

"I'm sorry to hear that. So, you are her next of kin?"

"Yes, we are."

"How are they? Can we see them?" Sophie asked.

"I'm told that other than a fractured rib and some bruises, Mrs. Vickers is all right. The cubicles are small, so only one support person is allowed with the patient."

"That's fine. Nana, you go to Brooke, and I'll stay with Lindsey."

"About Lindsey—"

The pounding of Sophie's heart returned, galloping out of control. "She's got to be all right."

"Lindsey suffered head trauma during the impact. We suspect an epidural hematoma. I've ordered some diagnostic tests to confirm or rule it out. As a precaution, I'm going to admit her to ICU for close observation. Once Mrs. Vickers has been discharged, you all can proceed to the ICU waiting area, and we'll keep you updated."

Sophie gripped Nana's shoulder. "I need to be with her. She must be frightened."

"Presently, Lindsey is unconscious. Please, give us some time to get her transferred and settled. I promise you can see her then. I'm also going to override the visitation policy and take you both to Mrs. Vickers."

Nana stood and held out her hand. "Thank you, Doctor. We appreciate that."

"Yes, thank you," Sophie added.

They followed him to Brooke's cubicle and listened as he repeated the update on Lindsey's condition.

Brooke cushioned her abdomen as she sobbed, tears spilling over her cheeks. Sophie's heart broke for her twin as she struggled to cry over the news of her child, her physical and emotional pain both apparent.

"We can give you something for pain or to help with anxiety," Dr. Dixon offered.

"No, I need a clear head, so I can understand everything as it happens. I'll be fine."

Nana had been right. Brooke was selfless. Now and when she had offered her kidney. Sophie moved closer and stroked her hair. "We're here for you, Sissy." The nickname slid out as easily as when they were little girls without a care in the world.

"I need my discharge papers, and then we can meet Lindsey in her room."

"Dr. Dixon, where can I collect them for Brooke?" Nana asked.

"I'll show you." They left the cubicle together.

"My Lindsey's strong. She's going to get through this."

"Of course, she will. We'll do whatever it takes to make that happen."

She must be going crazy, wanting to see Lindsey. She needs a distraction.

Pulling the only chair next to the stretcher, Sophie sat. "Tell me about Kent."

"What?"

"I want to know about the brother-in-law I missed knowing."

"An amazing man. You did miss out."

"Where did you meet?"

"At the postal store I managed. Kent hurried in one day to print a document and got into a fight with the copy machine. I came to his rescue."

"Love at first sight?"

"For him, maybe. He began stopping by every day for purchases he could have made elsewhere. Within a few weeks, he was bringing me coffee, asking me to lunch…"

"That happened fast."

"I turned him down the first three times."

"So the allure was there for him, but not you."

"Oh, the attraction grabbed me from the minute I saw him wrestle with that copy machine, but I had decided men weren't worth the pain they caused."

"Dean."

"Yeah."

Sophie stood and turned, not able to look at Brooke. "I'm sorry about cutting you out of my life. I want us to be close again—"

"I was hoping for that when I came back, so it's good to hear you say it."

She faced Brooke. "I'm working on it." Though she wanted to let it all go, a sliver of resentment remained.

The hospital sounds around them amplified while their conversation lulled.

Sophie returned to her chair. "What made you change your mind about men?"

"Kent was persistent. He told me we belonged together and finally convinced me. I'm so glad I listened. That man brought a dimension to my life that gave me such joy. I'll never find that with anyone else."

As she held Brooke's hand and listened to her heart, the last of Sophie's bitterness and angst dissipated.

"You have Lindsey, so you'll always have a part of Kent."

"When he died, most of me shut down. But the mom part had to continue. I had to love, protect, and provide for my baby. If I lose Lindsey, I won't have anything left to fight for."

"Stop it."

Brooke's jaw dropped at the curt words.

Sophie's voice softened. "Don't go there. We'll take today one step at a time. Your discharge, ICU, and whatever else. Nana and I will be with you through all of it. And I'm calling Ben, too. You're not alone this time, Sissy."

****

The calendar declared today a day of thanksgiving. Brooke had been thankful every day since the accident. The tests had ruled out a hematoma, and Dr. Dixon had reported Lindsey's injuries as serious, but not life-threatening. She had spent one night in the ICU with Brooke at her bedside. The next two days they resided on the pediatric unit until leaving the hospital yesterday. The discharge education process had emphasized rest as an absolute.

Brooke had taken the time to make Lindsey's spot on the sofa engaging with a brightly colored comforter, fluffy pillow, and her favorite stuffed animal, hopefully making it easier to follow the instructions. Lindsey had always been an obedient child, but it wouldn't hurt to make the process appealing. It seemed to be working. The munchkin appeared happy with her crayons and coloring book.

When they held hands around the table before dinner today, there would no doubt be words of thanksgiving for Lindsey's and her recovery from the accident. And Brooke would concur with a loud *Amen*. She placed her hand over the tender area of her abdomen, mindful of how differently things could have gone.

Ding Dong.

Along with muffled voices from the nearby front door came a whoosh of cold air affirming the season. Though fake, the gas logs did their job well and absorbed the cold air quickly.

"Ben, you're here!" shouted Lindsey.

"Is it okay I brought some dinner guests with me? How big is the turkey?"

"About a hundred pounds. Nana had to squeeze hard to get it in the pan."

Laughter filled the room. Nana joined the group with a bottle of Chardonnay.

"Mom, Dad, this is Sophie's niece, Lindsey, and her mother, Brooke."

"Nice to meet you, and thanks for inviting us today," Mr. Pritchard said.

Ben's mother knelt by the sofa. "Oh, you're a doll. I heard you were in the hospital. I bet it feels good to be home."

Lindsey nodded. "But I'm sad for the kids that are still there."

Mrs. Pritchard looked up at Nana. "Wow. A kid this young already thinking of others."

"She takes after her mother," Nana said. "Lindsey, you can say an extra prayer at dinner today for the children spending Thanksgiving in the hospital."

"Okay, Nana."

Once everyone was settled with wine, Nana stood. "Please excuse me. I have to check on a few things in the kitchen."

Brooke took a quick sip of her drink and set it aside. "Sophie and I are going, too. Ben, would you mind keeping my angel occupied? I'll send my sister back to you soon."

"Sure. We'll teach my parents the ABC game."

"Thanks," Brooke said as she pulled Sophie along to the kitchen.

****

The air was thick with the aroma of Thanksgiving. Sweet potato soufflé, roasted turkey, and yeast rolls. Sophie pulled the scent into her olfactory organ and paused to give proper appreciation for the holiday fragrance. Memories of long ago Thanksgivings when Gramps was still alive flooded her mind.

"You girls need something?"

"I'm here because sister dear pulled me away from my fiancé and his parents. Talk about appearing rude."

"No worries. Lindsey is a natural hostess. They won't miss us."

Brooke moved to a cabinet used for storage and opened it. She pulled out a box and handed it to Sophie, who stood motionless. "Go on, open it," Brooke prompted.

"I don't understand. It's not our birthday." Sophie opened the flaps and reached in the box. Her jaw dropped as she pulled out a gravy boat matching the pattern of Nana's good china.

"How? I used every search engine on the Internet and came up empty. And why are you giving it to me?"

"I wanted *us* to give it to Nana together. I just haven't had time to show it to you until now."

Sophie surveyed the serving piece. "The thought is nice, but it's not the same as Nana having the gravy boat Gramps gave her. Brooke, did you see this chip by the handle?"

"It *is* the dish he gave her."

"How is that possible? I threw the pieces away," Nana said.

"And I went through the trash and dug them out. At the time, I didn't know why. The urge to retrieve them was so strong I couldn't ignore it. After the article about the transplant came out in the *Smyrna Times*, I received a phone call from one of my high school girlfriends. We spent some time catching up, and that's when I found out Marilyn does glass creations. I asked how she was at repairing broken china, and she agreed to give it a try. The chip on the handle is the only giveaway about its past."

Speechless and with moisture gathering in her eyes, Nana sat.

"Here you go, Nana." Sophie placed the boat on the table in front of her.

She touched it gingerly. "I thought it was gone forever."

Sophie put her arm around Brooke. "Some things are meant to be." She turned and faced Brooke. "Like us. I'm so glad you're moving home to Smyrna. Now Nana and I will have the pleasure of watching Lindsey grow up. However, you should be aware there's a hazard to moving back."

Brooke frowned. "What's that?"

"With you living here, there's a huge chance the twin thing we had will kick in again."

"When that happens, I'll be the happiest twin on the planet. I believe I'm almost there."

Sophie pulled in a deep breath. "So this might be an ideal time to ask a favor."

"Give it a try."

"Would you be my matron of honor when Ben and I marry next May?"

Brooke focused on Nana. "What do you think?"

Nana burst into tears. "I've been waiting forever for this reunion. Worried I might not see it before I leave to join Stan in heaven." Nana pulled a handkerchief from her pocket and dabbed at her eyes. "I have so much to be thankful for today."

Sophie touched her sister's arm. "Well?"

"Yes, little sister." Brooke pulled her into a hug. "I'm honored and happy to accept."

The End

Rachel's Summer Squash Casserole

Ingredients

2 pounds yellow squash, sliced and cooked
Salt and pepper to taste
1 small onion, chopped
½ cup butter
1 carrot, grated
1 8-ounce container of sour cream
1 10.5-ounce can of cream of chicken soup
2 cups cornbread stuffing (I use Pepperidge Farm brand)
1 cup sharp Cheddar cheese, shredded

Directions

Preheat oven to 350 degrees.

In a large pot, cover squash with water. Add salt and pepper. Cook until tender. Drain and mash.

Sauté onion in butter. Add all other ingredients, except cheese.

Mix well and pour into a greased baking dish. Sprinkle cheese over mixture.

Bake for 30 minutes.

Rachel Jones

Rachel Jones—Labor & Delivery RN by night and writer by day—is an award-winning author who began her first novel at age fifty-seven. She composes stories of strong heroines, heroes with heart, and sweet romance. Her writing reflects her passion for performing arts, and a twenty-eight-year career in healthcare has influenced the threads of medical drama woven into her storylines.

A music enthusiast for most of her life, Rachel enjoys playing the piano and clarinet. Other creative outlets include sewing and cross-stitch. She lives in metro Atlanta with her husband of thirty-nine years and one large, spoiled Labrador retriever who has a full-size bed but sleeps wherever she desires.

You can learn more about Rachel and her books at http://rachelwjones.com

Layers of Love

Linda Joyce

Acknowledgments

Around a table is where I met with Caroline Tate, Director of Special Events for Atlanta Ronald McDonald House Charities. Her enthusiasm has added to the delight in creating this book for such a worthy organization.

I wish to thank Melissa Klein, Marilyn Baron, Rachel Jones, Constance Gillam, and Ciara Knight for joining me on this journey and for their labor of love in contributing a story for this anthology.

In my story, you will meet Clara. This character is in honor of my best friend from college who was a huge supporter of my writing. I miss her; however, I have so many wonderful memories to sustain me.

Love happens in so many ways around a table. May it happen for you, too.

Linda Joyce

Layers of Love

Chapter One

Holly quietly lifted her knife roll from the kitchen counter. Tiptoeing and heading for the front door, she skirted the dining table in the small apartment. Photos and contracts of various sorts, stacked neatly, covered the entire tabletop. A laptop in the middle occupied prime real estate. She paused. Guilt flickered. She'd promised Clara again last night to set a meeting time to listen to the updated business presentation she'd prepared.

"Aha! Stop right there." Clara stood in front of the door with one hand on her hip, the other raised to halt Holly's progress.

Holly froze. She'd been made. *Dang!*

The white-noise machine she gave Clara when they began sharing the Atlanta apartment had failed to cover her noise tracks. Her friend possessed superpower hearing—even heard a pin drop during middle school recess. Well, the sniffles of a hurting girl no one else detected. She and Clara had been friends ever since.

"I've a meeting with the new executive chef at work." Holly straightened and squared her shoulders, but on her most confident day, she had no chance of ever intimidating her friend. "I have to go."

Clara shook her head, her black curls swishing back and forth. "Holly Everett"—Clara eyed her—"I haven't landed a new job yet, so we need to work on *our* project. I'm investing in our partnership, but once I land a big corporate dream job, I'll be married to work. The only time I'll see you will be to grab your luscious cupcakes and go."

Holly straightened more, rising up on her toes. At five foot two, she still had to look up a bit to make direct eye contact. "Clara Peterson, I believe *today* will be the day you receive a great job offer due to that fancy MBA you have. So we'll celebrate this evening. I'll bring cake and champagne. Then I'll quietly suffer through your business proposition."

"Holly, I promise, this place is so perfect"—she purred the word—"for Layers of Love. I have the entire business plan nailed down in an easy-to-read picture presentation."

"Wait. Just because I can't follow a spreadsheet—"

"Okay, that was a sucker punch, but I'm resorting to middle school tactics to make you understand, this is a great deal for *both* of us. I need us to do this. I'm not doing it just for you." Clara's dark eyes lit with excitement. "The potential opportunities could make us both a lot of money. Cookbooks. Multiple locations. Maybe even franchising."

"Hold on there, Oprah Winfrey of the pastry world. I'm the talent and—"

Clara's cell phone rang from her bedroom. She held up a finger. "You hold that thought, blondie, and don't move. Let me check to see who's calling."

The minute her friend raced away from the front door, Holly exited, running down three flights of stairs, clutching her knife roll with her crossbody purse whacking her hip.

"Holly Everett!" Clara shouted from an open window in their apartment. "I have a second job interview this afternoon. Tonight, we *must* finalize our plans."

Showing her a thumbs-up, Holly smiled widely, placed the tools of her trade on the backseat of her car and slid inside. Joy for Clara mixed with the nervous butterflies turning pirouettes in her stomach. The command audience called by the new executive chef puzzled her. She expected changes at work, but worry skittered through her. The reputation of this chef—she'd discovered his nickname was The General—rivaled that of a seasoned military officer, and he had one volume setting—loud.

She started the car and drove, battling Atlanta's morning traffic.

She loved her job. Had worked at the hotel for five years since culinary school. Through those years of learning and perfecting her craft, Clara had remained her strongest supporter, even pushing her to start the side business of making specialty cakes for a select group of clients. However, butting heads and reining in Clara's starry-eyed, sky's-the-limit business plans proved to be part of the give-and-take of their friendship. While Clara had a creative mind for business, Holly made fabulous creative desserts. Her friend liked to brag to others how she had a cupcake designed and named after her— The Clara was milk chocolate cake with chocolate chips and filled with chocolate ganache, topped with a chocolate rose—to represent her beauty.

Holly pulled into the parking section designated for hotel employees. The Atlanta Buckhead landmark never wavered in sophisticated style and sterling reputation. With tools clasped to her chest, she wondered why she'd been ordered to bring them to the meeting. As a pastry chef, her most important utensils weren't these sharp instruments.

Once in the small locker room, she reached for a clean, starched white chef's coat with her name embroidered above the hotel's logo. The constant supply of coats was one of the perks she received when she took on the role of executive pastry chef. The youngest one the hotel had ever employed. As she pulled her brown hair into a ponytail, her attention snapped when a voice yelled, "Chef Everett!"

She entered the kitchen. Prep cooks dropped their gazes and busied themselves.

"Here, Chef." Holly scurried toward the office at the far side of the large kitchen. Her voice echoed in the mostly empty space. She crossed the threshold to his office where he stood looking down at brochures on his desk.

"Close the door."

After doing as asked, Holly stood with her hands behind her back and waited for him to speak.

"We're doing new promotional brochures. These are part of the GM's plan for marketing. I was brought in to raise the bar…the kitchen needs to make more money for the hotel."

Holly stood at attention as he continue.

"I want to feature you with a few of your creations—you do beautiful, unique cakes. But..." He lifted his gaze and locked eyes with her. "I'm told you refuse to be photographed."

Puzzled, Holly lifted an eyebrow. He hadn't asked a question. She was uncertain how to respond.

"Why?" He pointed a finger at her.

She fought the urge to turn away. "I...I'm uncomfortable being photographed."

"Well, you better get used to it quick. Mathew Roberts is the best there is, and I'll be setting up a photo shoot date. Not only will you be featured with your cake and your newest award from that baking magazine, you'll be hosting a local home-bakers cake bake-off. We'll have TV covering it. We're contracting to have a fifteen-minute infomercial video made, too. Parts will be used for TV ads."

All her nerves sprung to alert. She fought the urge to flee. Holly swallowed hard. "No, Chef." She'd found her voice, but it was shaky. "I get paid to make desserts. Eye-catching cakes are certainly my passion, along with unique flavors. After all, what's pretty without substance? That's what I do. I have no problem with my work on display, photographed, or videoed."

The older man drew back, looking down his nose at her. "I was told you would refuse. You understand"—he leaned, his palms planted firmly on his desktop—"I'm giving you a direct order. I run this kitchen operation."

"With all due respect—"

"Respect requires you to follow orders. Are you being insubordinate?"

When did I join the military? A kitchen is a place for creativity. He's turning it into a battlefield.

"Chef, I request that we go over the job description I was given when I was hired."

A slow smile lifted the corners of his mouth but never reached his eyes. "Miss Everett, I know what your job description says. The duties I'm assigning you fall under the heading of 'And all other duties as assigned.' Most chefs would jump at this chance to be the face of sweetness for this hotel."

But not every chef has scars like mine.

Her hand went to the side of her face. She fingered the line above her temple to her jaw. Theatrical makeup covered the physical scar, but the ones inside made her flush with shame. One of the reasons corporate baking attracted her was the ability to work in relative seclusion—no one would see her. She clasped her hands together to keep from tracing the thin raised line again. "What about if I switch positions with my next in command?" It would mean a demotion and a cut in pay but preferable to her scarred face plastered in print.

"No. But I'm not as bad as you might think," Chef said. "If you do not wish to complete this part of your duties as head pastry chef, then you will battle a sous chef for the chance to keep a job. Which is the reason you were told to bring your knives."

Holly's heart sank. She swallowed hard. In five years, she had barely practiced knife skills, hadn't worked a food line, hadn't kept up with emerging savory flavor profiles. Failing to meet The General's demands would mean she was fired.

"I want to inspect the sharpness of your knives. That will be telling. You have until Sunday to practice. Then you will compete with another employee by prepping and cooking for me. Three savory dishes. I'll let you know which ones. If your work doesn't meet my standards, then you will be out of a job. Or you may win, in which case, someone else will be fired. Or…"—he eyed her—"you could agree to do your job. You may go now."

Trying to keep her spiking emotions closeted, she nodded. But her rubbery knees threatened to collapse as she turned to leave. He expected her to battle one of the staff? They were family.

"Oh, deliver your knives here. I'll inspect them in a bit, then return them to you."

Holly nodded. When she set her knives on The General's desk, he had already departed. She made her way to the kitchen corner where laminated menus were taped to cabinet doors for all kitchen employees to review.

"Oh," she groaned, scanning the savory items. Which would be the better approach? To practice dishes she enjoyed eating or working on the more complicated ones Chef most likely would require? Thankfully, whatever she made for practice could be shared with the staff. But which chef would she battle? And why? Everyone on this side of the kitchen was committed. Dread rolled into a knot in her stomach.

"What's up?" Chef Lamar elbowed her as he stood next to her. "Your cake didn't rise?" The head sous chef sometimes helped her with her side cake business. The guy could pipe icing on a cake!

"Studying the menu. Evidently, my refusal to subject myself to hair, makeup, and brochure photos means I'm battling a sous chef to keep my job."

"Say what?"

She pivoted and stared pointedly at him. "Is there someone in your kitchen struggling in some way? For this savory battle, it appears the loser will be out of a job. This apparently is kitchen colosseum where the loser is fed to the lions—or, at least, the unemployment line."

"The General hasn't said anything to me." Lamar's forehead wrinkled. "When is this duel scheduled?"

"Sunday."

"It's Tuesday. That's only five days away. Honestly, Holly, my team is top notch. We put out five-star food. No slackers here."

"I know." She sighed. Her panic was rising like yeasty dough. "Well, I'll get to work on tonight's desserts. Maybe I'll get some practice time later tonight. The good thing about today— I'm headed to Pineapple Place for the birthday celebration. I've got to start those cakes, too. Come help me decorate there, if you have time. Amanda would love to see you."

She stalked to her area of the kitchen. Usually she loved this time of morning. Quiet. Soothing. Flowing energy always carried her along. Never did work feel hard or oppressive in any way. But now, her fingers trembled as she assembled the ingredients for a caramel ice cream, chocolate torte, and a grilled peach cobbler.

Focusing on the desserts for dinner service, she worked steadily. When a timer in the other part of the kitchen blared over the rising chatter in the kitchen, she glanced at the clock. Eleven a.m.

"Wow. Time flies." She scurried to pull five different sizes of cake pans. What would any princess love more than a cake castle? For her special friend at Pineapple Place, it had to be made from carrot cake. The girl could eat her weight in it.

"Baker Sue reporting for duty!"

Startled, Holly dropped one of the pans.

"Am I supposed to salute you?" Sue whispered, her hand jerking toward her temple.

"Stop that. No saluting. Grab the tub for the ice cream and pull it from the machine." Holly raced to the counter, set down the pans, and then washed the one she'd dropped. She had assembled all the ingredients for the carrot cake, except the carrots and pecans.

One of the busboys laid a large bag of carrots and a bag of shelled pecans on her workstation. "Lamar sent me over here with these." She nodded, and he wandered back to his side of the kitchen. She wanted to hug her friend for saving her the extra steps.

Over an hour later, the cakes were pulled from the oven. Holly sniffed the mouthwatering aromas and set the pans on the marble-topped island to cool.

While Sue worked on plating the few dessert orders for the lunch crowd, Holly grabbed the fondant and the fillings from the fridge and placed them in a small cooler. The ingredients for pastillage went into a large box. Heading back to her storage closet, she entered the small room and reached for a large, round metal disk. *Click.* The door closed, and the light went off.

"Chef Everett," a male voice said. Holly paused. It took her a moment to recognize the voice as that of her new boss. "I returned your knives. They're deplorable. Sharpen them this afternoon. Do not leave before I have a chance to inspect them again." The door opened a crack. The light turned on.

"But Chef—"

"You have nothing to say to me, Chef Everett, except 'yes, sir.' Is that clear?"

"No, Chef. I have an afternoon commitment I cannot miss. People are counting on me."

"These people are *more* important to you than your career?"

Holly blinked. She'd been down the same path they were walking. Injured. Scared. Sometimes feeling hopeless. This was her way to give back. He was going to force her to choose?

"Chef, I volunteer twice a month to provide a birthday cake for the families at Pineapple Place. They're counting on me. I've not missed a date in four years."

Chef lifted an eyebrow.

"It's good publicity for the hotel and the restaurant," she rushed to add.

"Is that what those cakes on your station are for?"

She nodded.

He stormed from the supply closet. Holly grabbed the disk and quickly followed.

"These?" He pointed. "Are for a birthday cake?"

"Yes." She tried to sound authoritative. Around her, the kitchen had quieted. Many pairs of eyes stared.

"No more! I won't allow you to waste work time or quality ingredients. This kitchen will no longer provide resources and your time for this personal endeavor on my time. Do I make myself clear?"

Holly lifted her chin. "Yes, Chef." Her voice was the only sound in the entire kitchen.

"Go. But remain after the dinner service to sharpen your knives to my satisfaction." He began to walk away. Three steps later he turned back to her. "Or Sue will be head pastry chef tomorrow." Then he crossed the silent kitchen.

"Hurry, Sue," Holly ordered. "I'm going to get my car and pull it to the back door. Help me load."

"Absolutely. But Holly, he can't possibly mean what he said."

"We'll talk about it later. I've got to go."

She, however, believed every word he uttered. He wasn't a general, but a tyrant. Why had he singled her out?

Chapter Two

Scooting into a spot near the door, Holly parked at Pineapple Place. Her pulse raced. What was she going to do about the duel? Lamar had a total of seven on his staff. Each needed a job, just as she did. But in five days, someone would be out. She gripped the steering wheel tightly, silently screamed, and then took several deep breaths, willing any possible calmness to settle through her. It was important she leave any angst at the front door. Here at Pineapple Place, she embraced the healing spirit offered through the camaraderie of the residents and in turn offered her talents to help them. Creating cakes two days a month had become the highlight of her life. Nothing from the outside world could be allowed to mar that.

She exited the sedan, squinting against the bright sun, and crossed warm asphalt to the entrance. The opening *swoosh* of the glass doors always grounded her.

"Chef Holly!" Amanda called. The ten-year-old rolled her wheelchair in Holly's direction. She wore a princess costume, the one for special tea parties where Amanda issued royal invitations. "I was worried you weren't coming."

Holly knelt down in front of the girl and leaned in for a hug. "I apologize for being late."

Amanda smiled. "Momma will be down in a minute with the aprons." Amanda's mother handled her daughter's injuries and recovery far better than Holly's parents had.

"I'll grab the cart to bring in the supplies. Do we have an audience today, or are we going it alone?"

Amanda shrugged. "Kids are upstairs playing. Some guy is hanging around with a fancy camera. Don't want him taking my picture. Miss Carol said a writer was doing a story on Pineapple Place. The photographer asked me the dumbest question."

"And what was that?" Holly suppressed a smile.

"He wanted to know *why* I didn't want my picture taken."

How many times had she been asked that same question?

"You told him what?" In her case, unlike Amanda's, the scar on her face was the last straw—it tore her family apart. Any photograph of her only brought up a bucket of pain. That she could do without.

"I pointed to the side of my face and said, 'Because of this.' He came close and looked but said he didn't see anything. Said I had the prettiest eyes and the cutest grin. That *I* should be on the cover of a magazine."

Holly smiled. She didn't know this guy, but she kind of liked him. That was the type of positive reinforcement her young friend needed.

"Amanda... I agree with him. It's your eyes and your smile. They light up the world. I would love to see you on a magazine cover. Well, let me get my stuff, and we'll begin."

After the individual layers of cake and containers of filling were set on the large countertop, Holly returned to her car to retrieve the box of supplies needed for making pastillage. She'd taught Amanda how to make decorations with the icing. As she balanced the box of supplies on one raised knee, she reached to close the trunk lid of her car.

"Hey there!" a voice behind her shouted.

She turned, and the box wobbled. Holly fought against losing her balance and tumbled forward into the guy. The box hit his camera. The jolt caused her to lose her grip. The box dropped. When it hit the ground, the lid on the plastic container filled with powdered sugar popped open. Sugar erupted, covering both of them—her work uniform and kitchen shoes and his dark gray slacks and a blue and white checked shirt. His shoe color was now indistinguishable.

"I'm so sorry." She bent to wipe powdered sugar from his shoes with the sleeve of her chef's coat. The sugar streaked.

"Please don't." He cupped her elbow, and the pressure urged her to stand. "Don't worry about me. Sorry I startled you." He hoisted up the box of supplies. "I came to help. Amanda's been telling me all about your fancy cakes. Says this is her birthday month, and the cake isn't only for her, but she's quite excited."

"You're clearly a photographer, but are you *the* photographer?" She studied him for a moment. Tall. Tan. Built like a golfer. Dark blond hair. Eyes were how she connected with a person. His were light brown and made her think they'd met before, but she couldn't quite place him. It would come to her... In the meantime, he had an ease about him that made her relax.

He nudged her forward. "Let's go."

Embarrassed, she swatted at her pants to shake the white powder from them, so as not to track it through the lobby on her way to the kitchen.

"*The* photog. I don't know what you're asking me," the guy said as they walked toward the front door.

"She belongs on the cover of a magazine," Holly stated.

"Yes, that was me. And she will, if I can make it happen."

All of her nerves pricked to alert. Holly stopped. "Amanda says she doesn't want to be photographed. *Don't* push her. She very sensitive about…she's just sensitive."

The man frowned as they reached the kitchen. He set the box on the counter near the cakes. "I think we got off on the wrong foot. Chef Holly, I'm Mathew Roberts."

"Oh." The news hit like a hammer slamming against a slab of chocolate, shattering it into pieces. Holly turned and walked to the sink to wash her hands. Just her luck to meet face-to-face with the photographer scheduled to do the photo shoot for the restaurant. He might not be the cause of her work dilemma, but he surely represented the photograph problem that would probably end her job. "Mr. Roberts, I'm really busy right now."

"I'm ready, Chef Holly," Amanda called out. Her mother trailed behind her. Mother and daughter wore matching pink cupcake aprons Holly had sewed for them.

"Hello again, Mr. Roberts," Amanda's mother said. The man smiled and nodded.

Holly tried not to roll her eyes at the guy taking up space in the kitchen. He seemed determined to want to make a point with her, but she wasn't interested. "Excuse me, Mr. Roberts, but only decorators are allowed on *this* side of the island. If you insist on watching, please do so from the other side."

She had a moment of guilt for being rude, but the man didn't seem to notice. He moved as instructed, continued to watch, and smiled at them.

Setting to work with Amanda and her mother, Holly created a batch of pastillage for the girl to make flowers. Her mother filled the layers of each tier of the cake with pineapple buttercream while Holly rolled out blue fondant.

The five tiers created a fairytale, blue castle shimmering with pearl dust. A gold crown topped the cake. Holly helped Amanda place the final flower decorations.

"It's so beautiful," Amanda's mother said as she moved to the other side of the island. "I'll go remind people to come for birthday cake."

"Exquisite art," Mathew said. "I've never had the opportunity to see a castle constructed before." He stepped closer and inspected the details. "It's beautiful, but at the same time, thoughtfully engineered."

"I don't know about all that." Amanda beamed. "But it'll sure taste good. Carrot cake is my favorite."

Holly put out her fist, and Amanda bumped it with hers. "Good job, Chef," Holly told the girl. Her young friend smiled bashfully at the praise.

A click caused Holly to turn. Mathew had his camera to his face. He snapped a few more shots.

Amanda's eyes grew wide and wild. She hung her head.

"Amanda"—Holly squatted at the girl's eye level—"will you go tell the nice folks in the office over there that we're ready to cut the cake?"

The solemn girl looked at her, and then, at Mathew. Holly's heart seized.

"Yes, Chef. I will."

After she wheeled away, Holly snapped her focus to Mathew. "I believe Amanda said she didn't want to be photographed. Please delete those pictures." Anger welled in her gut. Amanda hadn't known when she told the man no photographs, she'd saved Holly from making the same point. Now she intended to protect both of them from the rogue photographer.

"Wait. Look at them first. Perfect shots." Mathew held out his camera.

"No. Amanda told you straight up, no photographs. Delete them now. Isn't there some photojournalism code like there is for reporters? No photos means the same thing as off the record."

"Will you at least look first?"

"Mr. Roberts, no means no. And if you can't abide by the request, then please leave." She began to clean the marble countertop and drop supplies in the box.

Mathew shook his head. "Can't do that. This story is about the people and residents of Pineapple Place. And you're one of them. They told me you've been doing this for years. Twice a month. Never missed making a cake."

"Then I'll make my apologies. I need to get back to work anyway."

"Are you always so difficult? You can't leave. This is Amanda's celebration. She's very special. There's something sweet and magical about that kid. You can't help but smile around her. I can't leave because I have a story to cover. The magazine reporter wanted to interview you. I'm going to need a few photos to go with this story."

But he didn't understand when a kid was involved in a serious accident, one where they're injured—and, in Holly's case, a sibling died, too—they wanted to control the sphere of their world. No pictures meant no photos. Even from a famous photographer.

Yet, Mathew was right. She couldn't leave now. This was Amanda's special time. The party was just starting. But she could ignore him.

Chapter Three

The residents and staff gathered and sang happy birthday to the girls with birthdays that month. Amanda's mother made hot tea—what princess party would be complete without it? Then Amanda cut the cake.

A half hour later, Holly checked her watch. Fun time was over. Real life called.

"Sweetie." Holly knelt beside Amanda's wheelchair. "I need to head back to work. I'll see you next time. We're tackling pirates then."

The girl gazed at her thoughtfully. "This is the best castle made with carrot cake I've ever eaten."

"I'm delighted you enjoyed it. You've learned so much about making pastillage. Your decorations are lovely."

"Holly?"

"Yes, Amanda?"

"I've been thinking."

Holly nodded. One of the things she enjoyed about Amanda was her creative mind and the wondrous words of wisdom her ten-year-old brain conjured. "About what?"

"My dad told me every girl is a beautiful princess, that the outside is only important to those who can't see the inside. Love-light of the heart. He asked me to consider having my picture taken. All the better if it lands on a cover of a magazine, he told me."

Blinking, Holly gazed at the girl in the princess costume picking at her chunk of the castle as though she'd said the most ordinary thing. Amanda's father had to be a prince among men.

She stood and kissed the girl's forehead. "Your highness, I see the love-light of your heart. Let me know what you decide about the magazine cover. I think it could be a good thing. Now I'm going to scoot."

Later that evening, Holly had made it through dinner service, managing to stay out of The General's sight lines. The adrenaline of a dinner rush always got her blood pumping. It was a kind of high only baking provided. But now, staff members scurried, gazes down, to clean. Usually, they cranked up the volume on the radio and joked while scouring down the kitchen. Tonight the place echoed more like a mausoleum.

"Chef Everett!"

"Yes, Chef!" Holly had kept one eye on her boss all evening. Always aware of his location every moment since he took up residence in the kitchen. Her station was clean, and she was about to begin sharpening her knives.

"Chef Lamar!"

"Yes, Chef," Lamar called out from his work area across the kitchen.

"In my office."

As Holly neared Lamar, he cocked an eyebrow. She shrugged. Maybe The General would reveal the unlucky person forced to battle her. Dread puddled in her gut.

"Close the door."

"I will be checking your knives before I leave tonight, Chef Everett. Don't make me late going home to my family."

"Yes, Chef."

"Chef Lamar, I've decided you will choose which of your staff will battle Chef Everett. The winner of the battle stays. The loser is out."

Holly stifled a gasp.

Stoically, Lamar turned to glance at Holly and then faced The General again. "I have a decision."

"I like a decisive employee. Please tell Chef Everett the competitor."

"Me."

Holly's eyes widened. Her heart thudded double time. The sound of blood rushed in her ears. Her hands went to her stomach, holding back a wave of nausea.

What did Lamar say?

She fought from hyperventilating. All respected his kitchen skills. He had far more experience than she had. He was certain to beat her. She'd be out of a job.

"You?" Holly stared at him. Not a fair competition. So much for thinking she had a shot at keeping her job if she was paired with the most inexperienced sous chef on his team.

"Hmmm. Not the answer I expected." The General eyed them both.

Lamar stood straighter. His hands clasped behind his back.

Holly's thoughts swirled. She drew in a soft ragged breath. She'd thought Lamar was her friend. Her skills as a sous chef might be rusty, but she still possessed more knowledge and passion than the least experienced person on his team. Why would he do this? Why?

"I'm a man of my word. Chef Lamar has spoken. Chef Everett, you now know who you're up against. You're both dismissed. Oh, but one more thing. I want no discussion of this in the kitchen."

Scooting out of the office first, Holly returned to her work area and immediately began sharpening her knives. She turned her back to the rest of the kitchen to avoid any possible eye contact with Lamar. The sting of his decision cut deep.

As the clock ticked to eleven p.m. and the main kitchen darkened, Holly knocked on The General's office door. "Chef, my knives are ready for your inspection."

"There's a small cutting board with a few items in the walk-in." He didn't look up but kept his gaze on a spreadsheet. "Grab that, and let's see how you do. You'll show me your sharpness."

Slicing and dicing, Holly displayed her knife skills with the julienne cut, the brunoise dice, and the batonnet. Muscle memory developed during cooking school kicked in, and she was pleased with her performance.

"That's enough." The General picked up a julienned sweet potato. Examined it, then dropped it on the pile. "You followed orders." It was the first time all evening he'd made direct eye contact with her. "I believe you have the passion and the drive to beat Chef Lamar. If you win, you'll have a position as sous chef, but you won't be taking his spot. I have someone else in mind for that."

He thinks I can win? He's not only a tyrant, but crazy, too.

"But if I win, what about Lamar?"

"He's fired."

Shock zipped through her. She blinked several times. Whenever the man showed an inkling of compassion, he jerked it back.

Holly stared at the back of her boss as he walked away, certain he could hear the pounding of her heart in her chest.

No. No. This can't be happening.

Lamar was a friend, albeit on shaky ground at the moment. However, he had two children and a wife. He'd worked for the hotel for nearly ten years. He'd even helped her get the job and then supported her as she moved up the line. Still, she had to battle her heart out against him. Giving up wasn't an option.

Heartsick, she drove home. When she pulled in front of her apartment, she ached for a shower and her bed.

Ding. The screen on her phone lit with a message from Lamar.

—Call me. Let me explain.—

She shook her head. She wasn't ready to talk about it. Looking up, she noticed the light on in the living room. "Oh, dang! I forgot the champagne and chocolate-covered strawberries."

Trudging up three flights of stairs, she heaved out a sigh before unlocking the door. Inside, champagne and chocolate-covered strawberries waited on the coffee table. Clara sat at the small, round dining table, glasses on her nose, and a pencil in her hand tatting out a random beat as she studied some papers.

"You're late." Clara lowered her chin and looked over the top of her reading glasses.

"I've had a terrible day." Holly sank to the couch.

"No. Today is birthday-cake day. It's your high. Which is why I planned this for tonight. I counted on you being in a great mood. What happened?"

"Someone ripped my heart out today." Holly moaned as she kicked off her shoes.

Clara quickly joined her in the living room, sitting forward in a chair across from her. Her brow furrowed. She sucked on her bottom lip. "Tell me about it?"

"Relax. No one died. It's not that bad, but bad enough."

Clara's shoulders eased a bit. "Well, then maybe I'll have some good news to cheer you up. But first, what's got you cranked down so tight?"

"I'm probably going to lose my job next week."

"What?"

"The General, that's what I call the new executive chef, is making me battle Lamar." She tucked her feet close beside her and then rubbed on the long, thin scar on the side of her face. "I refused to pose for photos and to do some TV stuff—you know I hate having my picture taken—and instead of firing me for insubordination, he said I had to do this battle to keep a job. And not even in pastry, but on the line. Then he gave Lamar the option to pick which one of his—"

"Wait. He's taking you out of pastry to work for Lamar?"

Holly rolled her eyes. "Well, actually, I thought The General would pick my opponent and maybe choose the least experienced person on the line so I could work for Lamar, but noooo."

"And?"

"He made Lamar pick who would battle me." She shrugged. "He chose himself."

Clara straightened, shaking her head. "That makes no sense."

"Sure it does." Holly sighed. "He's protecting his staff. Lamar can beat me hands down."

"I see…and maybe that explains the phone call I had from him a bit ago."

Holly sat up. "Lamar called you?"

"Well…he knows about the spot I've made a deposit on—"

"You did *what*? Without talking to me?" Holly stood, then strode to the dining table. She spotted the lease agreement and snatched it up. Flipping through the pages, she stopped on the last one with a yellow tab and yellow highlighted line waiting for a signature.

"Before your brain explodes, I can get the deposit back. I gave them a thousand to hold the place, and we have until tomorrow to sign the lease or I get my money back."

"That was your graduation money from your family."

"Holly, come back and sit down. Lamar called and asked me if I was still looking for a place for Layers of Love. I explained everything to him about our—"

"Your."

"—plan. He didn't say why, but he offered to apprentice with you for free for a day a week for the first six months. Said his wife would even help run the counter. This is their way of supporting you."

"His way of assuaging his guilty conscience."

"Now his call makes sense. But, woman, this is the universe yelling at you to take a chance on yourself *now*." Clara was practically yelling at her. "You've already got a cake following, Holly. Listen, I'm so sure about this I'm willing to give up the corporate job offer I received today to prove to you Layers of Love will be an automatic success."

Surprise smacked Holly. "You got a job offer? The one you wanted?"

"Yep."

"And you'd give it up for me?"

"Ah-huh."

Holly shook her head and plopped on the couch. "You're too much, Clara. You can't do that. But a new business…I don't know. It's tempting. I don't want to feel like a quitter at the hotel…I'll have to sleep on your idea."

Clara opened the champagne and poured two glasses. "And while we're speaking of risk, I have another message for you." Holly took the offered glass. "He tried to be really crafty, but my momma didn't raise no fool."

Sipping the cool sparkling wine soothed Holly's throat. "Who's crafty?"

"Remember when you made that huge wedding cake for the socialite last year?"

"She's crafty?"

"No." Clara smacked her forehead with her palm. "She had that fancy photographer there. He kept trying to get a picture of you with the cake when you were assembling it."

"Fool even asked me for my phone number," Holly muttered.

"Right. Mathew Roberts. He called here looking for you."

"I remember that name. But the guy I met today doesn't look like the same guy I met last year. That guy dressed in green camo and had shoulder length, sun-streaked hair. He wore a bandana. The guy today, Mathew Roberts, dressed sharp, from his styled hair and button-down shirt to his polished black shoes." She chuckled, remembering them covered with a dusting of white.

"He called and asked for you, but I asked to take a message. He wanted to confirm he had the right Holly Everett and the correct phone number."

Holly eyed her roommate. "So he didn't say anything about a date. You're creating connections and stories where none exist."

"Not exactly." Clara sat back in the chair and crossed her legs. "I asked about the nature of his call. He said, 'Professional.' And then I said, 'Well, personal might get you further.'"

"Ohhhh." Holly groaned.

"He perked right up after that. Got a tinge of excitement in his voice. Started peppering me with questions about what you considered a perfect date."

Shaking her head, Holly closed her eyes. "You didn't. You didn't. He's the photographer the hotel is using for the big PR splash that I refused to participate in."

Clara placed her index finger in the middle of her chin. "Oh my. What have I done?" She blinked a few times. "I think"—her voice took on a deeper edge—"I might have gotten my best friend a date with a well-known photographer, whom I'll bet is quite nice to look at."

"That's it." Holly pushed to standing. "Enough. No photographs of me. No date with a photographer for me. And I'm not sure it's a good idea to move forward with a new business for me."

Glaring, Clara rose. "If not now, when?"

"When what?"

"When will you stop hiding behind the past? When will you invest in you? You don't have a wall, sister. You've got a deep moat. You're pretty, talented, and can be really funny...sometimes. But you won't give yourself or any guy a chance. Why?"

Holly shook her head and took a few steps away, heading for her bedroom. "When, what, why...you sound like a reporter. I need a shower. I said I'd think about it, and I will."

"I *need* an *answer* in the *morning*." Clara's voice was singsongy.

"*And* you'll *have* one." Holly left Clara alone with the champagne, strawberries, and the entire business plan for Layers of Love.

With every step to her bedroom, the events of the day plagued her. If she took a chance with a bakery and failed, she could find another job. But taking a chance on a guy...for that she'd have to drain the moat, and she wouldn't know where to begin.

Chapter Four

Ding. Ding.

Holly groaned and grabbed her phone. Who was texting so early in the morning?

—*Mrs. Baron here. Why didn't you tell me you were opening a bakery? I want to place several orders now. Before you're too busy. Call me to discuss.—*

"What?" Holly rubbed her eyes and looked at the time. Six-thirty in the morning. Mrs. B had to be on her morning two-mile run.

Setting the phone beside her pillow, Holly rolled over. Another half hour of sleep would make the day worth living.

Ding. Ding.

"Now what?" she moaned.

—*I want to put in my cake orders so I know I'm covered for the holidays. You should've told me you were opening a bakery. Let's talk about the anniversary party, Halloween cupcakes for the Auxiliary Club, and Christmas party. Mrs. Klein.—*

Before Holly could put the phone down, she received another text.

—*Layers of Love? You're taking new clients and didn't tell me? You must promise you will fill my orders. I can't have a party without one of your cakes as a centerpiece. And you know Randi is getting married! Wedding cake time! Call me. Now. Mrs. Jones—*

"Clara!" Holly shouted. "Clara, what have you done?"

More texts popped up. Ones from Mrs. Gillam and Mrs. Knight. Each demanding to place orders. Not one, but multiples.

"Clara! Claraaaaa!"

"What?" Clara banged the bedroom door open a few moments later. "Why are you shouting?" She stumbled across the floor and fell on the bed next to Holly, then grabbed a pillow and covered her eyes. "It's too early," she whined.

"Look. *Look* at these texts. What have you done?" Holly yanked the pillow away and shoved the phone in front of her friend's face.

Clara squinted and shoved Holly's hand away. "Mmmm. I told you I had a business plan." Clara grabbed the pillow back. "I created a newsletter for your current private clients. A short one-page blast about Layers of Love."

"And you just happened to forgot to mention this to me?"

Clara crinkled her nose, rose from the bed, and left as aromas of coffee filtered into the room.

"Be that way. Don't answer me," Holly muttered, turning the phone off and shoving it under her pillow.

Just about asleep, Holly jumped when Clara began screeching. "Holly! Holly!" she yelled from the other end of the apartment.

Scrambling out of bed, Holly raced to the living room. "Are you crazy?"

Dressed in a long robe, Clara offered a mug of coffee. "We're having a meeting *now*. I'm going to give you all the details of the lease, the business plan, even show you the proof for the business cards—which, by the way, you're going to love—and then you're going to sign on the dotted line."

"*After* I've had my coffee."

"Now." Clara stood rooted with her fists on her hips. "Take a seat."

Holly raised a warning eyebrow, but she did as instructed. Clara handed her a printout of an Excel spreadsheet. "This shows your estimated monthly expenses, including a salary for you."

"You've got it itemized down to flour, sugar, and vanilla? And what's this? Toilet paper?"

"There's a need for precise accounting of *every* line item."

Something about the way Clara cut her eyes away made Holly suspicious. "What aren't you telling me?"

Clara sighed. "I asked Lamar for his help."

"You…you what? He's going to cost me my job. You went behind my back." Indignation planted a flag in the middle of her chest. Her jaw locked. She narrowed her eyes and glared.

"Just listen. He lined up suppliers and vendors. We're getting a deep one-time discount thanks to him. We can open the doors at less than half the price the first month could cost because he worked with me on this. He *is* your friend."

Anger and affection for Lamar ping-ponged through her. Frustration was winning the battle.

"You *say* I have to make a decision today?"

"Well, if you answer in the affirmative, no real response is needed immediately. However, if it's negative, I need to know ASAP so I don't lose the thousand-dollar deposit I made."

Holly rose. "I'm going to work. I'm going to work on my skills. The General believes I can beat Lamar, so I have to try."

"Holly," Clara snapped. "Think about your future. Take a chance on you." She circled around the table and stood inches away. Holly held her breath, worried about what would come next.

Clara grasped her by her shoulders and shook her. "We believe in you. Now it's time for you to believe in yourself."

When Clara stopped trying to rattle her teeth lose, Holly shook her head. "No. I believe I can beat Lamar. That's the smart thing to do. Practice. Practice. I'm going to work now to do just that." She headed to the bedroom to change.

After battling Atlanta morning traffic, Holly arrived in the hotel kitchen and tied an apron about her pressed chef's jacket. Aroma of bacon filled her senses. She headed straight to her station and retrieved her knife roll. On her visit to the pantry and cooler, she pulled a box of risotto, two sweet potatoes, and a ribeye steak. "Paella would be more to my liking, but it's not on the menu," she muttered.

"Holly?" Lamar headed in her direction. "Could we talk?"

"Which of the savory dishes on the menu is the most difficult to cook? Have to talk later."

Lamar stood beside her. "It's not any one component of a dish that's difficult. It's getting everything to the plate hot and cooked perfectly that matters. Then, of course, there's plating. Presentation is important."

"It's not like I'm someone walking off the street. I've cooked in a kitchen before." When she reached for a knife, Lamar grasped her wrist. Slowly, she turned her head and glared at him. "You're impeding my progress."

He tugged on her wrist and led her outside. "You're going to listen to me." Holding up her hand, he said, "I'm going to tell you the five reasons you can't battle me." He tugged on her little finger. "One—you are very talented at desserts. It's your calling. Two—you already have a following, so building a business will be easier. Three—with Clara's business skills, Layers of Love will flourish. Four—opening the bakery will get you involved in life outside the kitchen. The last time you went out on a date was with my cousin Jason. Five—you can't possibly win against me. And even if you did, you'd be miserable as a sous chef."

Jerking her hand away, Holly tensed. "You want me to just quit? Chef told me last night he thinks I have more passion and believes I can beat you."

"But for what? To take a demotion and do a job you don't like?"

"You can't talk me out of battling you. It's something I have to do." She stormed back to the kitchen and washed her hands. Anger radiated from her core out to each of her fingers, causing them to tremble. She attacked peeling sweet potatoes. The only way she enjoyed them was in cupcakes or muffins. Being forced to peel and cube and roast sweet potatoes every day for lunch *and* dinner service would be like digging ditches—by hand.

Grabbing one of the peeled tubers, she placed it on a cutting board, then reached for the slicer knife on the counter. The anger zipping through her exploded into outrage. Raising the knife, she cleaved the orange root, splitting it in two. She sliced one half into thick pieces and began to chop. The blade of the knife slipped. Her thumb sprouted red. Shocked, Holly stared. Blood spurted. Light-headed, she blinked. Swallowed hard. Then crumpled to the floor. Her head hit. It was the last thing she remembered.

Chapter Five

Beyond the cubicle in the ER, people bustled about. Holly sat up, flinched at the noise, and squinted against the too-bright light over the bed. Any memory of crumbling to the kitchen floor eluded her. One minute, blood spurted, the next, Lamar's frantic patting of her cheek bordered on slapping. The spot still stung. Dazed, she'd said little when the EMS guys loaded her onto a gurney and delivered her here. The medical staff had been efficient.

She eyed the white gauze dressing on her thumb that made it look bulbous and clown-like. A shot had numbed all pain entirely, but the back of her head hurt where it hit the floor. Spots of dark red dotted her pristine white chef's coat. The stains would never come out. She flinched at what she remembered of the morning and kept her hand elevated as instructed.

Pain and anxiety, a potent cocktail, flooded her. She couldn't battle Lamar until she could return to work. Would The General fire her now? Lamar's words echoed in her brain. *Misery* screamed the loudest. Slightly rocking, Holly fought to settle her shaky nerves.

Never before had she reached a crossroad where a single decision would dramatically alter the course of her entire life. Once before, life crumbled and forever changed her. But she didn't have a say in that decision. When she was a kid, her father had abandoned her and her mother after the accident. It remained the most pivotal event in her life…until now.

"Miss Everett, you are released," the ER doctor said. "Remember to keep those stitches clean and dry for a minimum of forty-eight hours—four or five days would be best. Though you only have a mild concussion, take it easy. Rest. I would recommend a few days off work. I've written a note for that."

"I'll make sure she follows orders, Doctor." Clara breezed in smiling. She stood at the foot of the bed. A wave of relief washed over Holly. Her best friend was her BFF for a reason. The building tension in Holly's chest subsided a bit. An achy tiredness seeped through her. Sleep begged her to close her eyes.

"I'm going to take you home, Holly." Concern shone in Clara's eyes.

The doctor left, and a nurse bustled into the cubicle. "Here are your discharge papers."

"I'll take those." Clara folded them and stuck them in her purse. "Let's go, Chef."

The ride to the apartment took forever. Holly's head throbbed. Once home, Clara tucked her into bed. "Rest. I'll bring you some tea."

Holly reached for her friend. "Clara, wait. We have to talk about the business."

"Now you want to talk?"

Closing her eyes, Holly nodded. "I think the bounce my brain took has rattled things loose. I've decided to take fate into my own hands. I'm going to make a decision for me, about me.

I'm not going to allow fear and The General to dictate my direction."

The bed moved. Holly opened her eyes as Clara sat and stared wide-eyed.

"The smartest thing would've been for me to agree to the advertising campaign." Holly took a slow deep breath and then let it go. "If I'm going to put myself out there, why not do it for me? Why not be the face of my own business?"

Clara's eyes widened. Her smile widened more. "You're saying 'yes' to Layers of Love?"

Holly nodded. "Maybe it's the concussion talking, but let's do this."

"Oh, thank God!" Clara fell backward on the bed. "It's a done deal anyway."

Pulling the covers up over her shoulders, Holly turned on her side. "I'm going to nap."

"I'll wake you in a while. I have work to do now. This is sooo exciting." Clara squealed and danced from the room.

As Holly closed her eyes again, it was as though a movie flashed images in her brain. Clara smartly dressed in a suit directing a board meeting. Lamar barking orders in a kitchen. Amanda with her smiling face, glowing with goodness, learning decorating techniques in a bakery. Another face came to mind. Holly blinked twice. Mathew Roberts. Camera in hand, he adjusted a beret on her head and then snapped a photograph of her. She was beaming. Full of confidence. Full of joy. And something more…

Chapter Six

The next morning when the house phone rang, Holly rolled over. Her eyes fought opening. Her body ached. Flicking her wrist, she ignored the annoying sound, snuggling deeper into the covers. The chiming stopped after the second ring. Cradled in her cozy bed, she drifted between barely awake and sleep.

Bang. Bang.

"Make it stop," Holly groaned, pulling the covers over her head.

"Holly?" Clara whispered. "You awake?"

"After the banging and roommate hissing—yeah."

"Oh, good. The call's for you. You need to take it. *Important.*"

Holly fluttered her eyes open. Maybe The General was calling? Taking the handset from Clara, she looked at the number displayed. No recognition came, though it showed a 404 Atlanta area code. "Good morning. This is Holly." She shooed her roommate away with a wave of her hand.

"I hope I didn't catch you too early."

She blinked and tried to place the man's voice. It definitely was not her boss on the other end of the connection. "No. How may I help you?"

"Breakfast, if you're available. I called the hotel's restaurant. They said you weren't coming in today."

Recognition kicked in. She sat up straighter in bed. Mathew Roberts was asking to meet up with her? Her toes curled and wiggled. Her pulse quickened. She hadn't accepted a date in nearly a year—no one she liked enough to bother with. But she hadn't met a guy like Mathew in a long while. Like making a cake, deciding to date only happened if there was a chemical reaction. Of course, timing played a significant role in the rise and fall of baking—and dating.

"Thought I'd take a chance and call you at home," Mathew said. "I'd like to show you some of my work. Show you what I can do on the photo shoot with you and your cake. I want to make you comfortable in front of the camera."

Her hope sank like a cake fresh from the oven. Clara had suggested he might be interested in more than a professional meeting. Clearly his interest was only work-based. She considered telling him she wouldn't be participating in the restaurant's advertising campaign. However, that news wasn't yet official. Best to wait. But after her thoughts about him last night, she hoped a friendship might blossom into something more. His artsy vibe resonated with her creative side. Her heart opened with joy whenever that connection happened with another dedicated, creative person. Mathew Roberts was special.

She chuckled softly. "You had me until 'comfortable in front of the camera.' That's not possible. However, I would like to look at your work. Too bad for me, today isn't good." She looked at her clown-like thumb. Forty-eight hours before she could undo the mummified appendage and assess its healing. "How about Saturday for brunch?"

"That works."—Clara was right. He sounded optimistic.—"But I thought weekends were the busiest time for restaurants."

I have a date! I have a date!

She straightened her shoulders, hoping to sound more businesslike. "Under most circumstances, that's true. However, I have an extenuating situation, and I'm taking a few days off."

"Shall we meet at the Blue Cup Café? About nine a.m.?"

"I'll see you there."

"And Holly, come ready to be convinced. I'm quite persuasive."

The moment she finished the call, Clara strode into the room. "You have a date!"

"It's not what you think. He still thinks I'm going to be the face of sweets at the restaurant. This is a professional meeting. I'm going to look at some of his work."

"It's a date." Clara's lips pursed and nodded. "Tell me more. Where? When?"

Anything she said would be scrutinized, and a lecture would follow about etiquette and decorum. There was one sure way to get Clara off the topic of Mathew. "Let me get dressed. Take me to Layers of Love, and we'll start on the paperwork there."

Her roommate squeed and spun in a circle and then danced herself out of the room. "It's a brave new world!" she called from the hallway.

With morning rush hour mostly over, the drive to the future home of Layers of Love was short. Clara pulled into a parking space in front of a house-like, white brick building with a high-pitched roof and deep red shutters.

Holly eyed the building with delight. "This used to be *The Rising! Café*. I loved this place. Why is it up for lease?"

She followed Clara to the door. Once the key turned in the lock, Clara linked arms with her. "The owner has moved to a new location and is doing pub grub along with bakery items."

"I love the color-stained concrete floors and wooden tables. The chairs are okay. Everything is in working order?" Holly asked, eyeing the deli and bakery cases. She made her way to stand at the counter where customers would soon come to place orders. In her mind's eye, she pictured customers drooling over cookies, brownies, cupcakes, and cakes.

"Chef, are you doubting me?" Clara spread her arms wide and turned in a circle. "From the electrical, to the plumbing, to the working order of the ovens in the back—"

Holly raced around the counter and pushed on the swinging door to the kitchen. Despite a light layer of dust, the place was immaculate. She opened doors and drawers, checking for cleanliness and damage. The kitchen was properly organized with all the necessary equipment.

She spun around when Clara entered the kitchen carrying a poster. "Layers of Love. This is the logo."

Unbounded anticipation zipped through Holly. The positive possibilities for her future flooded her with joy. She checked her feet to be sure she wasn't hovering off the floor. "You, Clara, are fantabulous!" Closing the distance between them, she hugged her best friend. "When can I begin working?"

Clara's shoulders shook as she laughed. "You can start this operation going"—she checked her watch—"now!"

"Wait. How's that?"

Clara scrunched her face and twitched her nose. She opened her eyes, and Holly locked gazes with her.

"I kind of…already told them…we'd take it."

"That was a huge risk." Holly shook her finger at her friend.

"In my defense, Chef, all I have to say is that I had faith."

"Well, thank goodness for that." She hugged her friend. "Now I'm going to need more of your help. Lamar's, too. We're going to make samples to test out all the equipment. I'm going to contact Pineapple Place and see if I can do the pirate ship cake tomorrow."

"Holly, there's one more detail." Clara cocked her head to one side. "You have to resign from the restaurant. Now don't be mad…I drafted a resignation letter for you to sign. We can take it by there if you'd like."

Squinting, Holly paused. "I think I need to call first."

Pulling her cell phone from the back pocket of her jeans, Holly called The General.

"Yes?" he answered.

"Chef, this is Holly Everett."

"I heard about your…accident. Can't have chefs fainting in the kitchen over a spot of blood."

"Sir, I'm calling to tell you this is my two-week notice of resignation."

He snorted. "I'm not surprised. You're a quitter, Chef Everett."

Anger pricked her. Who was he to judge her that way? She swallowed back a snarky retort. She wouldn't stoop to his level. "I'll drop off my letter of resignation later today."

"Don't bother coming back. I'll have Lamar empty your locker and bring your stuff to you, including your knives. Don't let me catch you in my kitchen again."

The connection ended before she had a chance to say anything further.

"Well, that's that." Holly shook her head.

"We can swing by there—" Clara started.

"No need. I'll mail it to the HR department. We have bigger things to focus on." Now that the ugly was out of her life, she breathed a sigh of relief.

"Let me grab my box of stuff from the car." Clara left her alone in the kitchen.

The energy, the vibration, and the echoes of sound filled Holly. This was her new home. Excitement surged. Everything about taking this risk felt right. Any dot of lingering doubt had to be shoved aside. She would only grow from this experience. Grow into the next phase of her life as an entrepreneur. In fact, she already had customers lined up for catering orders.

Making her way into the café area, Holly sat at a table to get a customer's perspective on the place. Photos of her award-winning cakes framed as posters would decorate the shiny white walls. And the man to provide exactly what she needed would be meeting her for brunch on Saturday. Would he be surprised?

As her thoughts turned to Mathew, her cell phone rang. She checked caller ID and answered immediately. "Hello there!"

"Holly! I walked! I walked today!" Amanda squealed.

Tears flooded Holly's eyes. "That's the best news I've ever heard."

"Come see me. Soon I'll be standing in the kitchen, not using that hunky old chair."

"You practice up. I'm going to call Miss Carol and ask if I can make the pirate cake tomorrow. Will you be able to help?"

"Of course, silly. It's not like I can walk away from here."

"Not yet, Amanda. But very soon."

After she ended the call, Holly folded her hands in front of her on the table. The bulbous thumb made her hand look comical. But it had been a sign. Something that set her life in a new direction.

Gratitude washed through her. How had she managed to have the best people in her life? Clara had her back and her future. Lamar's support had brought her to this crossroad and showed her which road to take. Sweet Amanda gave her hope. As much as she encouraged the young girl, that same child encouraged her with her tenacity to heal. Baking was a labor of love, the focus of her life, yet the thought of a relationship...with Mathew? Even if they became only friends, that would be a blessing in her life.

But could she dare dream for more?

Chapter Seven

"I'm thrilled Miss Carol agreed to allow me to host the pirate cake birthday party early," Holly told Amanda as Lamar unpacked the few supplies they needed to finish decorating the cake. While she usually handled all the decorating at Pineapple Place, today, given her disadvantaged thumb, the cake was complete minus last-minute decorating touches. All due to Lamar working through the wee hours of the morning to make it possible.

After Amanda's decorations were placed on the ship, the party started. Everyone *oohed* and *aahed* over the cake. The birthday boys gathered to cut and serve. Holly stood back, soaking up the joy from the faces of the kids and the parents. Her contribution to them might be small given the health issues they faced; however, she had brought them smiles. That warmed her heart.

"Chef Holly." Amanda hobbled over on crutches. A thin rope trailed behind her. "I have a game for you."

"Me? A game?"

"Every pirate has treasure, right?"

Holly nodded.

"Instead of a treasure map, you must follow the rope to find your treasure." Amanda beamed. Her eyes glinted with mischief.

"Aye aye, Captain!" Holly saluted, her bulbous thumb bumping her forehead, and then she took the rope from Amanda. "Let's find treasure, Matey."

Miss Carol stood at the opening between the dining area and the large lobby. Smiling, she clapped. "Good luck!"

Rolling up the rope as she walked, Holly followed the lead. A niggling of apprehension bloomed. Surprises, especially public ones, made her skittish. But she couldn't possibly say "no" to Amanda.

She wound her way through the lobby, down a hallway, and then back again. The rope continued to the large tree house at the far end of the lobby, a realistic structure with an elevator inside. The rope wrapped around the tree house, then back toward the front door. More people had gathered near the threshold to cheer her on.

"Clara? What are you doing here?" Holly asked.

"Focus," Amanda insisted, still hobbling beside her. "You're going to be surprised, Chef Holly."

The rope disappeared beneath a closed door to a conference room. The window in the door had been covered, preventing any sneak peeks inside. Holly turned when Clara and Lamar came up the hallway. Raising an eyebrow, she caught each of their gazes. They shrugged.

"Open the door. Step inside," Amanda instructed.

After turning the knob, Holly pushed open the door. The end of the rope was tied to an easel near the window. A sheet covered it—the treasure? Mathew stood beside it. She smiled. His grin tickled her heart. This wasn't a happenstance meeting.

"Hello, Chef Holly." Mathew bowed with a flourish as though she were royalty. "Please come closer. Miss Amanda has a treasure for you."

Holly glanced at Amanda who blushed and reached for her hand.

"Chef," the girl said. "Please remove the sheet. Your treasure awaits."

Glancing at each of the faces in the room, Holly shrugged, crossed the space, and tugged on the sheet.

"Oh. Wow!"

In poster-size living color, an image of her princess castle cake took up the foreground. She and Amanda tossed sugar sprinkles into each other's mouths. The sugary bits had been manipulated to look like tiny stars. The smiles on their faces shone at least a thousand watts bright. Holly's chest tightened. She swallowed. Surprise and joy flooded her.

She glanced at Mathew, who winked.

What she noticed first in the poster was the cake. Then the smiles on the faces in the photograph. Taking a step closer, she had to look hard to see the scar on the side of her face.

"Know what I see?" Amanda asked.

Still too moved to speak, Holly waved her hand for Amanda to continue.

"Love-light of the heart."

Fighting tears, Holly scooped Amanda into a hug. Her crutches fell to the floor. As she hugged the young girl, Clara, Lamar, and Mathew joined in.

"Group hug!" Clara shouted.

Holly's eyes misted more. When the others stepped away, she set Amanda back on her feet, and Mathew helped the girl settle onto her crutches again.

"Thank you." She wiped her tears. "This gift… I treasure it. You can't know what this means to me." She hugged Clara and Lamar.

As she moved in Mathew's direction, Clara said, "Amanda, why don't we go snag another piece of cake? I think the chef and the photographer have some business to discuss."

Holly waited until she was alone with Mathew. "You were right." She stood in front of the easel and gazed at the poster.

Mathew stood next to her, his shoulder so close they almost touched.

"You're a tough sell. I'm glad this didn't shock you or put you off."

She turned to him. "I have a question for you."

Mathew's eyebrows lifted. "Yes."

"I need to know how much you charge for something like this. I'm opening my own bakery—that's confidential right now—and I want cake posters like this, frame and all, for the walls."

His expression turned pensive.

"What's wrong?" Holly asked.

This time he furrowed his brow. "My 'yes' was to answer the question I thought you were going to ask me."

"I'm not following."

Her gaze shifted when Mathew reached for her hand and held it in his. "I've been waiting for you to ask *me* out."

Surprise widened her eyes. Butterflies danced in her stomach. Had she heard him correctly? Her mouth dried and she swallowed, hanging on his every word.

"I didn't want to push," he continued. He smiled as his thumb made circles on the top of her hand. "Which is why I asked you to brunch. The reason—just a ruse."

Holly linked arms with Mathew. "Mr. Roberts, I think we need to return to the party. However, if you have a few minutes afterward, I have another question I'd like to ask." They strode out of the conference room.

"And Chef Everett, my answer is 'yes,' if the question is about dinner tonight."

The butterflies in her stomach danced more. "Seems I'm saying 'yes' to quite a few new things." She chuckled.

Amanda was right.

You really can see the love-light of someone's heart. It illuminates a person's entire life.

Somehow, Mathew had captured hers in a photograph for her to see.

And her life truly mirrored her art—both filled with layers of love.

The End

Linda's Carrot Cake with Orange Glaze

Dry Ingredients:

2 cups sifted flour
2 teaspoons baking powder
2 teaspoons baking soda
2 teaspoons cinnamon
1 teaspoon salt

Wet ingredients:

1 cup salad oil
2 cups granulated sugar
4 eggs
Plus: 3 cups grated raw carrots and 1.5 cups chopped pecans or walnuts

Directions
Preheat oven to 325 degrees. Oil a 10-inch tube pan with butter or shortening spray product.

Sift together dry ingredients into a bowl.

In a second, larger bowl, combine oil and sugar. Mix well. Add eggs, one at a time. Mix thoroughly after each egg.

Slowly combine dry ingredients into the wet mixture. Once incorporated, add carrots and mix. Then add pecans.
Pour into oiled pan. Bake at 325 degrees for about 1 hour & 10 minutes. Check with a skewer (metal or bamboo or wooden) to ensure center is done.

After cake is cooled, remove from pan. Take a skewer and gently poke holes in the cake. This will allow the Orange Glaze to dribble down into the cake.

ORANGE GLAZE:

1/4 cup cornstarch
1 cup extra-fine granulated sugar
1/2 teaspoon salt
1 teaspoon fresh lemon juice
2 tablespoons of grated orange peel
1 cup fresh squeezed orange juice
2 tablespoons of butter

Combine sugar and cornstarch in saucepan. Add juices slowly and stir until smooth. Add remaining ingredients. Once all ingredients are combined, cook over low heat until thick and glossy. Spread on cooled cake.

Linda Joyce

Amazon Best-Selling author and multiple RONE Award Finalist Linda Joyce writes contemporary romance and women's fiction featuring assertive females and the men who can't resist them. She lives with her very patient husband in a house in metro Atlanta run by a fifteen-year-old canine named General Beauregard who believes they are his pets. Linda's a closet artist who paints with a brush, yet longs to finger paint but hates getting her hands messy. She's addicted to Cajun food and sushi. Linda will deny she only leaves the house once a week and only then to get criticism from two other authors.

Learn more about Linda at her website: www.linda-joyce.com

Mississippi Catfish

Constance Gillam

Acknowledgments

A special thanks to Linda Joyce, Marilyn Baron, Melissa Klein, Rachel Jones, and Ciara Knight for giving me the opportunity to share a book project with them.

Connie Gillam

Chapter One

Spring 1931

The train's whistle rumbled through Vonie Baldwin's body as she fidgeted on the railroad platform in Vicksburg, Mississippi. She and Aunt Sadie waited under the shade of the station house, seeking relief from the already baking sun.

"Bertha made that coat?"

"Yes, ma'am."

Her aunt grunted, one eyebrow climbing toward her hairline.

At the mention of her mother's name, Vonie fought the tears that made her aunt's face blur. Instead of crying, she stroked the soft fabric of the fur-trimmed wrap. Even though the coat was much too heavy for the Mississippi heat, she loved it. It was the last thing her mama made for her before she died.

"That's your grandpa," her aunt said, pointing toward a tall, dark-skinned man who moved ghostlike in and out of the train's steam towards them. Vonie had never met her grandfather. She met her aunt Sadie for the first time when she'd come to Chicago for her mama's funeral.

"This here is Vonie," Aunt Sadie said when her grandpa reached them.

He stared down at her with her father's dark eyes, then he turned to Aunt Sadie. "Where's her things?"

She nodded toward the lone suitcase at Vonie's feet. "That's it. Pretty fancy, if you ask me."

Vonie's mother had painted pink and yellow flowers on the outside of the case. Her mama had made everything look so pretty. Vonie blinked several times. She wouldn't cry. She promised her father she'd be a good girl for her grandfather.

"Well, let's get goin'. The cotton ain't gonna plant itself."

The two of them followed him through the crowd and out to the street where a horse hitched to a wooden wagon waited.

The horse's ears twitched, fighting off the flies that buzzed around its head.

"You need me to drop you off?" Grandpa asked Aunt Sadie.

The woman shook her head. "Tom's here." She nodded to a wagon a ways down the unpaved street.

Vonie's grandfather lifted her and placed her on the bare wooden seat. He smelled of sweat and old man.

Without a word of goodbye to her aunt, Grandpa Baldwin pulled himself up beside her and picked up the leather straps tied around the horse's head.

"Giddy up." He whipped the straps until the horse started moving.

Vonie gripped the wooden bench, afraid she'd slide off and land in the middle of the road. Her teeth clattered together as the horse clip-clopped down the dusty, bumpy street. They quickly left behind the train station and the flat-face buildings and moved out onto an open road with nothing but trees as far as her eyes could see.

The sun beat down on her head. She felt the dampness under her hat. Under her coat, her dress clung to her body. Back home in Chicago, the bulbs her mother planted last fall were just beginning to poke their green shoots up through the cold soil. In some places, like Mrs. Carter's yard, there were still traces of snow.

"Take that coat off." Her grandfather's voice could rip the bark off a tree. It made her stomach ache. Not looking at him, she tried to unbutton her coat, but her fingers wouldn't work.

"Whoa." He pulled back on the reins, and the animal stopped. Pushing her useless fingers out of the way, he unbuttoned her coat and tossed it into the back of the wagon. The coat with its big blue buttons and dark trim landed among the many sacks. Tears pricked the back of her eyes when a fine layer of white dust settled over the coat. Remembering her father's warning, she clutched her fingers in her lap and said nothing. They were off again. She was cooler, but her rear end suffered mightily.

Just as she started to nod off from the heat and lack of sleep, they turned down another dusty road—this one bumpier than the last one. A fence made of twisted wire separated the road from the field. Up ahead a small wooden house came into view. The roof was gray and shining, and two columns held up the porch roof. One lone chair sat on the porch. As they drew closer, the porch seemed to lean in one direction and the rest of the house in the other.

Her grandfather stopped the horse. "Get down."

Vonie eyed the drop from the bench to the ground. How could she get off this wagon?

There weren't any steps.

Her grandfather mumbled something under his breath. Wrapping the reins around a piece of wood that rose up between the wagon and the horse's rear, he jumped off the wagon. He came around to her side, gripped her around her waist, and lifted her from her seat.

"Go into the house."

She did as he ordered.

The house smelled of fried meat. Her stomach growled. She hadn't eaten since early this morning.

Once her eyes adjusted to the darkness, she could make out a small fireplace to the left of the door, a bed in the far corner, and a dirt floor. A table with a bench on both sides sat in the middle of the room. A pair of men's overalls hung from a hook next to the bed.

One bed. Where would she sleep? She still stood in the middle of the room when her grandfather stomped into the house.

"Lost time going into Vicksburg. Need to get back into the fields." He went to the table and unwrapped a piece of burlap. Inside was a large piece of cornbread. He broke off a chunk and bit into it.

"Get out of your fancy clothes and cook up something for our dinner." Bits of cornbread flew out of his mouth. "Should be eggs in the henhouse, and there's milk in the root cellar." He dusted his hands on his pants after cramming the last of the cornbread into his mouth. "I'll be back at sundown."

He disappeared through the open door before Vonie could get the courage to tell him she couldn't cook.

****

From the shade of a large leafy tree, Vonie watched the children play tag. They weaved in and out of the tables being set up by their parents after the Sunday service. Tables groaned with fried chicken, greens, yams, and cake. Her stomach grumbled. She hadn't eaten a decent meal all week. But neither had her grandpa. When she'd told him the first night she couldn't cook, she feared he would drop over dead. Her gaze sought his tall, thin form. He talked with his daughter near the church's wooden steps.

Vonie's Sunday dress clung to her body. Her mama had made the dress for a spring day in Chicago, not the wet blanket heat of Mississippi. When she thought of the heat inside the church, she stepped farther back into the shade and coolness of the tree. People had squeezed into the small building for service until if one person sweated then the one next to them got wet. The only thing that came through the open windows was flies.

The smell of crispy chicken drew her out of the shade toward the food, but shyness kept her from going to the table. She walked toward her grandpa. His back was stiff, his voice low.

"—want you to take her," he said as Vonie drew near.

"I can't. I—" Aunt Sadie caught sight of Vonie, and her mouth clamped shut.

Her grandfather turned. His lips tightened, and his face crunched up into a frown. "Let's get some food." Vonie didn't know if he spoke to her or her aunt, but she fell in behind him.

Later that day, back at the farm, Vonie beat off the chickens. Their feathers floated all around her like a snowstorm. One of the hens flew at her head. She threw up her arm to protect her face and got pecked on the hand instead. They hated her, especially the redheaded leader of the bunch. She thought about the puckered scowl on her aunt's face. That woman hates me, too.

But it didn't matter who hated her. Today she had to get eggs. She didn't want to see tomorrow morning at breakfast the look that had been on her grandfather's face all week.

A short time later, she marched out of the henhouse with two eggs in her basket. She placed them in the cellar. For breakfast tomorrow, she'd make scrambled eggs. She knew how to make eggs. Her mother had taught her. She would give them both to her grandpa so he wouldn't be angry with her anymore.

Wiping the sweat from her forehead and the blood off her hands, she stared at the woods across from the cotton field. Its dark coolness called to her.

She glanced around the corner to the porch. Mouth hanging open, her grandpa slept, the Bible open on his lap. If she angled through the field, she would be out of his sight long enough to shoot across the road to the woods and not be seen. Keeping his relaxed body in her sights, she crept past the porch and tiptoed through the field, mindful of the baby plants pushing their heads through the soil. Vonie expected at any moment to hear her grandpa's voice shouting her name.

Silence wrapped its arms around her as soon as she stepped among the tall, slender pines. A slight breeze caused the trees to sway, sending a shower of yellow dust floating to the ground. Vonie coughed as she trudged through the thick bed of dry pine needles. She walked, enjoying the shade and cooler temperature. Her father had promised he'd come for her in a couple of months. She hoped he would come soon. She missed the Saturday night dancing she and her parents did in front of the phonograph.

The tinkling of water intruded on her daydream. Up ahead, she could see a break in the trees. She moved slowly through the thick pines until she reached the edge of the woods. A boy sat on the ground, his feet dangling over the edge of a drop-off.

He drew back his arm, and a line flew over his shoulder, and then, with a snap of his wrist, the line sailed out over the ravine, hitting the water with a splat. "Come on. Come on."

He didn't wear a shirt, and his shoulders were hunched beneath his brown skin.

Enjoying the peacefulness of the woods and the lapping of the water against the bank, she watched him fish for several minutes.

"Dag nab it." He jumped up and stomped up and down the creek edge. With a start, she realized he was a white boy. His bone-thin lips were tight. His hands balled into fists. Short brown hair stood up like he'd tried to pull it out of his head. His blue eyes were startlingly bright against his sun-browned skin.

She moved forward to get a better look at him. A twig cracked beneath her shoe. His head jerked in her direction. She froze. Her heart thumped wildly against her chest. He seemed to look directly at the spot where she stood. After a long few minutes, his shoulders relaxed, and he picked up his pole again. She released the breath she'd been holding.

This time, when he threw out his piece of string, within minutes the pole bent. His arm worked hard to draw the string back to him. He tugged and tugged until a big fish exploded out of the water, sunlight glittering off its wriggly body.

"Whoopee."

She smiled at his excitement. Tiny bumps danced across her skin. She'd ask her grandpa if he had a fishing pole, and tomorrow she'd come back and fish from this very spot. Maybe if she caught a fish the size of the one the boy had pulled from the water, she would make her grandpa happy. If he was happy, he wouldn't send her to live with his sourpuss daughter.

****

Sweat trickled down Green Thompson's bare back and into his pants. He itched and wanted to dive into the muddy water to cool off but didn't want to scare away the fish.

The eye of one dead carp stared back at him from its position next to him on the bank. That was his yield from last night's traps. Usually the traps had at least four nice size fish—enough meat for six mouths, if his older brothers didn't go back for seconds.

Just as he was about to cast his line back into the creek, snapping twigs and rustling dry pine needles sounded behind him. He gritted his teeth but didn't turn his head. His brothers liked to sneak up on him and try to scare the bejesus out of him. They usually sounded like a herd of bulls stampeding toward the feed, not like mice scurrying in the underbrush.

"Come on out. I heard ya."

When they didn't rush him, he turned his head to shout again. Standing just outside the line of pines, a skinny colored girl with a fishing pole watched him.

Green looked at the pole and then back at her. Ain't no way she was gonna fish in his spot. "Git."

When she didn't move, he picked up a pine cone and threw it in her direction. It only hit her because she dodged it. He'd aimed to miss. With his sisters, just the hint he was going to throw something sent them scurrying away.

But this girl, about the size of the older of his two sisters, didn't budge. So what was he going to do now? He didn't fight girls. He didn't fight no one. According to his brothers, that was his problem. He stared at her long and hard, giving her the look he sent his sisters when he couldn't stand their whining and begging any longer. It didn't work on this one. He would have said she dug in her toes, but she wore shoes, which was strange. No one wore shoes in the summer. They saved them for school, if they went to school, which he only did once or twice a year.

He turned his back to the girl. He'd run out of tricks. Recasting his line, he decided not to pay her any attention.

After several minutes, she edged past him and took up a spot down the creek bed.

The pull on his line drew his attention away from the girl and onto what tugged at his pole. The bamboo stick bent until he thought it might snap. After jumping up, he dug his bare toes into the dry soil. His trembling arms strained to hold on to the catch. The pull on the pole suddenly released, sending him crashing to the ground.

As he lay stunned, a shadow moved over him. The colored girl stood within touching distance. She stared at the ground. He raised himself up on his elbows. An old waterlogged boot, its tongue hanging out like a tired hound dog's, lay near his feet.

She studied the boot and then glanced at his face. "Wonder where the other one is?"

His anger evaporated like morning mist off the creek. He'd expected laughter, not a question asked with such a serious tone. She was an odd bird with her two braids framing either side of her nut-brown face. Who cared where the other boot was?

"Don't know." He stood and picked up his fishing pole. At least, it hadn't broken. From the slant of the sun, he still had a couple of hours to reel in some carp or catfish.

She didn't move back to her spot but watched him as he baited his line. "What are you doing?"

Kneeling on the ground, he glanced up. She didn't talk like anybody he knew. Her honey-colored eyes watched his fingers.

She pointed at the worms. "Why are you putting them on a hook?"

Green blew his irritation out through his mouth. Girls were all the same—dumb. "The fish like the worms." He stood. "What bait are you using?"

"None."

He closed his eyes. Well, let her fish with nothing on her pole. When she got tired of not catching anything, she'd go away. He smiled at the thought. Walking back to the creek edge, he tossed his line in and prayed.

"I'm Vonie. What's your name?"

Green breathed deeply, and then he let the air out to the count of ten. He didn't answer.

"I live back through the woods."

He concentrated on the water, waiting for tiny bubbles, which meant a fish was just below the surface.

"I'm from Chicago, living with my grandpa, Thurman Baldwin."

She kept babbling, and Green kept his attention on the water. Her words faded into the background as he let his mind wander. What if he didn't catch anything? He hoped his rabbit snares had snagged something. His Ma and brothers wouldn't be too happy with a meatless dinner.

****

Later Green trudged through the sumac trees and the scruffy underbrush to avoid their pasture land that lay just beyond the house. Two small carps hung from his belt loop. One lone rabbit carcass made the burlap sack thump hollowly against his leg. He hoped his sister had put beans on for dinner; otherwise, they would all go to bed hungry tonight.

Lottie, his five-year-old sister, sat on the porch, combing the hair on her corncob doll. Singing off key, she fussed over the doll as though it were a real baby.

Green sniffed the air. Without looking at him, she said, "Sissie didn't cook nothing. She said you were gonna catch a bunch of fish."

Sissie was the older of his two sisters. At eight, she fed the two laying hens and the one pig, kept the house and porch swept, cooked, and kept an eye on Lottie. At twelve, he was right smack-dab in the middle between the girls and his two older brothers.

"Well, I didn't. So she better think of something quick, or we're going to starve." Green hated to admit the blame was on him, and he'd let his mother down.

A flutter of cloth caught his attention. Sissie stood in the open door of their two-room cabin, batting away the flies that buzzed around her head. She stepped out onto the porch and pinned him like a bug with her sour expression. "It's too late to cook beans." Her eyes darted toward the garden patch on the side of the cabin. Seedlings the height of his middle finger struggled in the dried cracked soil. Nothing in the garden was big enough or plentiful enough to feed six people.

"We got potatoes still, don't we?" Green asked.

"A few. Don't know if they're enough for all of us. What you got in that sack?"

He glanced down at the burlap bag attached to his waist. "Rabbit." He held up the two small fish. "And carp."

Sissie came off the porch. "Lottie, go down to the well and get some water." Turning toward him, she said, "Skin the rabbit and scale and cut the fish. I'll throw the meat in a pot with potatoes and whip up some skillet bread. You hunt up some wild onions."

Relieved the weight of his failure had been taken off his shoulders, Green didn't put up a fuss about her bossing him around.

Later that evening, Billy, Green's oldest brother, empty bowl clutched in his meaty fingers, stood over the cast-iron pot.

"They ain't no more food." He glared at everyone sitting around the table as though there were a thief among them.

"Sit down, Billy," their mother said. She swept a lock of white-streaked yellow hair off her face. Her faded blue eyes swept around the table, daring anyone to say anything about the lack of food. Her gaze settled on his other brother, Sam, who was too busy glaring at Green to notice his mother's anger. Green buried his face in his bowl. Tomorrow, he wouldn't come home until he had enough meat to feed his family.

Chapter Two

The sun at Vonie's back was setting fast as she rushed through the woods. Fear and frustration tightened her stomach in spasms. She'd had visions of returning home with so many fish she couldn't carry them. Instead, she returned home empty-handed—she'd even left that makeshift fishing pole back at the creek.

Everything had gone wrong, from the string tied to the pole being too short, to falling into the creek. The boy had made it all look so easy. He hadn't shown up for her to ask for his help. Well, maybe he wouldn't have given her his help, but she could have watched him and learned.

"Vonie." Her grandpa's rough voice echoed through the woods.

She stopped, heart slamming against her ribs. The birds had stopped singing at the sound of her grandpa's angry voice.

"Vonie."

Maybe she could sleep here for the night. Something rustled behind her. She whirled, but the darkening woods appeared empty. Wisps of air skittered across her neck.

She burst out of the woods as though her dress were on fire. Her grandpa had moved from the porch to the fields and watched her run toward him. When she came to a stop in front of him, he said, "Where. Have. You. Been?" The words shot from his mouth like hail to bruise her spirit.

She opened her mouth to reply, but the words stuck in her throat, only a rush of air escaping. She pointed behind her. She didn't even have her pole to help give truth to her story.

He turned away and started back toward the house. One word floated back to her, "Sadie."

"I went fishing." The words came out in a gush of fear. She ran to catch up with him.

Turning around, she ran backwards to keep level with his long angry stride. Her words didn't stop his progress toward the cabin or toward the wagon that would take her to her aunt Sadie's place.

She tripped over a root and fell on her rump. She barely felt it. She scrambled up to chase after her grandpa. She had to make him change his mind. Tears burned at the back of her eyes. "Wanted to fish for our dinner." The words came out in stops and stutters. He slowed and then stopped.

Hands on his hips, he towered over her. His eyes were dark as coal and just as hot. "Do you know what could happen when you are away from this place without me?" His chest rose and fell.

She shook her head. She knew there were things that lived in the woods, things that only came out at night. She'd felt their eyes on her when she'd been back there. "Animals?"

He blew out his breath and looked away from her. "Yes, animals. But not the four-legged kind. These walk on two legs, like you and me. I want you to stay out of the woods and away from the creek. You understand?"

Vonie nodded. She would have promised him her soul if it meant staying here and not going to her aunt's house. Her father's sister had said some hateful things about her mother. And her mother not even cold in her grave. Vonie didn't want to live with someone who mouthed unkind things about the dead or the living.

"Yes, sir."

He walked away from her. She trailed behind him, her feet dragging through the dirt, causing a small dust storm. The ache in her chest had nothing to do with going to her aunt Sadie's house. With that promise, she'd lost something. She couldn't put a name to it, but it hurt just the same.

****

Green checked the traps he'd set the night before—two medium-size catfish, better than yesterday but not as good as he'd hoped.

At midday the colored girl hadn't shown up. What was her name? Bonnie? No. It didn't matter. Maybe she'd lost interest. Good. He wouldn't have to run her off. He knew her grandfather. The mean-looking old man who, like Green's mother, also sharecropped for Mr. Durham. Durham had the big house up the road. Sometimes when his boys were back from college, they'd hang out with Billy and Sam. His brothers thought the Durham boys really liked them. Green knew better. His brothers were being used. When their pranks went bad, it was always Billy and Sam who got in trouble.

"I didn't catch anything yesterday."

Green's heart leapfrogged in his chest. The girl had crept up on him like a field mouse.

Dang. He hoped he'd seen the last of her. He fiddled with his lines, hoping his silence would drive her away.

"My grandpa would be very angry if he found me here."

She paused as though waiting for Green to say something. He had nothing to say to this strange girl with her city way of talking.

His silence didn't seem to bother her.

"I figure as long as I'm back before sunset he won't know I'm not at home."

Hope the plow doesn't break or he runs out of water.

Maybe her grandpa catching her away from home would be a good thing. The old man would take a belt to her hide. That would keep her away from his creek. It wasn't very Christian of him, but his mother gave him only one job—to make sure the family had meat on the table. He didn't want to let her down. His pa had let the family down when he left. Green wanted to be a better man than his father.

"My grandpa doesn't want me. He's going to send me to live with my aunt. But she doesn't want me either. I don't think she likes me."

The sadness in her voice caused Green to glance up from the trap he was tying to a tree. "Where's your ma and pa?"

Her gaze moved away from his to stare out over the water. Her brown eyes shimmered like his ma's did when she kissed the girls goodnight.

"My mother died last month. My father works on the railroad up in Chicago. He's gone most of the week."

"Oh." Green couldn't think of anything to say. He saw his mother every day. The thought of never seeing her again made his throat close up.

"What are you doing?"

"Setting traps."

"What are those?"

Green took a deep breath and let his irritation flow out with the release of air. "Strings I leave in the water overnight to catch fish."

Knowing the next word coming out of her mouth would be "why?" he answered before she could speak. "The best time to catch fish is around sunset and sunrise. I bait my strings and put them in the water in the evening. I got other chores and can't be out here all the time, so the traps help."

As he moved down the creek bank tying string to the overhanging trees, she followed him like his shadow. He was fine with that as long as she didn't talk. He stooped to open his bait bag. The squeal she let out hurt his ears.

"What are those?" She pointed at the bait in his hand.

"I done told you once. They're worms."

"But these are different. They're all black and wiggling and…and nasty."

She stepped back, getting too close to the edge of the creek. He'd enjoy seeing her fall in, but then he'd have to go in after her. Instead he moved farther away from the bank, knowing she'd follow.

He rolled his eyes. Dag. She was as dumb as his sisters. "They're a different kind of worm. They live on trees we got at our place. Catfish really like them."

"Yuck. I'm not eating catfish anymore."

She was in a dress again, her skinny brown legs like sticks. "Don't you have no pants?"

Frowning, she looked down at her legs. "Girls don't wear pants."

"My ma and sisters do. It keeps their legs from gettin' eat up." He pointed to the red welts on her legs. "Mosquitas."

Her fingers went to the red marks and started to scratch.

"Don't. You'll leave marks. Use some vinegar."

"Vinegar? Grandpa doesn't have vinegar. There's barely food to eat."

"Is that why you're trying to fish?" He didn't look at her but stared at the last trap. No one liked to admit there wasn't enough food to eat.

"Well…yeah. And if I make myself useful, maybe he won't send me away."

"How you gonna fish if you're not supposed to be here?"

For the first time, they looked each other in the eye. She looked away first. "I don't know. Plus, I'm not good at it. I didn't catch anything yesterday."

Green's lips twisted. It wouldn't kill him to teach her a thing or two about bait 'cause based on her reaction to the worms, it was a sure bet she hadn't used any yesterday.

"Put worms on the end of your hook."

"Worms? I can't—"

He walked away. Either she would, or she wouldn't.

****

Vonie propped open the door to the hot, smelly shed. She squinted until her eyes adjusted to the darkness. Then she began her search for a bag that would hold the worms she'd discovered while weeding the garden.

When she found what she needed, she dumped the seeds it contained in a dark corner, praying her grandpa wouldn't find them.

She weeded fast, and when she finished, she had half a bag of wiggly, disgusting worms in her sack. She took off for the creek. Along the way, she picked up her fishing pole, string, and hooks she'd hid in the woods earlier that morning.

When her grandpa saw the fish fried up big and flaky, he'd forgive her for disobeying him and would tell her she never had to leave.

She drew up short when she reached the water. Her stomach twisted like when she'd expected sweet potato pie for dinner and there wasn't any. She'd expected to see the boy, but he wasn't there.

Shedding her shoes and socks, she sank her toes into the warm soil. The dirt felt hot and strange between her toes. She'd held her breath as she reached into the sack and almost dropped the whole bag when the slimy things moved against her fingers. It took her several tries to get one worm on her hook. She threw the string out toward the center of the water just like the boy had done. Sitting on the creek bank with her feet hanging over the edge, she found some of that peace she'd seen in the boy's face a few days ago.

She'd almost fallen asleep when a mighty tug happened on the line. Her heart jumped into her throat, and her palms kept slipping on the pole. She had a fish, but what did she do now?

She took her eyes off the water and glanced toward the woods. Where was he? She didn't know what to do.

Vonie stood, holding tight to her stick. The water rippled violently as her fish tried to wiggle off the hook. Her arms were getting tired. She thought about how her grandpa's eyes would go from dark and cold to warm with love when she cooked this big fish up. She started running along the creek, trying to keep the fish from pulling her pole into the water. Just when she thought she couldn't hold on any longer, the pull on the line eased. She lifted the line straight out of the water. Her breath left her lungs in one sad gasp. There was no fish at the end of her line. The hook was there, but the worm was gone. She stared at the hook so long she began to see double.

Don't cry.

Clamping her teeth together, she dug her hands into the bag again and pulled out another big, fat worm. This time when she threw her string into the water, it took just a short while before something pulled on her line again.

Please.

This time the tug wasn't so strong. It took her five minutes to bring her catch to the bank. A small fish about the size of her father's palm stared up at her with a begging look in its eyes as its body wiggled weakly.

She couldn't keep it. But how would she get it off the hook to throw it back in the water? Biting her lip, she tried to gently remove the hook. It wouldn't give. She twisted first one way then another without success. She glanced down at the poor fish. It didn't move. She'd killed it.

****

As Green's bare feet trudged through dried pine needles, he prayed his traps held enough fish to make a decent meal. His rabbit snares were as empty as his belly had been last night.

His steps slowed as he reached the edge of the trees. Heat rushed into his face. The girl was back at his creek. He squinted, trying to see what she was doing. Curiosity got the best of him, and he moved closer. She was bent over something on the ground—a small carp.

"What ya doing?"

She turned a serious face up to him. "I was going to throw it back, but...but it's dead."

Green laughed. "How ya gonna cook 'em if they're still alive?" When he saw the tears in her eyes, he had the good sense to stop teasing. Her sad expression made him swallow a joke he'd heard from one of his brothers' friends about do-gooders.

Her small brown fingers were in the fish's mouth. He knew immediately what had happened. She had tried to remove the hook but didn't know how. And she was making a mess of it.

"Here, let me show you." He bent on one knee, stuck one finger in the carp's mouth, and gently removed the hook.

"So what are you gonna do? It's too late to throw it back."

"We could bury it," she whispered.

Green rolled his eyes. "Toughen up." His words were echoes of the ones his brother Billy shouted at him. He softened his tone, but couldn't soften the message. "If you gonna put fish on the table, the fish are gonna have to die."

He let her brood over that bit of wisdom and went to check his traps. From six lines he had three nice size catfish. Not great but enough to provide a better meal than the one they'd had last night. He needed to get back home to tell Sissie to cook up a mess of those turnips from the cellar.

As he walked back up the bank toward the girl, he considered for one brief moment letting her have one of the catfish. Naw. He was going soft. His brothers would never let him live that down if they found out.

"You can throw it back in the water. Let the creek be its grave."

She appeared to consider his words. After picking up the carp, she walked to the bank's edge. She closed her eyes, and her lips moved silently. She was praying.

Green's family didn't have much time for church or preachers or prayers. They worked seven days a week to put food on the table.

The girl tossed the dead carp into the creek. He couldn't see the water from his position behind her, but he imagined the carp sinking slowly into the muddy water. Shaking his head at the waste of good meat, he picked up his catch and turned to make his way back home.

"Will you teach me to fish?"

The softly spoken words made Green stop just before he stepped back into the woods. He cursed in his head. He'd learned to keep the words to himself 'cause his ma would have washed his mouth with lye soap if he'd spoken them out loud. No, he didn't want to teach her to fish. He didn't have time for her crazy ideas of burying perfectly good food. But when he opened his mouth to say no, yes floated out.

Chapter Three

The boy wasn't at the creek the next day when Vonie arrived. She shifted from one foot to the other. She couldn't do this without him, and she didn't have all day to wait. Her grandpa had watched her last evening like a rooster.

She eyed the woods on the opposite side of the clearing. His home must be in that direction.

The laughter in his voice yesterday had hurt her feelings. He'd made her feel like a baby. At ten-years-old, she wasn't a baby. She would keep any fish she caught. She'd have to confess to her grandpa what she'd been doing and suffer the consequences of her actions, her father's favorite phase when she'd been bad.

The idea of going through the woods again made her stomach hop like frogs in water. Before she could change her mind, she took off.

With every snap of a twig, her body jerked. The walk seemed to take forever. Finally, she spotted a house as the trees began to thin.

An awful screech—like cats fighting—made her stop. Her heart beat like a snare drum on one of her parents' favorite phonograph records. The sound kept going on and on. Curious about the source of the racket, Vonie stepped a little ways out of the woods and closer to the house.

A little girl with flyaway brown hair sat on the step that led up to a house similar to Vonie's grandpa's. She sang to scraps of what looked like corn husks. How could so much noise come out of one small person?

As though the girl heard Vonie's thought, she looked up and stared straight into Vonie's eyes.

Both of them froze. The girl was the first to break the spell. Turning her head, she called to someone inside the house. Vonie took a step back into the woods. She hoped the boy would appear, but she was ready to run if a grown-up did.

A bigger girl came out. This one stepped off the porch. Shading her eyes against the sun, she glared in Vonie's direction.

"Whatya want?" Her voice carried across the yard with the tone of a mother talking to a dim-witted child.

Vonie's already hot face flushed hotter. Maybe she didn't need the boy's help. She could teach herself how to fish. It might take a little longer, but she could do it. Without answering, she took another step back into the woods.

The younger girl walked over and said something to the older one. The older girl, without taking her eyes off Vonie, shook her head. The smaller of the two started walking toward Vonie.

"Lottie, come back here."

Clutching one of her cornstalk dolls in her hand, Lottie ignored the order and continued walking. When she stood within a few feet of Vonie, she could see the girl had the boy's bright blue eyes. The girls must be his sisters.

"You don't look different," Lottie said.

Vonie couldn't stop the frown that puckered her face. Different?

"Sam and Billy said colored people are different from us."

Vonie's body jerked. Maybe this hadn't been such a good idea. She'd had very little dealings with white folks outside the grocer at the end of their street back in Chicago. Their neighborhood was filled with other colored people from Mississippi and Alabama, like her mother and father.

While she'd listened to the girl with the cornstalk dolls, the other sister had come closer. The girls watched her with more curiosity than meanness in their eyes.

"Is your brother here?" Vonie asked. Her voice came out in a whisper. She wiped her sweaty hands on her dress.

"Billy—" Lottie's sister clamped a hand on her shoulder.

"What do you want with our brother?" the older sister asked.

Vonie cleared her throat, but the words still came out like the croak of a frog. "He was going to teach me to fish."

Lottie looked up at her sister. "She means Green."

"I know who she means," the other girl snapped. She turned her cornflower blue eyes on Vonie. "He ain't here."

"Okay—" A flicker of motion made Vonie glance toward the house. A broad-shouldered man leaned casually against the one of the post, watching them.

Vonie suddenly needed to pee. She backed up farther. "I'll be going."

"What are you girls doin' out there?" the man shouted.

"That's Billy," the older sister said. "You'd better go. Now."

Vonie didn't need anyone to tell her twice.

She turned and ran.

****

Green side-eyed the girl sitting on the bank next to him. Breath slower, the scared look had left her face. She seemed calmer than earlier when she'd burst out of the woods. It didn't escape his notice she'd come from the direction that led to his house.

He'd shown her how to bait her hook and how to cast her string out toward the middle of the water. Midday wasn't the best time to fish, but she had to get back home before her grandfather returned from the field.

Her voice broke the silence and probably scared away half the fish. "My name is Vonie Elizabeth Baldwin."

He sighed. Why'd she have to speak? "I'm Green. Green Thompson."

"I met your sisters."

So she had been at his house. He wondered why. "I figured as much."

"You're lucky."

Was she trying to talk the fish to death? "How come?"

"You've got sisters."

Green only grunted. There were times when he'd gladly trade Sissie and Lottie for a pack mule.

"And I think I saw your daddy."

Green sat up straighter. His heart banged in his chest so hard he couldn't catch his breath. "You saw my pa?"

Her gaze stayed locked on the water, but a frown wrinkled up her forehead. "I think it was your father—big, hair almost yellow as the sun."

Green's body collapsed in relief. "My brother, Billy."

His brother was a bully to anyone smaller and weaker. He also didn't like colored people, which might explain why she'd burst out of the woods like the demons from hell were after her.

Green's hand tightened on his pole. "Did he say anything to you?"

"I ran before he came off the porch."

"Good."

She had the sense to not say another word about his crazy family and even crazier brother.

The sun peeped through the pines on its slow journey toward the day's end.

"Whatcha going to say to your grandpa when you bring fish home?"

Green could have sworn she stopped breathing she went so still. Her eyes filled with tears.

"I don—" Her body stiffened, and her gaze flew to her pole. "I got a fish."

He abandoned his pole and came to stand close to her. He drew her to her feet. "Don't pull too hard. Let him have his head."

Her line dipped once, twice in the muddy water. Each time she was dragged closer to the end of the creek.

"Hold steady. He'll get tired, and you can bring him in." He could tell by the scowl on her face she didn't know what he meant.

He put a steadying hand on her pole. The tightness and the pull told him she had a nice size fish. "Easy, easy."

"I can't—"

"You can." He could hear her fear in the wildness of her voice and the fast rise and fall of her shoulders.

When it seemed she would lose the pole, he put both his hands over hers. His arms trembled by the time they brought the catfish onto the bank. Not the biggest he'd seen, but a respectable size, probably two pounds. He grinned at her. "It's a nice one."

She glanced at the flopping fish and then at Green. "Now what?"

"We gut it."

She shuddered and swallowed several times. He knew the signs. She was about to puke. He had to take her mind off fish innards.

"You take it home to fry up for supper."

She mumbled something he couldn't understand. "What?"

"I can't cook."

He stared at her in disbelief. "All girls can cook."

"Well, I can't." Her eyes flashed. He almost smiled. This was the first time he'd seen some spirit in her. Maybe not the first time. She had been pretty stubborn about fishing at his creek.

It would be blasphemy to allow her to ruin this fine piece of fish. He glanced at the sun. Maybe three solid hours before full-on darkness. "Come on."

He led her back through the woods to his house. When they reached the clearing, he said, "Stay here."

At the house, he made sure neither Billy nor Sam was around, and then he went in search of Sissie. He found her weeding the garden, Ma's big floppy hat on her head. "I want you to teach Vonie how to fry fish."

Hand on her hat, she rose from a crouched position. "Who's Vonie?"

"The girl I met at the fishin' hole."

Sissie got that look when something didn't sit right with her. One side of her face crinkled until her left eye almost closed. "You mean that colored girl?"

Somewhere in the last day or two Green had stopped noticing the color of Vonie's skin. She was just that irritating girl who wanted to fish in a place he considered his.

"Yeah, that's her. Will you help her?"

His sister stared at him with her sharp blue eyes until he squirmed.

"Why are you helping her?"

He didn't know. It wasn't because he liked her. He shrugged. "It's the Christian thing to do." His words sounded more like a question than a fact.

Sissie shook her head. "You're a heathen. Rev. Jonas even said so."

"Well, maybe I'm changing."

She pursed her lips, staring him down. "I'll do it this one time. And if she don't learn, don't ask me to keep trying."

"Thanks." But his sister had marched out of the garden, heading for the woods where Vonie waited.

****

"And you said Mrs. Thompson brought over this here fish?"

Vonie's grandpa stuffed more food in his mouth as he talked around the best fried fish she'd ever tasted—besides her mother's.

"Yes, sir," she lied.

Forcing Vonie to watch, Green had cut the fish open and pulled out the innards, then sliced it. Sissie had rolled the catfish in cornmeal and egg and fried it in animal fat.

"Hmmm. Don't see much of her. Always seems to be in the fields. I'll have to go around after church and say thanks."

Vonie's heart fluttered like a bird caught in a cage. "I—I thanked her. Like you said, she's busy and you're busy…"

Her grandpa stopped eating and eyed her. Vonie forced her food down a suddenly dry throat.

"I know it's different here from Chicago, and my boy couldn't wait to get out of here, but there's beauty in Mississippi."

"Yes, sir." Why he was telling her this? She listened politely because her father would expect it. But honestly, this was the most godforsaken state she'd ever seen—not that she'd been in many.

"There's beauty, and there's danger. Take Helen Thompson's boys."

Vonie sat up straighter.

"Those fellas are the devil. They get in more trouble than you can imagine. The only reason they're not in jail now is 'cause Mr. Durham needs them to work their mama's land."

Vonie thought about the big, yellow-haired man Green had called Billy. She didn't need Green or her grandpa telling her this Thompson was evil. She felt his meanness clear across the yard. And the way Green had spoken about his brother told Vonie he knew his brother was evil.

"I know Ms. Thompson has girls about your age, but don't go visiting. Don't want you anywhere near those boys."

Vonie wanted to tell him not all the Thompson boys were bad. But she didn't dare say anything about Green because her grandpa would want to know how she knew him.

"I want you right near the house in case there's trouble. You understand, girl?"

"Yes, sir."

He rose, dusting crumbs off his overalls. "Come Sunday maybe we can go by Sadie's place, and she can introduce you to some of the girls around there. Would you like that?"

"Yes, sir." Vonie wanted to be near her aunt like she wanted to drive a nail into her foot.

"Good." He walked to the door. "Clean up and get yourself to bed. Another day tomorrow."

As Vonie scraped the scraps into the slop bucket, the scent of tobacco floated into the cabin. She covered the bucket with a cloth to keep out the flies and placed it by the door. Tomorrow morning she'd feed the slops to the one pig her grandpa owned.

Her grandpa had created a little area for her in the corner of the cabin. Two large burlap bags had been thrown across a rope secured by nails to opposite corners of the cabin. From the shed, he'd brought out an old cot that smelled of damp, dark places and provided a sheet that he said came from Sadie's place.

The one good thing about her space was it included the only window in the cabin. So at night, like now, she could lie on her bed and stare up at the stars and hope her mother was looking down on her from heaven.

Chapter Four

The letter burnt a hole in Green's pocket. His mother and brothers couldn't read, so he had tried to decipher the letter's meaning. He stumbled over some of the words and downright didn't know the others.

The sun beat on his bare shoulders as he gathered his catch from the traps. He glanced toward the woods, wondering when Vonie would show up. From the way she rambled on about her life in Chicago and the citified way she spoke, he figured she could read. He prayed she could read. His family didn't get many letters, so this one must be important.

He heard the crunch of leaves and dried pine needles coming from the woods and turned, hoping to see Vonie. Her face lit up when she spotted him. He couldn't stop the smile that crept over his face. Why was he so happy to see her? Relief because she'd be able to read the letter? Maybe, because it sure wasn't to listen to her chatter and chase all the fish away.

"I brought some more bait." Grinning, she held up a burlap bag, but then she caught sight of his catch. "You leaving?"

"I can stay for a little while, but I need to check my other traps soon."

Her mouth drooped. "Oh."

He dug his toes into the soil and stared down at his footprints. Glancing at her from under his lashes, he asked, "Can you read?"

She nodded. "Can you?"

"No." He rushed on before he could lose his nerve. He could fish, hunt with a gun and a crossbow, swim, and use an axe, so telling her he couldn't read didn't sit well with him.

Reaching into his back pocket, he pulled out the folded letter. He brushed at the dirt that had found its way into the creases. "Will you read this?"

She took it from him, opened it, and he figured she started to read it silently.

"Would you read it out loud?"

"Dear Mrs. Thompson, this letter is to inform you that Abe's Grocery will no longer ex— extend you credit. You have 'til the end of this month to bring your bill cur...current." Vonie frowned. "I think that means pay him all the money you owe."

She continued reading. "Two dollars will be added to your remainder for each month you carry a balance. Sincerely, Abraham Brody."

A weight like a felled tree settled on Green's chest. No more credit? What would they do for flour and meal, and more importantly, ammunition?

With a worried expression on her face that matched his feelings, Vonie handed him back the letter. "Sorry."

Suddenly Green didn't feel like fishing. His mother, who carried such a heavy weight on her shoulders since his pa left, wouldn't be able to take any more. Her body, which had been so strong, now seemed weighed down by a big boulder on her back. Thirty-four was old, but she looked more like someone's grandma—even her hair had started to turn white.

"What are you going to do?" Vonie asked.

Green could only shrug. If Pa was here, he'd be able to talk to old Abe—man-to-man like. But he wasn't here, and Green didn't want him back. He, Billy, and Sam were the men of the house. They'd have to think of some way to satisfy the grocer.

****

The sweet smell of licorice and lemon drops usually snagged Green's attention. But today the big man behind the store's counter had Green's full attention. With his white beard, Mr. Brody looked like Santa but not as jolly. The old man bared his teeth at the two ladies at the counter, like he was smilin'. His daughter actually added up the ladies' purchases while he looked on. Mrs. Brody, who was also behind the counter, didn't join in the conversation between her daughter and the customers but kept her gaze on something out in the store.

Green's toes dug into the bottom of his shoes to keep his feet from slipping out when he walked. Sam's shoes were too big, but they were the only ones Green had. Sweat ran down his back and stained the one nice shirt he owned. The hand-me-down almost fit him.

He repeated the words he and Vonie had practiced yesterday. Good afternoon, Mr. Brody. I'm—

"What do you want in here, gal? You got money?"

Mrs. Brody's loud voice jerked Green out of his mental rehearsal. He followed the woman's gaze until he found Vonie standing almost hidden among the bolts of ugly colored cloth.

"Yes, ma'am."

Afraid he'd forget everything they'd practiced, he'd begged her to come. She'd agreed but almost changed her mind when she saw how they were going to get to town—old Betsy, his family's ten-year-old horse.

Now Vonie marched to the counter and showed Mrs. Brody the coins in her palm. The old lady harrumphed in her throat. "What do you want?"

Vonie pointed to the lemon drops.

"Next." Mr. Brody's voice boomed out like a crowd of people waited to see him rather than just Green.

Shuffling forward, he was careful to bring his shoes along with him. Wouldn't do for the shoes to fall off.

"Ah, Mr. Brody, I'm—"

"I know who you are. You're one of them rowdy Thompson boys."

"Ah, no, sir. I mean, yes, sir. I mean—" Green's face felt as hot as Sissie's cooking fires.

"What do you want?"

Green had caught the attention of everybody in the room—the women who'd been talking with Mr. Brody's daughter, Mr. And Mrs. Brody, and Vonie.

He swallowed, and the speech he and his friend worked on yesterday vanished from his pea-sized brain. In desperation, he shot her a quick glance. She mouthed the word fish.

He nodded and licked his lips. "I fish and hunt…"

The grocer's lips tightened. Green stumbled over the speech in his hurry to get the words out before he lost Mr. Brody's interest. "I was wondering…"

"Mind your business, gal," Mrs. Brody said to Vonie as she handed over the bag. "Now git."

"I'm a good fisherman. I hunt rabbits. Sometimes I get lucky and get a turkey. I... I could bring them into the store, and you could sell them to your customers."

Mr. Brody opened his mouth. Green could tell by the frown on his big forehead and the deep breath he took that stuck out his broad chest the man was going to say no.

Green could sense the interest of the women who'd been at the counter before him. He turned to them. He'd do whatever it took to get Mr. Brody to agree. "I know these young ladies would like to have fresh catfish for their evening meal. Flaky, hot fish to serve their families."

Mr. Brody seemed to notice for the first time they'd drawn a small crowd. "Well, I don't know…"

Vonie still stood at the counter, her bag of lemon drops clutched in her hand. She beamed her approval. Puffed up by her encouragement, he continued to address Mr. Brody's customers. "Would you ladies be interested in fresh fish? If Mr. Brody's not, maybe I can deliver to your door."

Vonie had told him how her mother had ironed clothes for the grocer in their neighborhood to pay down the bill the family had run up. She'd suggested he give the grocer some of the meat he caught. He hadn't thought the plan would work. She'd come along to give him encouragement and make sure he didn't chicken out.

"Now wait a minute," Mr. Brody said. "I never said I wasn't interested. Maybe young Mr. Thompson and me can work something out."

****

Vonie swung her bag of lemon drops as she made her way through the woods toward the creek the next morning. She'd saved her candy to share with Green to celebrate yesterday's success. Mr. Brody had agreed to give Green a chance. Based on how well the meat sold each day would determine if Green could bring more. Mr. Brody would reduce the family bill by how much of the meat was sold each day. So each day had to be good.

She'd finished her chores quickly, so she could be at the creek early to help Green get as many fish as possible for the next day. If there were a lot of fish in the traps, his day would be set. If there were too few, he wouldn't have time to catch more, so she'd agreed to help him fish. She and her grandfather only needed one large fish a day. Green had said he'd give her any extra rabbits or small game he caught.

Vonie hated lying to her grandfather. She would have to tell him the truth about what she did when he was in the pasture. Would that be the end of her fishing days and her time with her new friend? Would her grandfather send her to live with Aunt Sadie? She prayed to God that wouldn't happen. But she had lied, no two ways around it.

She burst out of the woods with a smile on her face and her candy held up in offering. Her smile died, and her hand dropped. Green wasn't alone. Four men who stood around him in a circle turned toward her as she bumbled out of the woods.

"Well, Green, what do we have here?" She recognized the voice and the speaker. It was Green's brother Billy. Three other males watched with grins on their faces.

"Go home, Vonie." Green's words came out broken and strange.

His face and mouth were red and swollen. They'd been fighting. Four against one. Green's brothers had been fighting their own brother?

With a singsong voice, Billy said, "Yeah, go home, little Vonie."

Her heart beat so hard against her chest she couldn't breathe. These were the two-legged animals her grandfather warned her about. She wanted to run, but she didn't want to leave Green alone.

"Boo." One of the other boys stomped his feet at Vonie.

She took off running. Tears blurred her vision as she stumbled through the pine trees. She fell once and thought she heard someone behind her. Without turning around, she picked herself up and stumbled on. Her breath came in ragged gasps, and her legs wobbled like a newborn kitten.

She didn't run for the house but straight for the pasture where her grandfather plowed. She stomped on the tender shoots of cotton as she ran. Her grandfather, who'd dropped his plow, watched her race toward him. She threw herself at him. His body was hard, unbending. He didn't put his arms around her but allowed her to cry into his sweat-stained shirt.

"What happened?"

Now she'd have to tell him what she'd been doing. And as sure as the sun rose, she'd be gone in the morning. Gone to live at Aunt Sadie's house. She didn't want to leave her grandfather, and it wasn't because her aunt didn't like children. Her grandfather treated her like a young lady, not like a child.

He'd allowed her more freedom than she'd ever had before. Yes, she hadn't done right by that freedom, but he'd offered it. Now she'd have to face the consequences.

She dropped her arms and stepped back. She swiped at the tears, delaying the moment she'd see disappointment on his face.

"They're beating up Green."

Her grandfather frowned. "Who the Sam Hill is Green?"

"Green Thompson. He taught me to fish."

His body stiffened, and his frown deepened. "The fish we had for dinner the other night?"

For a moment, a sense of pride made her smile. But the glower on his face wiped the smile from hers. She nodded. "Green taught me to fish."

"You've been hanging around those white boys?" The thunder in his voice made her take a step back.

She almost said Green wasn't white, but she caught herself because he was white. She'd just forgotten that small fact.

"Just Green," she said in a small voice. "He's nice, and his sisters are nice. It's just his brothers…"

Her grandfather peered into her face. "Did they hurt you, girl? Lay a hand on you?"

She shook her head. "No, but they're beating up my friend."

"Go back to the house. I'll deal with you when the day's planting is finished."

"But what about Green?"

Her grandfather snorted through his nose. "What about him?"

"We need to stop them from beating him up."

"Those are white boys beating on their own. We don't get involved in that. You git back to the house, and I'll deal with you later."

Vonie knew what "deal with her" meant. Her feet dragged with guilt and fear as she made her way back to the house.

****

The rooster crowed, but Vonie didn't rise from her cot.

Eyes closed, she listened to her grandpa move around the room beyond the burlap bags. He'd kept his promise. Pain still throbbed from the welts on her legs.

She wanted her dad. Silent tears trailed down her face into the corners of her mouth. She wanted to be back in Chicago in their small two-room apartment that shook when the train thundered past. But how could she face him? He would be so disappointed in her. She let him down, let her grandpa down, and let Green down. She'd made Green a promise to help him fish, but when next Sunday rolled around she would go to live with Aunt Sadie.

"Vonie. Time to get up."

She wanted to ask why, but instead swung her legs off the cot and stood.

The rising sun hit her in the eyes when she stepped onto the porch. The old rooster strutted around the yard like he owned it. When he saw her, he squawked and flew at her head before backing off.

She ignored him. Her gaze drifted to the woods, the woods she'd probably never explore again. Why had Green and his brothers fought? She'd always envied other children who had brothers and sisters. They had each other and were never lonely.

"Whatcha cryin' about, girl?"

She hadn't heard her grandpa come out onto the porch. "Nothing." She swiped at the steady stream of tears that kept coming.

"I know you miss your mother."

Vonie's head jerked in his direction. He'd never said one word about her mother dying.

"Did you know her?"

He nodded. "She was raised on the other side of Vicksburg. I didn't think she was the right woman for my boy, but he had a mind of his own." Her grandpa looked at her. "Like you."

Did he hate her because he didn't like her mother?

Her grandpa leaned against the other post and stared out over his partially plowed land.

"When your father left and went to Chicago, I thought it would break his mother's heart."

Vonie glanced over at him. His eyes had a faraway look, as though he were seeing her father, his son, walking away from this place never to return.

"You miss him, don't you?" Vonie whispered.

He coughed and straightened. "Course I miss him. He's my only son. Just like you're his only child. Couldn't let anything happen to you. He'd never forgive me. I'd never forgive myself." This last part was said more to himself than to her.

"Does that mean you like me a little?"

His thin body jerked, and his face scrunched up into a frown. "Like? Course I like you. Where'd you get the idea that I didn't like you?"

She shrugged. "You're sending me away."

He straightened and cleared his throat. "Need to get out to the field."

But now that Vonie had him talking she couldn't let him go back to being the silent man he'd been before. "Were you lonely here by yourself?"

One foot raised to step off the porch, he stopped. "Too busy to be lonely."

"I was lonely. But I met Green, and he's taught me a lot about fishing. I'm going to miss him. Just like you miss my dad."

"Those boys are bad."

"Not Green. I think he only introduced me to his sisters because he didn't want his brothers to know about me. When they were beating up on him, he didn't say go for help, just told me to run." Her gaze drifted to the woods for a second. "Like he wanted me to get far away from what was happening."

Her grandpa only grunted. For the first time, Vonie realized she'd never seen him smile.

Deep lines slashed into his face on either side of his mouth. His loneliness hit her in her stomach and brought more tears to her eyes. How long had he worked this farm by himself without her grandmother, without her father?

"My dad told me about this place. About the creek, about the summers."

Her grandpa shifted his gaze from the field to her face. "He walked away from this place and never looked back."

She saw the sadness in his eyes. She couldn't leave him here on this farm by himself. He needed her, just like she needed him. But how did she make him see it? "He sent me here so you wouldn't be lonely."

Her father had sent her because he didn't have anyone to care for her. But maybe he was also thinking about his father.

"Now you're sending me away."

Her grandpa stepped off the porch and without turning started to walk away. "Who said anything about sending you away?"

****

Green's body throbbed with every step he took. His left eye was swollen shut, and his view of the woods was limited by what he could see out of his right eye.

He ached, but his brother Billy ached more. Tired of being Billy's punching bag, Green had given as good as he got. He did this more out of fear for Vonie. If he couldn't take up for himself, how was he going to take up for his friend? To Green's surprise, Sam had jumped into the fight on his side. The Durham boys had stood back and laughed, calling them a bunch of backwoods hooligans.

It had been two days since he'd seen Vonie. He'd been able to keep up his deliveries to Mr. Brody, but it had meant fishing late into the night. Sam had gone with him to the creek the previous evening. Green would have liked Vonie's company better.

He'd told his mother about Vonie. She'd suggested he go to his friend's house and introduce himself to her grandfather. So here he was, heart pounding in his chest, staring at her house. What if her grandpa ran him off with a shotgun? Even this big catfish might not make him welcome.

The house looked tired in the late afternoon sun. Chickens pecked at the dirt, looking for food, and a lazy hound slept under the porch. When Green drew close, the door opened. Smiling, he lifted the catfish. His heart sank when Mr. Baldwin stepped out on the porch.

The old man looked him over, from his swollen eye to his busted lip, but didn't say a word.

Green cleared his throat. "Evening, sir. I'm Green Thompson, a friend—" He stopped. What if Vonie hadn't told her grandpa about him and the fishing? Maybe she hadn't shown up at the creek because she didn't want to fish with him anymore.

"Is that catfish for us?" The old man nodded toward the fish in Green's hand.

"Yes, sir."

"Well, we can't cook it with you standing out there in the sun." Vonie's grandpa opened the door wider. Green took a deep breath and stepped into the house.

Vonie stood in the middle of the room. Her eyes widened when she took in his face.

"You should see Billy." He tried to smile, but the movement caused his lips to ache.

She shot a glance over at her grandfather, who watched them from the door. "Grandpa, this is my friend, Green."

"Is that what you are? Her friend?" Vonie's grandfather asked.

Green's gaze held Vonie's. He couldn't stop the smile that spread over his face. "Yes, sir. I'm her friend."

The End

Constance's Southern Fried Catfish

Ingredients
6-8 catfish fillets
1 cup of cornmeal
1 cup of flour
½ teaspoon salt
¼ teaspoon pepper
1 teaspoon Bay's seafood seasoning
2 eggs

Directions

Mix cornmeal, flour, salt, pepper, and seafood seasoning together in a large shallow bowl.

Whip the eggs until frothy in a separate bowl.

Dip each fillet in the egg mixture first. Hold upright to remove excess egg.

Then roll the fillets in the cornmeal mixture. Shake to remove excess.

Immerse fillet in a skillet half filled with hot oil or a Dutch oven.

Fry to golden brown about five to six minutes.

Serve catfish with coleslaw, hush puppies, and French fries.

Constance Gillam

Books and music have always been my life. Some of my earliest memories were of walking to the library on my own at age seven or eight. (Those were the days when children weren't snatched off the streets.) I read every chance I got.

In a quest to find myself, I've worked as genetic counselor, health underwriter, bank proof operator, phlebotomist, real estate agent, and medical technologist. In the end, I've come back to the profession I've revisited most often, being a writer.

I write contemporary thrillers, historical fiction, and dabble in young adult. My husband and I live in the Atlanta area with our three children and grandchildren.

Website: www.constancegillam.com

No More Lonely Hearts

Marilyn Baron

Acknowledgments

I'm very honored to be part of this worthwhile project with such talented authors. I'd also like to thank my mother, Lorraine Meyers, for a lifetime of encouragement and support. She lives in a place very much like the fictionalized Eternal Springs. True, they don't have a Senior Match program, but she enjoys a variety of activities, great food, and a friendly and safe atmosphere. Here's to significant others and second chances and finding that special someone or something no matter where you are on life's journey.

Marilyn Baron

No More Lonely Hearts

Chapter One

"Welcome to Eternal Springs, Mr. Traynor. I'm Olivia Bartlette."

He must be dreaming. The beautiful woman in front of him extended her hand, as if inviting him to dance. He took her hand in his and got lost in her fathomless green eyes. He heard strains of music in his head—*Night and Day*—and thought, *you are the one.* No, the sounds he heard came from a quartet playing Big Band music during cocktail hour in the main lobby of the community advertised as luxury carefree living for active seniors in suburban Atlanta. His parents used to dance to that song. He had been about to take a stranger into his arms. What had gotten into him?

A vision in red, Olivia Bartlette appeared so unexpected in the sea of leathery faces, blue hair, and seniors zipping around on walkers. And he fell under her spell. Everyone told him, warned him, not to fall for the next woman he met, but the women he met in his line of work were off limits. As an airline pilot, a captain, the cockpit ruled his world.

He hadn't dated since his divorce. He enjoyed married life, sharing his life with someone. Sleeping alone, eating alone, left him feeling disconnected from the world. He hoped his loneliness didn't show. He'd almost forgotten how to talk to a woman, except his mother, and without her hearing aids, she couldn't carry on much of a conversation.

Get out of your head, Traynor. And say something intelligent before the lady thinks you're a complete idiot.

"Mr. Traynor was my father. Please call me Nick."

"Nick, then. I'm Olivia. Do you have any other family? What about Mrs. Traynor? I like to connect with all family members."

"There was." Nick paused. "She's not in the picture anymore. It's just me. Me and my mother. She has dementia, and I see the decline in her health. After my father died, well, I couldn't just leave her alone. I've tried a number of in-home caregivers, and none of them worked out. So now you see why I'm here, trying to find the best place for my mother. I'm gone for days at a time, and I can't look after her the way she needs to be cared for."

Nick stood, transfixed. Something about Olivia made her glow.

Stop spilling your guts, man. Let the woman get a word in edgewise. Get it together, Traynor.

"Yes. Well then, Mr. Traynor, Nick, you've come to the right place. How did you hear about Eternal Springs, if I may ask?"

"Another pilot friend of mine placed his mother here, and he says she's never been happier. It's like night and day."

The song he'd heard the quartet playing in the lobby came bubbling up in his brain. *Night and Day. She was the one for him.*

Olivia chuckled. "We get that a lot. At Eternal Springs, we offer the full continuum of care."

Her laughter lifted his spirits like one of his planes taking off.

Nick held up a brochure and some pamphlets. "I've read all the brochures, all the materials you sent. I've talked to the director, and I know all about the three levels of care you offer. Independent Living, Assisted Living, and then possibly skilled nursing care.

"Yes, well, we don't need to discuss those other levels at this time." Olivia touched his arm. "As long as she has an aide and doesn't wander outside. We will try to keep her in independent living as long as possible. Our community is fully accredited and highly rated."

Nick laughed. "You should be. The prices are pretty steep. But I understand there's no such thing as a free lunch, as my mother always says."

"On the contrary, lunch *is* free at Eternal Springs." Olivia winked. "Or rather lunch is included in the resident's fee. No other facility in the city offers that option. And our food is excellent, as you'll see in a minute when we go into dinner. We lured the chef away from Chez Allison."

"That's impressive."

Olivia impressed him more. Knowledgeable. Competent. And he could barely take his eyes off her. Her charm was magnetic.

"And we always ask our residents for their favorite recipes. If you wouldn't mind, please email them to me before you bring her to lunch. We'll have a surprise in store for your mother."

"Mom was a great cook, but why do you need her recipes?" Her request triggered a niggling suspicion about her intentions.

"Actually, it was Chef's idea. In addition to the gourmet meals he prepares, he feels it gives the residents a flavor of home if they taste the dishes they used to prepare. Food entices memories of happier times."

"Clever." Nick scanned his memory. "Several recipes come to mind. She throws in a couple of secret ingredients."

"Such as…"

"She always said she'd take those secrets to the grave, but I don't think she'll mind sharing. Her best dish is Spaghetti Carbonara."

"Oh, I love Italian." Olivia's eyes lit with delight. "Before I forget, here's my card." She pulled it from her blazer pocket.

Nick read Olivia's credentials. "Activities director, psychologist, matchmaker." He shook his head in surprise. "Matchmaker?"

"Only unofficially. That's another difference that sets our community apart. We actually offer a matchmaking service called Senior Match here at Eternal Springs. We don't believe love stops at a certain age. We try to help the residents find happiness wherever they can." She leaned in closer. "We have a very high success rate. Our motto here is 'No More Lonely Hearts.'" She winked.

Nick swallowed hard. "I'll take some of that." Nick teased, trying to get his heartbeat under control. He hadn't ever had such a visceral reaction to a woman.

"I'm sure *you* don't need a matchmaking service."

"You'd be surprised."

Is she flirting with me?

"What about availability?" Nick studied her more as he tried to keep the conversation on track. The twinkle in her eyes suggested she might be flirting. "I understand there's quite a waiting list to get in."

Olivia nodded. "It's true. Our portfolio is extremely limited. But one unit just became available a few days ago. It's a rather nice corner unit, very spacious with floor-to-ceiling windows and a magnificent view of the lake. Plus, there's a great amenities package."

Nick tried to stop assessing Olivia's amenities. He blinked several times. Looking directly at Olivia was like staring straight into the sun. But as beautiful and sincere as she appeared, getting too close to the sun could cause him to get scorched. He'd been burned before and preferred to avoid a repeat performance.

"What happened to the person who lived there?"

"Sadly, she passed on. However, we provided excellent care, and she wanted for nothing. Shall I show you around?"

While the news of someone's passing triggered sadness, Olivia managed to snap him back from his thoughts. Her high heels clicked on the marble floor as she headed to the dining room. Puzzled by the instant attraction, he wanted to follow her anywhere. He greedily inhaled her scent of fresh oranges and lemons in spring…and something that reminded him of a day at the beach. A peace and calm he hadn't experienced in months settled over him. It sure beat the stress he'd been experiencing while trying to find the right place for his mother. He'd managed to find someone to stay with her during his visit to Eternal Springs.

"After dinner, I'll take you on a tour, show you the space that's available, and go over all of the activities we offer. You could even talk with your friend's mother, Mrs. Scott."

"I'd like that."

Olivia led Nick to a table. He pulled out her chair and waited until she was seated.

"Thank you."

The server brought over menus.

"Dinners are four courses with wine. There's a European-style breakfast, daily happy hour with hors d'oeuvres and drinks in the afternoon. And we offer in-room dining if a resident is under the weather. We offer nightly entertainment—live acts, lectures, movies, bingo, and more."

The amenities sounded incredible. And opportunities to gaze at Olivia provided a little extra bonus. Nick cleared his throat and then turned his attention to the menu. "What do you recommend?"

"Honestly, there's not one bad thing on the menu. I always love the pasta."

"That's what I'll have."

While the food ranked high, his dinner companion ranked even higher. He enjoyed her lilting laughter.

"This was great," Nick said during desert. "The dinner *and* your company. My compliments to the chef. These days, I'm more accustomed to airline food. This was a cut above some of the finest places I've dined in town. The service was impeccable."

"I'm glad you enjoyed it." Olivia lowered her gaze. She oozed charm.

He didn't want the evening to end. Olivia's smile always reached her eyes. The candlelight made her even more enchanting. He had to bring himself back down to earth. This wasn't a date, after all. "My mother is used to the best, and I think she is going to like it here."

"We try to pamper our residents."

When they finished dinner, Olivia led him to the luxurious carpeted common area off the lobby with wall tapestries, a piano bar, and a hallway to the various rooms that identified activities taking place during the day—chair yoga, book discussions, bridge, and even jewelry making.

"Is there any activity you don't offer?"

Olivia chuckled. "If not, we'll add it. This is not your ordinary place, Nick."

He winked at Olivia. "And you're not an ordinary activities director."

Olivia blushed as an elderly couple approached them. "Oh, look. Here's your friend's mother, with her significant other."

Nick moved to shake her hand. "Mrs. Scott, so nice to see you again."

"Do I know you?"

"I'm a friend of Brian's."

"Betty, this is Nick Traynor." Olivia grasped the woman's hand as she spoke to her. "He's thinking of moving his mother to Eternal Springs."

"Oh, hello. This is my husband, Al."

Nick's mouth opened, and then he stopped. "Nice to meet you, Al."

Al shook Nick's hand.

"Well, we're off to catch the eight o'clock movie. See you later." Mrs. Scott and Al walked away.

Nick scratched his head. "That was confusing."

"Don't be surprised that Betty doesn't recognize you. Sometimes she doesn't know her own son."

Watching the couple dodder away, Nick tried to understand. "Did she remarry? I went to Mr. Scott's funeral. I thought Mrs. Scott was still a widow."

"She is. But to Betty, Al looks like her dear departed husband."

Is this what he had to look forward to with his mother? An ache stabbed his chest. "Brian's father was tall and had a full head of hair. This man is short and bald and looks nothing like him. However, Mrs. Scott looks a lot younger than the last time I saw her, which was five years ago."

Olivia cleared her throat and flashed a smile. "Must be something in the water. After all, this is Eternal Springs."

"Are you trying to tell me you've discovered some kind of Fountain of Youth?"

"When someone stays active and happier longer, they feel younger," Olivia said.

"Sounds like a lot of hocus-pocus to me."

"It may be magical, but there's nothing fishy going on here, if that's what you mean." Olivia's voice took on a slight edge. "We engage in a number of approved techniques to keep our residents youthful. The power of suggestion is very strong, even if memories fade."

"Let me show you the swimming pool." Olivia pointed to the double sliding glass doors. She took a few steps in that direction.

She's trying to change the subject.

"I'm not sure I understand," Nick said, remaining rooted.

Olivia turned back to him. "Betty is simply seeing her new friend through different eyes. Al resembles her deceased husband. That makes her deliriously happy. Now she has peace of mind."

"Are the residents hallucinating?" Nick asked.

"No." Olivia crossed her arms over her chest. "We do not allow illegal substances here."

"Then what's the secret?" Nick demanded.

"Belief. You have to believe. It's obvious, you're a doubter, Mr. Traynor."

"Nick."

"Mr. Traynor, perhaps this isn't the right place for your mother. Maybe you require a more conventional facility." She turned to walk away.

Nick caught up with her and tapped her shoulder. "Wait, Miss Bartlette, or is it Mrs. Bartlette?"

"It's Miss," Olivia said, pointedly.

"Please don't punish my mother because of me. I'm an idiot. I think my mother could be very happy here."

Nice going, Nick. Great job of upsetting this angel of a woman.

"I would need to meet her and have her evaluated to see if she's a good candidate for Eternal Springs."

"When may I bring her by?"

"First thing Monday morning?"

"Okay. I know how competitive these places can be, and I don't want my mother to miss out."

"You have no idea." Olivia's eyes widened.

"What do you mean?"

She leaned in and whispered. "Next year, we're going off-planet."

"What!" Nick exclaimed.

"Oh yes, we're going to be the first to offer interplanetary excursions. It will be the penultimate experience. We call it our Seniors-in-Space program."

"Seriously?" Nick shook his head in amazement. She appeared totally levelheaded and in control of all her faculties, but this was more mind-stretching than he could grasp.

"Of course not." Olivia broke out laughing. "But you should have seen the look on your face."

Nick shoved his fingers through his hair. He wasn't usually so dense. Olivia had turned him around. He blew out a breath. "This is all new to me, which is why I sound like an idiot. I'm sorry. I appreciate everything you've shown me. I know you're working past your regular hours, so thank you for your time."

"It's all part of the job. We work hard to meet our residents' needs, both physical and emotional, to provide a worry-free experience for the caregiver."

"Looks like you've covered all the bases." Nick paused. Thought about his own needs. About take-out dinners or delivery pizza whenever he wasn't flying. Sometimes cereal was his standby dinner. He shoved his hesitation aside and engaged his courage. "*Miss* Bartlette. I am wondering…would you have dinner with me sometime? The more I get to know you, the more secure I'd feel about placing my mother at Eternal Springs."

Olivia drew back. "That sounds like a pickup line."

Nick raised his hands in surrender. "You've got me. But I must get my mother's situation squared away sooner rather than later. So, how about a date? When do you get off tomorrow?"

Her face remained neutral. Had he overstepped? Would she refuse? "I am off at five o'clock."

"I'll pick you up tomorrow at five and take you *out* to dinner. I apologize for being rude. I hope you'll give me and my mother another chance."

Olivia stood. "All right, Mr. Traynor. Five p.m. tomorrow."

Nick stood up and shook her hand. All very professional.

But tomorrow night would be another story. While he had to secure a place for his mother, he very much wanted to get to know Olivia Bartlette better. He intended to turn on the Traynor charm.

Surely, he had some left.

Chapter Two

All day Olivia busied herself with the residents, but every other thought turned to Nick. Tall. Handsome. Well-traveled. And he genuinely cared about his mother and her well-being. Family meant everything to her. Especially for someone growing up in foster care, as she had.

Now Olivia sat across from Nick at a cozy Italian restaurant, complete with red-checked tablecloth and a candle in the center of the table.

However, the conversation had turned...more friend-like than date-like. Or maybe he didn't consider this a real date. Maybe he was vetting her to make sure Eternal Springs was the right place for his mother. That would be disappointing. His care and concern for his mother demonstrated his respect for women. He acted like a complete gentleman. Something she'd had little of lately. When he turned his full smile on her, butterflies danced in her stomach.

"More wine?" Nick poured before waiting for her response.

But Nick had listened when she said she loved Italian food. In her limited dating experience, that was unusual. Points for him.

"Nick, this may sound forward, but what happened to the former Mrs. Traynor?" Olivia adjusted the napkin across her lap.

Nick grimaced. "I don't like to talk about it."

"Well then, we won't." But her curiosity pushed hard. Really, she did want to know. She placed her elbows on the table and rested her chin on her laced fingers.

"She left," Nick said quietly. "Left me for my best friend after my mother came to live with us. She'd changed. My wife, not my mother. Started bidding for international flights, the same routes as my best friend, a captain on the same airline. And she stayed away for longer and longer periods of time, until one day, she didn't come home at all."

As a psychologist, she was used to people venting. The problem was she could become interested in a man like Nick Traynor if he was truly over his past. The man was tall, rangy, and to her, devastatingly handsome. He was kind. But complicated.

Betrayed by your wife and your best friend. That had to be rough.

She had to give him credit; he tackled the five stages of loss. But he wasn't her patient. She was interested in dating him, not trying to psychoanalyze him.

Olivia twisted the strands of spaghetti carbonara around her fork and onto the oversized spoon, scrutinizing him.

"The husband is always the last to know," Nick said. He dabbed his mouth with his napkin, then rested his forearms on the table and flexed his hands several times. How much anger was lurking within him?

She put her fork down and sipped the sweet Moscato d'Asti. Curiosity consumed her. She gazed at Nick and worried about the answer to the question pressing on her mind. "Nick," Olivia said. "I have to ask. Are you still in love with your ex-wife?"

Nick narrowed his eyes. "What makes you think that?"

"Talking about her seems to have triggered your anger. And you've done nothing but talk about her the entire night. I thought this was supposed to be a date."

Nick frowned. "I'm sorry. I didn't realize. Let's talk about you. Do you like to cook? Any hobbies?"

Olivia's spirits rose. She leaned in, her hands resting on either side of her plate. "I love concerts—country music, good books, and dream of traveling."

Nick chuckled. "I think my mother will really like you. The two of you have very similar tastes."

"Well, the important thing is, will she like Eternal Springs? Have you talked to her about your plans? Does she want to move?"

"I'll bring her in Monday. Let her see what a great place it is. I think that will convince her. My house is right in the neighborhood, so it's convenient. I could visit her whenever I'm in town. I will feel better knowing she's safe while I'm away."

"That's the important thing."

Nick leaned forward and tapped his fingers on the top of her hand. "Now tell me more about Olivia Bartlette."

Olivia took another sip of her Moscato. Talking about herself was like trying to tame her curly hair to straight. Possible, but not her favorite task. She was trained to listen to others, but the wine lowered her inhibitions. Relaxing warmth was spreading through her. "There's not much to tell."

"Have you ever been married?" He leaned back and rubbed a finger over an imaginary spot on the tablecloth, but his eyes never left hers.

Olivia pursed her lips. "No, but I've come close."

"Really? Tell me about it."

She sighed. "We were engaged. But along the way, we discovered we weren't compatible." She shrugged.

"In what way?"

"He was heavy metal, and I'm country music. The bad boy and the good girl. A flash in the pan for this girl. After a while, the passion faded. And reality settled in. We parted."

"Sorry, but I guess, a good thing for me." Nick smiled, and again, she felt the flutter of butterflies.

"What about you?" She took another slow sip of wine.

"I'm more of a nineteen-forties guy. My mother always listened to Big Bands. That's all I heard growing up. But tell me more about your story."

"The story is boring. We're friends. The breakup was amicable."

"So behind the twinkling eyes, the warm smile, and the college degrees, you're a country girl at heart?"

Olivia's cheeks heated. "Metaphorically speaking, yes."

He poured more fizzy liquid into her glass. It was going to her head.

"Are you trying to get me tipsy?" She was halfway there.

"Is it working?"

She laughed. The more she was around Nick, the more comfortable he made her feel. He was sweet and possessed a good sense of humor. All of it added up to a significant attraction. But where could it lead?

"Mr. Traynor, you're a smart man. A pilot with the lives of many in your hands. What do you think?"

"I think...I think I want to tempt you with dessert."

You could tempt me with a kiss, Nick Traynor.

"Thank you, but I'm full. And I do have an early day tomorrow."

Nick paid the check and drove her home. As he walked her to the door, he said, "My mother and I will see you Monday morning."

"I'll look forward to it." Olivia waited. Would Nick kiss her goodnight? Looking up at him, she smiled.

He shifted on his weight while they stood together under the porch light.

"Oh, dang." He pulled her into his arms. Kissed her thoroughly.

"Passion," Nick whispered.

Olivia's eyes widened. Her knees wobbled. She couldn't speak. He'd left her mindless.

"Apparently that myth about a toe-curling kiss is true." Nick chuckled.

Olivia blinked and touched her lips where his had just been.

"I'll take that as a yes," Nick said, opening the front door for her. Still stunned, she stepped inside.

She watched as he strode back to his car. Niggling doubts about his feelings for his ex-wife tried to sprout, but she shoved them aside.

"The man can kiss," she said breathlessly. "Monday can't come soon enough."

Chapter Three

"Look, Mom, on that welcome board." Nick helped his mother into the lobby with her walker.

"Welcome, Mrs. Barbara Traynor," he read.

"For me?"

"Yes, isn't that lovely?" He needed to remember to thank Olivia for that nicety. "Mom, do you have your hearing aids in?"

"Yes," she snapped. "I'm not a child."

"I know, Mom, but this is the third pair you've lost this year." His train of thought evaporated when Olivia approached. Did Friday night's kiss have the same impact on her that it had on him? Sleep had eluded him most of the night.

"And here's Olivia now."

Olivia reached for his mother's hand. "Welcome to Eternal Springs, Mrs. Traynor."

"You may call me Barbara."

"Barbara. We have a busy couple of hours. First, we'll take a tour and see the space that's available. Then I've arranged for you to sit in on some classes. Lastly, we'll have lunch so you can meet some of the residents."

"I told Nick I don't need to move anywhere. I'm perfectly happy where I am. When my husband died, I moved in with

Nick. Now he wants me to move again. I don't think I'm ready."

"Well, this is just a visit, Barbara. You don't have to make any decisions. Nick just wanted you to evaluate some of your options."

He appreciated the way Olivia maneuvered the conversation to the positive. He followed as she started the tour with his mother, introducing her to key staff members before showing her the available suite.

"Oh my. Look, Nick. This is lovely. I had no idea. Look at all this space. Would all this be for me? Or would I be sharing it?" The surprise in his mother's voice gave him hope.

"No," Olivia assured. "It would be all yours." She winked at Nick.

"Barbara, a stress-relief coloring class just started if you'd like to participate."

Mother looked at him questioningly. "Go on, Mom. Maybe you'll meet some people."

Olivia guided them to the arts and crafts room where she helped Barbara into a chair. Afterward, she walked him to the lobby. When he looked at her, she radiated the same soft glow that she had at their first meeting.

She motioned for him to sit next to her on an oversized sofa. "After class, we'll pick her up and take her to lunch. There you'll discover that special surprise I told you about."

"This is nice of you. Do you go to this much trouble for all the visitors?"

"Absolutely." Olivia's angelic smile lingered on her lips.

"You mean I'm not getting special treatment?"

She nodded. "We treat all of our clients with the same respect."

"Hmm. What if I want to be more than a client?"

Olivia flashed another smile. "Then you might want to do something about that."

"Will you go out with me this Saturday night?"

"What did you have in mind?"

Nick leaned closer until their shoulders brushed. "Dinner and a movie."

"I'd like that." Olivia smiled. "But do you have any other questions about Eternal Springs?"

"No, I'm ready to sign on the dotted line, *if* I can get my mother to agree."

"I hope she likes it here. I would really hate for her to lose that suite. It's the only one available now. Plus, we celebrate all the holidays here with big parties. Relatives are invited."

"I'm sold."

Olivia looked at her watch, then rose from the sofa. "It's time to pick up your mother."

Nick followed Olivia walked into the arts and craft room. His mother was coloring and talking to one of the other women.

"Hi, Nick," his mother said. "You'll never believe who I ran into. I didn't know Shirley Weston lived here. We were just catching up."

"That's great. Wow. That's an amazing picture."

Olivia leaned down. "I'll take it and leave it at the front desk until you're ready to go home," Olivia said.

"Thank you."

"And now, Barbara, we're going to lunch."

Nick retrieved his mother's walker.

"I don't need that, Nick. I can manage on my own." His mother waved him away.

"Mom, look around. Everyone uses a walker. It's safer. It will make me happier if you use it."

Barbara rolled her eyes. "Okay. But I'm only doing it for you."

Nick glanced at Olivia, and she shrugged.

When they arrived at the dining room, a member of the wait staff discreetly removed Barbara's walker, escorted her to a table, and placed the walker nearby. Another server appeared and poured water into glasses, then asked for their beverage order.

"I'll have an orange soda," said his mother.

"One orange soda coming right up." The server smiled as he handed over menus.

"This is very fancy." His mother eyed the menu. "It must be expensive."

"It's our treat," explained Olivia.

"You don't have to worry about money," Nick reminded his mother.

"Look," Barbara exclaimed. "They have my challah egg casserole on the menu."

"Yours?" Nick asked.

"Yes, it says right here, 'Barbara Traynor's Challah Egg Casserole.' And my spaghetti carbonara. My cranberry brisket. Oh my." Barbara's eyes teared up.

Nick perused the menu and flashed a grateful glance at Olivia. He had emailed her the recipes over the weekend.

After the server returned with Barbara's orange drink, he took their orders.

"I'll have the Barbara Traynor Challah Egg Casserole, please." His mother closed the menu with a smile.

"I'll have the Barbara Traynor Cranberry Brisket," Nick added.

"And I'll have the Barbara Traynor Spaghetti Carbonara," Olivia said.

"Excellent choice, Mrs. Traynor."

"Please, call me Barbara."

His mother is flirting with the server?

"And thank you." She waved at the server.

"Mom, what do you think so far? Do you have any questions?"

"What if I move here and then decide I don't like it?"

Olivia patted her hand. "It's a month-to-month lease. You can leave whenever you like."

Olivia answered more questions until the server delivered their food to the table. Nick paused as his mother took a bite of her egg casserole.

"This tastes just like mine!" Her eyes were wide with surprise. "And you used the sharp cheddar just the way I make it."

"This carbonara is delicious," Olivia raved. "The pasta is al dente, and it's made with bacon, not ham, the way I prefer."

"And this brisket. Tender. Flavorful. Mom, it tastes just like yours."

A man in a white chef's coat approached the table. "Is everything to your liking?"

"Where did you learn to cook like this?" Barbara asked. "Your recipe tastes exactly like mine."

"It is yours, Barbara. Just like it says on the menu," Olivia explained.

"Mom, I gave them your recipes," Nick confessed.

"What a surprise. Thank you all." She nodded at each of them.

"Our pleasure," said Chef. "We want you to feel at home here."

"I already do." Barbara smiled warmly.

After lunch, Olivia took Nick and Barbara to the pool area.

"This is like a country club," Barbara said. "You even have monogrammed towels."

"Hey, can I move in?" Nick joked. "This is the life."

Olivia laughed. "We get that a lot. Do you have any particular talents, Barbara, in addition to being a great cook?"

"My mother is an amazing singer," Nick said.

Barbara blushed.

"Well, we have a singing group here," said Olivia. "And every night at cocktail hour we have a band or some form of musical entertainment for dancing and, of course, a pianist is always on hand, and he loves it when the residents sing while he plays."

Barbara's face lit up.

"Mom, what do you think? Do you think you could be happy at this place?" Olivia's warmth toward his mother endeared her to him. She exuded sweetness and caring that he wanted in his life. As corny as it sounded, she could be the wind beneath his wings.

Hi mother looked at him. "I guess we could try it."

Nick hugged his mother. "Mom, you won't regret it."

"It sounds like you want to get rid of me."

"Of course, I don't. But I'm often out of town. You know how I worry about you. This will ease my mind. All of your needs will be provided. I'll be visiting often. And think of all the new friends you'll make."

"Mrs. Traynor, you won't be disappointed."

Barbara beamed.

"Well, Olivia, lead the way," Nick said, relieved that his mother would be properly taken care of in his absence. "I think you have just found your newest resident. I couldn't be happier."

Olivia hugged Nick's mother. "Welcome to Eternal Springs!"

Nick smiled at his mother and Olivia. He hoped to have a moment alone with the beautiful woman when he signed the papers for his mother's care.

And he fully intended to top his last toe-curling kiss.

Chapter Four

Nick entered Eternal Springs, signed the guest book, and scanned the lobby for Olivia. Last night's country music concert had rocked his boots—the new ones he and Olivia purchased. Everything about her brought him joy. When he wasn't with her, he was thinking about her. After six months of dating, his thoughts and emotions turned serious. Toward the future. A future with Olivia.

He spotted his mom and moved toward her. "How's my favorite girl?" Nick kissed his mother and helped her to a seat on a couch.

"I thought Olivia was your favorite girl."

"You're both my favorites. I'm going to order a drink and get some popcorn. We'll sit awhile before you go in to dinner." Nick ordered a cocktail and returned to his mother.

"It's been six months. How do you like it here, Mom?"

"I'm very happy. I have some nice friends."

"Olivia tells me you're going to the theater this weekend in the Eternal Springs van. Are you remembering to use your walker?"

His mother frowned. "Yes."

"What did you do today?"

"I went outside and walked around. I like to see the end."

"The end?" Nick scratched his head. His mother was losing more words with each passing day. What could she possibly mean?" Then it dawned on him. "Oh, the sunset."

Her face brightened. "Yes. Will you stay for dinner?"

"I'm taking Olivia out. We've been dating six months now."

"That's very nice. I like Olivia. She's a lot better than what's her name."

Nick laughed. He barely remembered his ex's name these days. "I couldn't agree more."

"Is it getting serious between you two?"

Nick nodded. Olivia was great. He had marriage on his mind and was ready to shop for rings. Although he didn't want to crowd Olivia by moving too fast…why wait longer for true happiness?

His mother patted his arm. "That's what I wanted to talk to you about."

"Olivia?"

"No—Stanley."

Nick straightened in his seat. "Stanley?"

"Yes, he's a resident here. He lives on my floor in a very nice suite. We've been dating for a month."

"Dating?"

"Yes, I met him through Senior Match."

"Senior Match?"

"A dating service for seniors."

"I know what it is. What I want to know is who is this Stanley person? Does he have a last name?"

"I know I love him."

"You love him? After a month?"

"When you're my age, you can't afford to wait around. Life is short."

Despite the fact that he had been thinking along those same lines about Olivia, he was not happy about this new development with his mom. "Am I going to meet this Stanley fellow with no last name?"

"His name is Stanley Morris. He's sitting over there." She pointed and waved.

Nick glanced in that direction. Sitting on a chair was a wizened old man, sprouting a few tufts of gray hair, wearing a plaid sports coat that looked straight out of Goodwill.

"That guy?"

"Yes. Don't you think he looks like your father?"

"Mom, he doesn't look anything like Dad. First of all, Dad was over six feet tall, and he had a full head of hair. That guy looks like a gnome."

"No, I see a lot of Dad in Stanley."

"Well, Dad is dead. This guy looks like he's at death's door. So there's that similarity."

Barbara smacked her son on the shoulder. "You'll like him once you get to know him. I'm going to take you over to meet him. I want you to be nice."

"I'm always nice."

Nick followed his mother as she slowly made her way across the room with her walker.

"Stanley Morris, I want you to meet my son, Nick."

Stanley struggled to rise. Once on his feet, he extended his hand, which Nick reluctantly shook.

"Barbara has told me a lot about you. It's nice to meet you."

Nick frowned. What was he supposed to say? Ask the guy what his intentions were toward his mother? How could his mother be in love with a man she just met? After all, she forgot what she did fifteen minutes after she did it.

When he looked up, his mother and the geezer were holding hands.

Crazy. This is not happening.

What did Olivia know about this? Why hadn't she told him?

"So," Nick started, but couldn't think of a single thing to say to Stanley.

The man stared at him expectantly. "Your mother is the most beautiful woman I've ever met. She reminds me a lot of my deceased wife, Lucille." Stanley drew out his wallet and began regaling them with tales of life with his late wife.

Jeesh.

"We're very happy," his mother added.

Suddenly, he imagined his mother sneaking into Stanley's suite for a romantic rendezvous.

No!

He couldn't even contemplate that.

The band began playing a popular song from the 1940s.

"Babe, they're playing our song," said Stanley. "Would you care for a spin around the dance floor?"

They already have a song? He's calling her babe?

Stanley and his mother drifted toward the middle of the room and started to dance. She left her walker behind but was supported in the arms of her—what was he? Friend?

Boyfriend? What did old folks call significant others these days? Between the two of them, they couldn't take a steady step, but they seemed to be fine on the dance floor, holding each other up.

"Mom," Nick called out. "Be careful. Don't fall."

Olivia sure had a lot of explaining to do. Though he'd been gone a week, every other week for the last month, they had talked on the phone. Surely, at some point, she would've mentioned this. Disappointment settled into his gut.

"Don't worry. Your father is a great dancer," his mother called back.

She thought she was dancing with her dead husband? Stanley probably thought he was tripping the light fantastic with his dead wife. How much would dementia complicate the situation?

"Hey, you," Olivia purred, sneaking up behind him, putting her arms around his neck, and planting a kiss on his cheek.

"Do you see that?" He pointed to his mother and Stanley parading around the room.

"Yes, isn't it lovely?" Olivia gazed wistfully at the dance floor.

Nick bristled. "Lovely? Look at the two of them."

"I am. Don't you want your mother to be happy?"

"Yes, of course, but—"

"Then why can't you be happy for her?"

"Because she can't remember the word *sunset*. She thinks Stanley is my dad. What's going on here?" Nick demanded.

Olivia laughed. "Love."

"When I first met you, you talked about that Senior Match program. I didn't think you'd use it on my mother."

Olivia squared her shoulders. "I didn't *use* it on her. She chose to participate in the program."

"She can't choose! She can't remember. She can't think. What have you done?" Anger rose, and he swallowed against it.

Olivia held up her hands. "Nick, lower your voice, please. You're alarming the residents."

"I asked you a question."

"And I'm not going to dignify it with an answer. You're obviously still a doubter."

"I am doubting my decision to move my mother here."

Olivia pursed her lips. "Are you doubting anything else?"

Anger clouded his brain. He couldn't think. "I need to say goodbye to my mother." Nick walked onto the dance floor and interrupted the happy couple just as his cell phone buzzed. Reaching into his jacket pocket, he pulled it out and read the text.

"Mom, I have to go. One of the pilots is sick. I've got to fill in. It's an emergency. Don't forget your walker when you go in to dinner." He kissed his mother.

"I thought you were taking Olivia out."

Furious, Nick glanced over at Olivia. "Tell her I'll call her."

When I cool off. And do some serious thinking about this relationship.

Chapter Five

Sitting at her desk at Eternal Springs, Olivia picked up the framed photo of her and Nick. The one they took at the country music concert in their new matching cowboy boots. Since they had started dating, she'd introduced him to country music. He'd gotten her hooked on Sudoku puzzles, often finishing hers when she was stumped. The man had a precise mind.

"Why haven't you at least called?" She sighed.

His world was facts and data—wings, weather, and whirlwind trips. Their discussions that boarded on disagreements involved gray areas she saw in life. Like coffee, it could be warm, hot, or cold and still taste good. Why couldn't he see how others could be more than always introverted or extroverted? People were like onions. They had layers. And Nick storming off showed a layer of himself she hadn't seen before. His care and concern for his mother was an attractive feature, but this angry outburst and radio silence caused her concern.

"It was probably for the best that you flew off to Paris…"

She placed the framed photo back on her desk. If they could grow and move past this snag, maybe someday she'd be able to travel to Paris with him. At the very least, it would take an apology from him.

"Knock. Knock."

Olivia looked up. Barbara was smiling at her from the doorway.

"Come in." Olivia motioned for the woman to enter.

"I'm sorry to interrupt your day, but I was wondering if you have seen my son, Nick?"

"I haven't. Have you heard from him?" Olivia stood and walked around her desk. She motioned for Barbara to sit in one of the chairs.

"How could I hear from him if I can't see him? I want him to meet Stanley."

It couldn't be a great day for Barbara. Her memory was slipping. Olivia patted her hand. Rather than correcting Barbara's memory, she said, "I'm sure Nick will be back soon. I hope he'll be delighted to meet Stanley."

Maybe he'd want a do-over with me? To not even call or text…it wasn't like him at all. Most ungentlemanly of him. Not much of a good friend, either. Three days of silence proved to her how intertwined Nick had become in her life. But this demonstration of his anger…could there be a possible future with him?

****

The three-day layover in Paris gave him time to try to settle the chaos in his head. How could Olivia not tell him about his mother and Stanley? Better yet, was she responsible for them…what could he call it? Dating? He shuddered at the thought.

As he continued to walk, the crowds at the Eiffel Tower diminished only a bit with dusk approaching. He imagined people making their way to cafés for coffee, and later, dinner.

He took in the beauty of his surroundings. Atlanta couldn't compare. Though the SkyView Ferris wheel at Centennial Park lit the night sky, it was nothing like what Paris offered.

Overhead, a daredevil zipped three hundred feet up. The only time he enjoyed being that high was on takeoff and landing a plane. He observed several couples strolling arm in arm, a few holding hands.

One particular young couple caught his eye. They appeared to be drunk on love as they meandered several feet in front of him, whispering and giggling. The young man leaned close and whispered something in the young woman's ear. She suddenly stopped, turned to face him, and then tried to pull away. The young man held fast to her hand. While he couldn't understand everything the young man said in French, it was clear he was trying to explain. The woman repeatedly shook her head. Whatever he was offering, she wasn't buying.

"Just apologize to her," Nick muttered.

After several rounds of tugging, the young woman jerked away and stormed off. He stopped as the young man cried out, "Margaux. Margaux." His voice filled with anguish, but the young woman ignored him, disappearing into the crowd ahead. A stab of pain for the young man hit Nick's gut. That too familiar feeling of hurt when someone he loved walked out of his life.

"Sad, yes?" A voice came from behind him.

He turned to see an older woman dressed all in gray, except for a vibrant scarf circling her neck and the tails hanging down. She had an air of sophistication and worldliness he didn't often encounter.

"Yeah, sad." Nick nodded.

"The young, so impetuous. Think being young is forever. But we know different, yes?"

Nick cocked his head. "Pretty much."

"But…I think if the young man is smart, he will act." The woman nodded, as she, too, noticed the young man still rooted in the same spot with his shoulders slumped.

"Act?" Her words puzzled him. Aeronautical charts he could read, but reading people…he didn't excel at that.

"Oh, yes. Which is why the gods gave us champagne and chocolate. So foolish men could woo the women they love. Love is ageless." She chuckled.

"Never thought of that." Nick shifted uncomfortably beside the woman. He wasn't accustomed to speaking with strangers so candidly.

"Food for thought," the older woman said. "And Paris is the city of love. *Au revoir.*" She lifted one end of the dangling scarf and waved it at him as she walked on ahead.

Nick stuck his hands in his pockets. The truth had never landed in his lap like this. It was as though lightning had struck him. How foolish he'd been. He couldn't get back to Eternal Springs and Olivia fast enough. But would Olivia forgive him?

Chapter Six

Nick punched the alarm to make the blaring music stop. But it blared with the same intensity as his head and heart declared he'd better fix things with Olivia. He hadn't seen or spoken to her in a week. That ended today.

He'd been sleepwalking through life before he met her. Now that he was awake, *wide awake*, he needed a plan to win Olivia back. He had to act now.

Before he left town, before he'd learned about his mother and her Stanley, he'd been thinking in terms of marriage. Though he and Olivia had only dated six months, he'd known from the start she was *the* one.

Nick stepped into the bathroom, shaved, and showered. He put on a white polo shirt, navy slacks, and loafers. Every thought focused on Olivia. Her smile. The twinkle in her eyes. The curve of her lips, especially when she laughed.

He ate a quick bowl of cereal and gulped down some coffee. If everything went according to plan, this would be one of the last breakfasts he'd eat alone. If Olivia agreed, soon they would enjoy leisurely mornings and sumptuous breakfasts together. Now that he had a plan, the next steps were clear.

Nick drove his white Lexus sports car to the neighborhood jewelry shop. He walked into a dizzying selection of rings, just like the landscape when he flew across the Atlantic. He paused for a second, having no idea how to choose the perfect one for Olivia. His Olivia.

A young woman approached. "You look a bit lost. May I help you find something?"

Nick exhaled. "Yes, thank you. I'm looking for an engagement ring."

"Then you've come to the right place." The woman led him to a glass-enclosed case filled with so much glitz, it was almost blinding.

The saleswoman pulled out a navy blue velvet cloth and began explaining the Four Cs of diamonds—color, clarity, cut, and carat weight.

That was data his mind could easily process. His heart said she deserved the very best he could afford.

"Are you looking for a classic white diamond? Or perhaps a canary yellow? Those are more rare, but very fashionable. And do you have any idea what cut you want—round, oval, pear, princess, marquise, emerald, radiant, heart-shaped?"

"No idea," answered Nick, his eyes wide on visual overload.

"Let's start with the price point. How much are you looking to spend on a ring?"

"It must be nice." How did picking a ring turn out harder than flying several hundred passengers across the Atlantic? "Olivia is a simple woman, though beautiful, elegant, and refined. I want something that reflects her personality. Something as breathtaking as she is."

"Well, let's look around and see if anything catches your eye."

Nick looked at stones and more stones in cases and more cases until his eyes glazed over. He had always considered himself decisive, but buying jewelry was beyond him.

"I think I know what you're looking for." The woman led him to another case. She brought out a ring. "This is a flawless square-cut diamond in a platinum setting."

"That's it!" He took the offered ring and gazed at in the light. Color danced inside it. "That's exactly what I'm looking for." Excitement raced through him as an image of him bending on one knee and surprising Olivia with his intention filled his mind. Wide-eyed and surprised, Olivia would tell him she wanted so spend her future with him, too. He couldn't wait to present the ring to Olivia. But would everything go like the scene in his head?

"You have one very lucky fiancée."

"I sure hope she feels that way. Wrap it up, please," Nick instructed.

He walked out of the shop with a signature gift bag and the ring he hoped would convince Olivia they were destined to be together.

Stopping on the corner, he called Eternal Springs. "Is Olivia Bartlette available?"

"Yes," answered the receptionist. "Would you like me to transfer your call to her office?"

"No, thank you. Not necessary. However, I would like to make a dinner reservation for two guests of Barbara Traynor, my mother. She's a resident there."

"Of course, Mrs. Traynor is one of our favorite people."

Nick ended the call. He needed to haul it to Eternal Springs in time to put his plan into action to surprise Olivia.

Yet, as much as he was a hundred percent certain he loved her, he didn't hold that level of confidence in her decision about him. There was no flight plan for him to follow now. Flying from point A to point B was much easier than navigating the journey of the heart.

Chapter Seven

Nick parked in the Eternal Springs lot and walked inside. Hopefully, he could make it to the elevator and upstairs to his mother's apartment without running into Olivia. He took the elevator up and knocked on his mother's door.

"Come in," his mother called.

Nick sauntered inside the foyer. "I'm here to take you to dinner, Mother."

The aide attending his mother smiled, pointed to the living room, and then followed him into the room.

"Nick, I'm in here."

His mother sat in her chair, working in her adult coloring book. "Look at this picture I drew."

Nick walked over and hugged her. "I missed you, Mom. Beautiful picture. You're a regular Chagall. "

His mother broke into a wide smile.

Sitting in a chair across from her, he asked, "So, Mom, what did you have for lunch?"

"I don't think I ate lunch today."

Puzzled, Nick turned to his mother's aide. "Did she have lunch?"

"Yes, an omelet, a glass of orange juice, and a pastry for dessert."

His mother's short-term memory flickered more, and not in chronological order. She showed significant change since she first moved to Eternal Springs. Once, he'd called the front desk and demanded to know why she wasn't taking meals. As time went on, he realized she just didn't remember having eaten.

When he had questioned Olivia about his mother's memory—like how she couldn't remember something from fifteen minutes ago, but remembered everything about the past, including lyrics to the songs she sang—she warned him that his mother's memory would continue to slip.

"Think of her memories like footprints in the sand. You see the imprint, and seconds later, the waves crash over them and wash them away like they were never there," Olivia had patiently explained.

He turned to his mother's aide. "I'm taking my mother down to dinner, and then I'll bring her back up to her room."

Since his mother was dressed for dinner, he retrieved her walker, helped her down the hall, and onto the elevator.

"Mom, what did you do this afternoon?" He pushed the button for the lobby.

"I'm not sure." She smiled up at him, but he'd seen the checklist showing her week's activities on the coffee table.

"How's Stanley?"

His mother's face lit up. She apparently had no trouble remembering him. "Have you met Stanley?"

"I did. I saw you dance together, remember?"

"Doesn't he look like your father? Your father is such a good dancer."

"Yes, he was. And so is Stanley."

The words from the older woman in Paris echoed in his mind. His mother deserved to have happiness with a significant other who reminded her of her husband. What harm was there in that? He had been stubborn and closed-minded about it. But worse, he'd been hurtful to the woman he loved. Maybe a diamond engagement ring was just as good as champagne and chocolate. Could she see past his flaws to the truth in his heart?

He felt the ring box in his pocket. Everything had to go according to plan. He intended to propose to Olivia with his mother present. Her presence might reduce the risk of Olivia storming away. His mother was an important part of his life, and if not for her, he might not have met Olivia.

"Here we are, Mom." He walked beside her into the dining room as she stumped along with her walker. They were escorted to a reserved table where the server handed them each a menu and left a third menu at the table.

His mother ran her finger down the length of the menu, muttering under her breath.

"Mom, you love sea bass. How about that served on a bed of spinach?" She nodded, and Nick gave the server their orders.

"Mom, stay right here for a minute. I'll be back." Nick headed to the receptionist and asked them to page Olivia, requesting she come to the dining room. He planned this for five o'clock—the dining room opening and the end of Olivia's workday.

Returning to the dining room, he tapped his fingers on the edge of the table, waiting for Olivia to appear. It was only a week ago, but it seemed a lifetime since he'd set eyes on her.

While that wasn't good for him, thankfully, Paris had turned his thinking around.

Out of the corner of his eye, he noticed Olivia the second she walked into the dining room. She paused. He stood up and waved. The woman he loved had answered the page. Just maybe she'd answer his important question with a *yes*.

Her brows furrowed as she frowned. There was sadness around her eyes. Then she pivoted and started to walk away.

"Olivia!" He waved. His heart skipped a beat.

She can't leave!

She frowned and clenched her fists but moved in his direction with an expression of steely determination.

"Barbara, you're looking lovely this evening. I'm sure you're glad to have company this evening." She patted his mother's arm.

"Olivia, it's great to see you." He pulled out the chair next to his, offering it to her. "I hope you'll join us for dinner."

"Barbara, I'm so sorry. I have other plans. I have somewhere to be and won't be able to stay."

Barbara blinked and looked from Nick to Olivia, then back to him again. "Olivia, please stay for dinner."

Mom had her lucid moments.

"As I explained, I already have plans."

"Please," Barbara insisted.

Olivia narrowed her eyebrows at him, though she sat in the chair he was holding out for her.

Nick's heart nearly beat out of his chest. He swallowed hard and cleared his throat. "Olivia."

She glanced at him, but her expression held no trace of leniency toward him.

"I owe you an apology," he continued.

She harrumphed.

"I shouldn't have walked out on you without an explanation. I shouldn't have left on a trip without telling you. I should not have remained silent for a week. I now realize my words were hurtful, and my behavior was rude. However, I'm asking for a second chance. I hope you'll forgive this pilot who flew a bit off course. But now, I've corrected my flight plan."

She remained silent, but he heard the *tap-tap-tap* of her shoe on the marble floor.

Olivia hadn't jumped up and run away. That had to be a good sign. He pressed on. "You're right. I was a doubter. I doubted the power of love. What you're doing for the seniors here, and my mother, is wonderful. I reacted badly at seeing my mother with a man who wasn't my father."

Olivia remained mute. She wasn't going to make this easy. He didn't blame her. Earning a second chance with the woman he loved outweighed his discomfort. "I had an emergency and had to sub for a pilot who was ill. I took that opportunity to let my anger cool. And I discovered how much I missed your presence in my life. I love you."

Olivia's expression softened. "I love you, too. I want to accept your apology, but how do I know you're serious? After all, how much does a week away change someone?"

Nick stood. He reached into his pocket to retrieve the package he had just for her. Then, just like the image he'd carried in his head, he got down on one knee in front of Olivia.

When her expression shifted from solemn to surprised, his spirits lifted more.

Nick held the box up for Olivia to see.

"What is this?" she gasped.

"A symbol of my love and affection for you."

"I don't want anything from you, Nick Traynor."

"Olivia, please…open it."

When she opened the lid, her hand flew to her mouth.

"Nick?" She stared at him, wide-eyed.

He reached for her hand. Her fingertips trembled in his hand. "It's an engagement ring, Olivia." She panted little breaths. Her eyes misted. But she held back.

"Finally!" exclaimed Barbara.

Tears traced a path down Olivia's cheeks.

"Nick…You can't just walk out on me for days without a word and then expect to come back into my life with a r-ring, no matter how perfect it is."

"Sweetheart, I'm a flawed man. I hope you can forgive my behavior. I've discovered that I'm orbiting around your world, and there's no place I'd rather be."

Olivia dabbed at her eyes, but tears continued to trickle.

Silence filled the dining room. No one moved, not the residents or the servers.

"I just don't know…" Olivia lifted her gaze to his.

Nick rose. "Olivia, I love you. I need you. Please do me the honor of marrying me."

She sniffled and looked longingly at him, then the ring.

He held his breath. Never before had he made a complete fool of himself, but only a grand gesture could show Olivia his true feelings. Would she refuse him? Would she?

"It's breathtaking, Nick," she whispered.

"Just like you," he said.

She wiped the corners of her eyes again. Then she tentatively put out her hand. He slipped the ring on her left ring finger. It was a perfect fit.

Now could he help her see that they, too, were a perfect fit? He would spend each day proving it to her, if she'd only let him.

"This isn't a *yes*," she said.

"Of course not." He smiled. His heart soared. Olivia loved him.

She fluttered her finger and held up the ring to the chandelier and watched it sparkle.

"We've only had one fight, and it hurt me so much," Olivia whispered.

"But sweetheart, you want everyone in the world to be happy and find love. We love each other. But what advice would the matchmaker offer? And shouldn't she be happy, too? I know I can make you happy. I love you, Olivia. Isn't love everything?"

Olivia looked down at the ring and then up into his eyes. "I do," she said softly.

Barbara shrieked, pounding on the table. "It's a *yes*!"

"She loves me," Nick shouted, and then he swept Olivia off her feet and kissed her.

Everyone in the room clapped.

"I have my two favorite women, the women I love, around the table. This calls for a celebration," Nick exclaimed. "Champagne and chocolate for everyone."

After dinner, as Barbara, Nick, and Olivia walked out of the dining room, a band in the main lobby began playing the song Nick had requested.

Strains of *Night and Day*, the song he heard when he first met Olivia, greeted them. Nick took Olivia in his arms and whispered, "They're playing our song." He strolled her around the reception area, kissed her with a passion he'd never experienced before, and sighed. Nick beamed at his bride-to-be. He couldn't remember being so happy. No more lonely nights, no more lonely hearts. Hope springs eternal at Eternal Springs.

The End

Marilyn's Spaghetti Alla Carbonara

Ingredients

4 eggs, lightly beaten
1 pound package of spaghetti
1 sweet onion
1 garlic clove
1 stick of butter (8 tablespoons)
Olive oil to coat pan
1 pound thick-sliced bacon, diced
Fresh ground black pepper, to taste
Chopped Italian parsley to garnish
4 tablespoons of grated Parmesan cheese

Directions

Sauté the diced bacon in a skillet until crisp. Drain on a paper towel.

Chop onions and garlic and sauté in olive oil until brown.

Drain on a paper towel.

Beat eggs in a bowl.

Cook spaghetti (with 1 tablespoon of salt and 1 tablespoon of olive oil) according to directions on the package until al dente (don't overcook); drain well in colander.

Put cooked spaghetti back into pot on low heat.

Stir in eggs until they coat and scramble on the spaghetti.

Add stick of butter and stir.

Toss in bacon and stir.

Toss in grated Parmesan cheese and stir well to mix.

Season with freshly ground black pepper to taste and garnish with parsley.

Serve on a platter.

Marilyn Baron

Marilyn Baron writes in a variety of genres, from humorous coming-of-*middle*-age women's fiction to historical romantic thrillers and romantic suspense to paranormal/fantasy. *THE VAMPIRE NEXT DOOR* is her twelfth novel published with The Wild Rose Press. Her novel, *THE ALIBI*, will be released later this year. She's received writing awards in Single Title, Suspense Romance, Novel With Strong Romantic Elements, and Paranormal/Fantasy Romance, and was a Finalist for the 2017 Georgia Author of the Year Awards in the Romance category for her book, *Stumble Stones: A Novel*. A public relations consultant in Atlanta, she graduated with a BS in Journalism and a minor in Creative Writing from the University of Florida. She loves to travel and sets many of her books in places she's visited.

Read more about Marilyn's books at www.marilynbaron.com

Table for Six

Melissa Klein

Acknowledgments

I wish to thank my sisters—those of birth, marriage, and choice—and acknowledge their significance in my life. Over the years, these women have demonstrated true friendship and love by dividing my sorrow and multiplying my joy. Many of those times have been around a table much like the one featured in this story. I'm eternally grateful for those moments of comfort and kindness.

Melissa Klein

Table for Six

Chapter One

Jessica Martin toed the wide-planked boards, setting the porch swing in motion. "I found the place with no problem. No GPS or anything."

From the other end of the call, her brother, Ryan, laughed. "Might that have something to do with the fact nothing in Mills County, Georgia, ever changes?"

"Nope. Totally my superior memory." One that refused to allow a painful childhood to fade into the past. "Three turns off the highway and I was pulling into Aunt Myrtle's driveway."

"What's it look like?" Tension radiated through the connection. "Matt and I didn't go back to her place after the funeral."

Her younger brother's efforts at honoring the woman who'd put a roof over their heads outpaced hers. Jess couldn't bring herself to pretend she mourned the woman—wouldn't be there now if it weren't for the Will. "Roof looks good. Porch could use a coat of paint. Inside…"

She gazed through a window into the kitchen where she'd toiled most of the day. "I had to dig a tunnel from the back door through the kitchen to her bedroom." She wedged the phone between her ear and shoulder and took a sip of lemonade. "Do you remember her being such a pack rat when we were kids?" After graduating high school, Jess hung around Millsboro long enough to raise Ryan and Matt. Then she escaped the faded yellow cottage and Myrtle's benign neglect, never looking back.

"I recall she kept all her magazines in the attic and enough yarn to knit an elephant a sweater, but nothing like you're describing. You sure you don't want to just hire some folks to come clean the place out?"

"I need to do as much of the work as I can if we're going to walk away from the sale with enough money to pay off her debts. Once I get the junk cleaned out, I can better assess how much work needs to be done inside before we can put the place on the market."

"Are you up to all that?"

Jessica rubbed her thigh, her fingers tracing scar tissue. "You worry too much. I'm as healed as I'm going to be." While in Afghanistan the previous year, her Humvee had driven over an IED. She'd been "lucky," having lost only her left foot and hearing on the same side.

"You know Matt and I would help if we could. He's got a new job, and my Trisha's due any day now…"

"I know." Both her brothers had settled down while the army had kept her on the move. Just the way she liked it. "I guess it's a good thing I'm between jobs." Following her discharge, she'd drifted around the country visiting friends and searching for work. Nothing had come through so far, but an interview as a civilian contractor in Huntsville, Alabama, the previous week seemed promising.

"Have you run into anyone we know?"

"No, thank goodness." She twisted her torso, trying to stretch the kink in her back. "Don't plan to either. I drove back out to the highway where they have one of those megastores, thinking I'd be less likely to see folks from the old days." Those who remembered the town's charity case.

Movement from the house next door caught her attention. A slender girl with long, dark hair stepped out of the screened-in back porch and flung a metal pan into the yard. It made a couple of bounces before landing in front of a doghouse. A beagle snuffled over to investigate, nosed the contents, and then returned to his house. "The meat loaf's so burned even the dog won't eat it." The girl sank to the concrete steps, drew her knees to her chest, and cried.

"Ryan, let me call you back later."

"Everything okay?"

"Yeah, it's fine. Just the neighbor kid."

Curiosity had Jessica's brain whirling. As an intelligence specialist, observation and analysis had become engrained into her personality. The girl appeared old enough to be on her own, but why, in this microwave-ready world, would she be cooking? Why wasn't she watching TV or hanging out at the community pool on the first week of summer break?

The back door opened, and three more girls poured out into the yard, the youngest barely out of diapers. "What are we going to eat now, Alice?" the next oldest asked.

Another, around seven or so, crossed her arms. "I'm not eating another tuna sandwich. You put too much mayo in it."

The youngest tugged on Alice's shirt. "Mac and cheese, mac and cheese."

The older girl scooped up the toddler. "Chloe, we don't have any of the instant kind, and I don't know how to make it like Mamma used to."

Jessica eased off the swing and crossed the narrow space between the postwar homes. "I have a leftover pizza you're welcome to."

Alice pushed the girls behind her. "No, thank you, ma'am."

"It's pepperoni." Jess fought the urge to close the distance between her and the girls. Did they have enough food in the house? They looked clean. No visible bruises.

"We're fine." Alice jutted out her chin, her hard gaze daring Jessica to say otherwise.

The next oldest peeped around her sister's shoulder. "But—"

"What did Dad say?"

The hairs on the back of Jess's neck stood to attention. What kind of man left four young girls on their own? The same kind of person who expected an eleven-year-old to tend to her younger brothers for days on end.

The whine of tires against asphalt stopped the conversation. A truck door banged shut. "What's Daddy doing home?" Alice shot her sister a glare. "Did you call him, Ella? I told you we were fine."

A man wearing a Mills County Fire Department uniform rounded the corner of the house. He embraced the older girls in turn before taking the toddler from Alice. "Want to tell me what happened this time?"

Her memories rewound time, smoothing the creases at the corners of the man's eyes and lightening the hair curling around his ball cap from brown to blond. Of all the folks she most wanted to avoid, Sam Taylor ranked number one. He held the top spot for regrets as well.

With any luck he'd be so engrossed in his girls, he wouldn't notice her. She took a backwards step, hoping to slip away.

"Penny got into the fingernail polish."

"Ella broke the Internet."

"Chloe bit Mrs. Jenkins."

He turned to Alice. "This true? I thought you promised to help."

The girl clenched her fists. "We don't need anyone to look after us. I can do it."

Sam leaned in, cupping his daughter's cheek. "We'll talk about that later." He then turned his attention to Jessica. "Thank you, ma'am, for seeing after my girls. I assure you…" Recognition widened his eyes. "Jessica? Jessica Martin."

For a split second, she considered denying her identity. "Yeah, Sam. It's me."

His smile broadened. "What are you doing back here?" He stepped across into Myrtle's yard, sending her heart into overdrive.

She licked at lips that had suddenly gone dry. "Fixing up my aunt's place. My brothers and I are going to sell it."

"The girls and I sure do miss her. She was a big help to me."

Her eyes widened. Must have been some other person because the description didn't match the woman who'd raised her and her brothers. Myrtle put a roof over their heads, food in their stomachs, and not much more.

The toddler squirmed her way out of Sam's arms to join her sisters in a pinecone war. "Stop that. Someone's going to be crying here in a second."

"I should let you go." She backed away.

"You're welcome to join us for dinner. I've got the makings for a meat loaf. We can catch up while it cooks."

"Actually, I don't think you do." She pointed to the mound by the doghouse. "Your oldest gave it her best shot."

Sam let out a breath. "All right, everyone, into the truck. We're going to Hamburger Heaven."

A chorus of cheers arose from the girls. Alice scooped up the youngest and then herded the others toward the front of the house.

"There's plenty of room in my SUV." Sam shot her a lopsided smile—one that had once made her weak-kneed. "I'd love to hear how you've been all these years."

"Thanks." Her heart pounded. The last thing she needed to do was spend time with the only man she'd ever loved. "But I've got tons to do here."

His smile evaporated, making her wish things could be different. That she was different. Or more accurately—that she was same girl she'd been all those years ago.

"I've been inside Miss Myrtle's house. You're going to be here for a while."

"All summer from the look of things." Given the number of boxes from the Home Shopping Network and the lack of upkeep.

Sam's familiar smile returned. "Fantastic. We'll have plenty of time to catch up then." He followed his girls around the corner of the house and drove away.

Jess stood frozen in place, trying to decide whether the prospect of renewing her friendship with Sam was a good or bad thing. Time hadn't done much to change the kind, decent man she'd give her heart to. Her war wounds ached as she limped back inside. She popped a pain pill, something she hadn't needed in weeks. "It's this place," she said to the cluttered kitchen. "It awakens every injury I've ever had." Jess rubbed at the center of her chest as she realized Sam might be able to do the same to her heart.

****

Later that night, Sam clipped the baby monitor onto his jean pocket and slipped out the back door. He stepped onto the porch, his boots rapping against the ancient boards. Through the kitchen window, he could make out Jessica's silhouette as she moved about. He knocked on the screen door. "It's me, Jess."

She opened up, her pretty brown eyes wide with surprise. "Hey. What's up?"

He shifted his weight from foot to foot, rethinking his decision to come over. After all, they hadn't spoken in over fifteen years. What made him think she wanted to talk now? "Got time to take a break?"

"I guess." She glanced over her shoulder. "I'd invite you in, but…"

"That's okay. We can sit out here." He pulled the monitor from his back pocket. "Not sure of the range on this thing anyway."

"How was dinner?"

He waited for her to take up a spot on the swing and then joined her. "Lively, as you can imagine from the few minutes you spent with my girls. Penny spilled her drink, and Ella decided she's a vegetarian."

A smile touched her lip. "Hamburger Heaven is a bad place to make that determination."

Something inside him stirred as they shared a laugh. A warm ease spread through his veins. "Too true, but that's my Ella." Following the death of his wife, there'd been few things outside his girls to bring him joy. "It'll pass. Next week she'll want to shave her hair. It's her way of dealing with losing her mom."

"Ryan's kept up with things here in Millsboro more than Matt and me. I was sorry to hear about Lindsay's death."

"Thanks." He swallowed past the lump in his throat. "It's been hard on all of us, Alice especially. She tries to take over for her mother, looking after her sisters, laundry, cooking."

Jessica stiffened, her hand tightening down on the swing's armrest. "That's a lot to expect from a girl of...what is she, thirteen, fourteen?"

He nodded. Alice's behavior had been the topic of discussion during several grief counseling sessions. "She turned thirteen in January. That's one of the reasons I came over here. I remembered how it was when you and your brothers came to live with Miss Myrtle. I didn't want you to think I was doing the same."

Jessica's gaze turned to the backyard. She pointed to a wire strung between two dogwoods. "I've hung many a load of laundry out on that clothesline."

"That was no way for you to spend your teen years." And certainly not what he wanted for Alice, despite her insistence she could take care of her sisters.

Jessica cocked an eyebrow. A gesture, even in the low light and as dense as he could sometimes be, he could clearly understand.

"From the time Lindsay got sick, I've hired eight different housekeepers and sitters. We've gone through two since school got out. They all quit after a couple days."

"What in the world? Over four little girls?"

Sam nodded. "The one today didn't last a week. My girls are a handful, especially Alice. She sees every woman who steps across the threshold as a threat to her mother's memory."

"What are you going to do?"

Wasn't that the question of the year? "I have the next two days off from the fire department. That will give me time to make some arrangements. I suppose I can put Chloe and Penny in daycare. There are enough day camps to keep Ella occupied, and all Alice wants to do is read. The hardest part is finding someone who can stay overnight when I'm at the station."

"I'll do it."

He waved away her offer. "I wasn't suggesting. I know you've got enough on your plate cleaning out Miss Myrtle's house."

"I know you weren't hinting."

"That's too much to ask." He took to his feet, pacing the length of the porch. The past few minutes had been like time had rolled backwards. He'd let his thoughts spill right on out of his mouth, just like in the old days.

"It's not. Remember back during the summer between junior and senior year?"

How could he forget? Despite everything she was going through at the time, it had also been when he'd fallen in love with Jessica.

"I still owe you for all the times you let me hang out at your house. A little babysitting will only be a partial payment for that."

"A little babysitting. Were you paying attention this afternoon?"

"You're overnight at the fire station every third night, correct?"

He nodded. "Yeah, twenty-four hours on, forty-eight off." He squeezed her hand. "Thanks."

"So, no big deal. I did Intel for ten years in the army. How difficult can four little girls be?"

The tendrils of connection wound their way around his heart. The years of separation evaporated until they were Jessie and Sam, two joined-at-the-hip friends. But like history, people had a way of repeating themselves. Once her obligations to her brothers were complete, she'd joined the army and never returned to Millsboro.

What was keeping her from doing that again?

Chapter Two

How hard can four little girls be?

Jessica's query of two days ago echoed in her brain. Just collecting Sam's brood had her longing for combat boots, ACUs, and MREs. With fourteen hours until Sam returned in the morning, a successful handoff of four living children was possible—if they made it through the car ride home.

"Meany, meany, butter beany." A wet and sunburned Ella taunted her older sister, who refused to relinquish her front seat position.

Alice thumbed over her shoulder. "Get in the back with the other babies."

Ella shifted her attention to the rear seats of Sam's SUV. "Shotgun." A day at swim camp should have tired the ten-year-old but hadn't. She yanked Penny out of the way by the seven-year-old's braid.

Penny fought against her sister's grip, baring her teeth. "Stupid head."

At least Jess had been allowed to yell at the soldiers under her command. She cut her eyes at Ella, who quickly let go of her sister's hair. "Reach a compromise peacefully, and there'll be Popsicles when we get home." The positive reinforcement tactic had worked with her squad of equally physical eighteen and nineteen-year-old soldiers, so perhaps seven-and ten-year-old girls would also be motivated by the carrot-versus-stick method. The argument settled to a simmer as both girls climbed into seats and buckled in.

Now she turned her attention to securing Chloe in her car seat. Jessica wrestled with the complicated harness system rivaling that of a parachutist. There were straps, clips, and buckles coming from numerous points in the seat. "Where does this piece go?"

From her spot in the front seat, Alice looked over her shoulder. "You're doing it wrong."

Obviously. Jessica inserted one of the medal tips into a buckle hoping to hear a click. "Like this?"

The teen huffed out a breath and climbed out of the front seat. She elbowed Jess out of the way. "It fits in here, and then you pull this strap."

"Thanks." By the time they'd finished, Chloe was beginning to fuss. Within a block, her whimpers turned into full-blown screams. Nothing in Jessica's military career had prepared her for this scenario. "Let's sing something." In the pre-handheld gadget days, she and her brothers had frequently entertained each other that way on car rides.

"Let's not and say we did." Following the snarky comment, Alice turned her face toward the passenger-side window.

A retort poised on the end of Jessica's tongue, but she bit it back. "Who knows 'On Top of Old Smokey'?" Apparently none of the girls did or any of the other tunes Jessica sang solo in her attempts to soothe the fussy three-year-old.

Back inside the house, things weren't going any better. Alice again nudged Jess out of the way, reaching into the freezer for the promised treats. She led the girls back onto the screened porch just off from the kitchen, making sure they had plenty of paper towels for drips. "Y'all stay out her while I nuke us some dinner."

As much as Jess admired the teen's childcare skills, she couldn't let the rudeness continue. "Hold up." Jess blocked Alice's path to the fridge. "Your dad left instructions for me to make you girls spaghetti and meatballs."

"I got this." She planted her hands on tiny hips and stuck out her chin. "Why don't you go on back home? I'll call you if we set the kitchen on fire or anything."

Jess's temper flickered, but she had to give the girl props. Alice would be ruled by no one. Could she be coaxed, especially if Jess treated her more like a peer than another child to manage? "I made your dad a promise. That's why. I don't mean to suggest you're not doing a good job looking after your sisters. I know some parents who could take lessons from you."

Alice released her breath in a huff. "Fine. Have at it." She stalked into the living room, making as much noise as possible as she turned on the TV.

Jess savored the minor victory, sensing it might be her only one. After locating the pasta and meatballs, she searched the pantry for tomato sauce to complete the meal. Sam had a decently supplied cabinet of canned goods, but not the one vital ingredient. "That's not going to work," she muttered to herself. She wasn't going to the store, either. Knowing Alice, she'd take the opportunity to barricade the door. "Let's see what we can do for plan B." She opened the fridge, looking for what she could cook as a substitute. Thankfully, Sam had all the makings for an equally easy dish. After assembling all the ingredients, she began pulling the meat from the rotisserie chicken and dicing it.

"That doesn't look like any spaghetti I've ever seen."

Jess turned slowly as if the girl were a deer that might flee. "I thought I'd make chicken squares. I hope you girls eat that."

"Yeah." Alice craned her neck to see into the kitchen. "It's one of our favorites. Our mom used to…" She bit her lip and turned her gaze to the floor.

Jessica's heart ached for the girl who obviously still mourned her mother. *If I offer to teach her, she'll turn me down.* An alternative took form, one that might allow the prideful teen to acquire the instruction she desired without seeming to come under Jess's tutelage. She slowed her prep, talking aloud in the hope Alice would catch on. "Now that I've got the chicken off the bone, I'm going to mix in a package of cream cheese. Sometimes I sauté an onion and mix that in, but I figured the little ones might not like that."

"Do you have to measure everything to make it come out right?" Alice took a step closer to stand at the edge of the counter.

"No, I just eyeball it." She opened the package of tortillas and began spooning in the chicken and vegetable mixture. "I could write down the recipe if you like."

The teen took a backward step, making Jess think she'd pushed her luck too far. As she left the room, the girl looked over her shoulder. "Just tell me the oven temp and how long to cook it. That's all I need."

Half an hour later when the timer went off, Alice collected her siblings, making them wash their hands in the kitchen sink. While Jess dished up the plates, the girls crowded around a tiny table in the center of a large breakfast nook. "Be sure to cut Chloe's into small pieces," Alice said as she hefted the toddler into the high chair. They even said a sweet prayer to bless the meal. Jess relished the silence that followed almost as much as she did the food. All too soon the girls were at it again.

"Stop kicking me." Penny pushed at Ella's shoulder.

In response, the ten-year-old crossed her eyes and stuck out her tongue. "You kicked me first."

Just as Jess was about to intervene, Alice stood from the table. "Enough." She moved behind her sisters' chairs. "Bath time, you two. Ella, you're first since you're dirtiest." She pulled the chair away from the table and "helped" her sister from her seat.

Ella dug in her heals, resisting being removed from the kitchen. "But I've been in the water all day."

For all the whining and flailing about Ella was doing, Alice managed her younger sister with a great deal of patience. "Which is why you need to wash the chorine off. It's bad for your skin." Once she got Ella on her way upstairs, Alice turned her attention toward the two youngest girls. "Penny, you watch Chloe while I clean the kitchen."

Jess had been lost in her thoughts, recalling the battles she'd fought with Ryan and Matt over personal hygiene. She shook herself loose from those memories to attend to the children in her present care. "Don't worry about kitchen duty. I've got it."

"No." Alice waved away the offer. "You cooked, so I'll clean."

Her thoughts still on her own teenage years, Jess couldn't help wondering why the girl wasn't jonesing to escape responsibility. "Don't you want to be out with your friends? It's summertime. You should be having fun."

Alice cocked an eyebrow as if Jess had questioned Katy Perry's popularity. "Dad needs me."

"Your dad is lucky to have you." While Jess loved her brothers and tried to protect them as much as she was able, Aunt Myrtle had never fostered any sense of loyalty or affinity.

A flicker of a smile crossed Alice's face. However, before Jess could relish the moment, a fat drop of water hit the top of her head.

Another fell on Alice. "What the heck?"

Jess looked at the ceiling to see a dark circle forming. "Is the bathroom above us?"

Alice shook her raised fist. "Ella, I'm going to kill you." She took off toward the living room and up the stairs.

Jess checked the kitchen for any apparent dangers. "Penny, keep an eye on Chloe." Then she took off after the teen. When she reached the hall bathroom, she had a moment to understand why the previous babysitters had quit. Bubbles climbed the bathroom walls a good five feet, and the tile floor held at least an inch of soapy water. There wasn't time to count to ten or try any other patience-extending tactic. "Ella, shut that water off and drain the tub. Alice, quick, grab the biggest towels you've got."

Eight towels and forty minutes later, they had the bathroom disaster cleaned up. The girls were in their pajamas, and the kitchen was tidy. Jess sank to the living room sofa where the three older girls were watching TV. "I vote we all turn in."

Ella turned, her bottom lip protruding in a pout. "Are you going to tell Dad?"

Jess would give her eyeteeth to avoid another meltdown, but she wouldn't lie. "I have to, sweetie. Not to get you into trouble, but because he'll need to fix the ceiling."

Huge tears spilled down her cheeks. "He's. Going. To. Kill. Me." She punctuated each word with enough emotion to make any Hollywood actress proud.

Jeez. What kind of discipline did Sam use?

Alice rolled her eyes. "Stop being such a drama queen." She turned to Jess. "The most he'll do is take away her TV privileges."

"Oh, okay." It never crossed her mind that Sam would physically abuse his daughters, but it was good to hear nonetheless.

Alice narrowed her gaze, making Jess think she hadn't done enough to keep her thoughts from her face. "I know you think we're some type of charity case or that Dad doesn't know what he's doing, but you're wrong."

"I'm sorry if I gave you that impression. I thought otherwise. See my brothers and I grew up—"

"My dad told me about how Miss Myrtle used to be. About all you were responsible for."

"It's all in the past." Or more accurately, there was no point in talking about it if Sam's girls had different memories of her aunt. "I'm glad Myrtle showed you some kindness and that your growing up is better than mine."

"Well, it is. My sisters and me—I mean, my sisters and I—are just fine. We don't need a mom, and we sure don't need some drill sergeant watching after us. My family is fine the way it is, just the five of us."

Jessica's eyes widened. Message received and understood. "All right, then, I'll let you get your sisters settled in for the night. I'm going to camp out here on the sofa in case there's an emergency, but otherwise, I'll let you handle things." She listened to the soft sounds of the girls getting ready for bed. Within minutes they turned off the lights, and after reading for a while, Jess did the same.

Sometime during the night, Chloe stirred and cried out. Jess padded to the foot of the stairs in time to see Alice cross the hall from the room she shared with Ella. Returning to the sofa, Jess caught Alice's sweet soprano voice singing through the baby monitor. Whether it was all the day's activity or the girl's singing, Jess, too, drifted off again. At least for a while.

"I wet the bed."

Jess sat up and scrubbed the sleep from her eyes. Before her stood Chloe, whose mermaid pajamas were soaked. "I see. Let's get you cleaned up."

By the time she had the three-year-old settled and the wet bedding in the wash, the sun was peeking over the horizon. Rather than return to the sofa, she made her way to the kitchen to start the coffeepot for Sam. With the girls still in their beds, she had a moment to absorb the cozy ambiance. A crafter's hand was evident in the cheery, yellow cabinets and stylized fruit paintings on the wall. When the coffee was ready, Jess took her cup to the bistro table the girls and she had crowded around the night before. She ran her hand along the mosaic top made from broken china. While the table was certainly a work of art, it wasn't at all practical for a growing family.

When Sam's shift change came and went, Jess assumed his station had caught a call. Per their plan, she started breakfast for the girls and mentally recalculated her day's plans for Aunt Myrtle's house. A knot formed in her stomach. "How difficult are the little minions in the morning?" Not only did she have to feed and dress everyone, there was the time crunch of getting them to their respective places. All while dealing with Alice's constant snark. "Food worked before. Maybe the way to a kid's heart is through her stomach." She gathered the ingredients for French toast, hoping a good start to the day outweighed the syrupy mess sure to come.

****

Sam stopped on the back porch long enough to kick off his boots before heading into the kitchen to relieve Jessica from babysitting duty. He'd texted with Alice throughout the evening, so he had an idea how much he owed his friend. What he wasn't prepared for was the sight that met him in the kitchen. His heart seized and grief opened afresh. Jess faced the stove while the girls chattered happily at the table—a scene that had greeted him many mornings until his wife's death. He shook his head to dissolve the memory. Lindsay was gone. This was Jess, a woman in his life temporarily. Her efficiency didn't indicate a commitment.

"More bacon, anyone?" Jess asked.

Sam swallowed past the grief. "I could eat."

"Daddy!" His girls sang their greeting, which took the edge off his pain and the horror he'd witnessed overnight. As many years as he'd worked for Mills County Fire Department, he'd never grown accustomed to the loss of life.

"How are my princesses this morning?" He kissed the girls in turn. "Everyone sleep well?"

Jess cocked an eyebrow. "You okay?"

He nodded. "Just tired."

"Ella overflowed the tub."

"Penny spilled syrup."

"Chloe has a runny nose."

Sam reveled in the chaos as he accepted a plate of food from Jess. Wedging into a spot at the table, he talked between bites. "Alice, did you remember to take the trash to the curb?"

"Yes, sir." She wiped her mouth with a napkin. "We're done with breakfast. I'll get everyone dressed and ready to go." She bustled her sisters from the table, carefully wiping Chloe's mouth as she released her from her high chair.

"Daddy, you smell like smoke," Penny said as she passed. "Did you put out a fire?"

Sam shuttered his eyes to block out the images. "I sure did, sweetheart." He planted a kiss on the top of her head. "Be good and listen to your sister."

After the girls left, Jessica joined him at the table. "Rough night?"

"How'd you know?"

She shrugged. "I recognize battle weary when I see it. House fire?"

"Fully involved when we got there. Multigenerational family, three stories, four kids, not a smoke detector in the place."

"Did everyone…"

"Nope. As bad as it was losing Lindsay, at least we had time to prepare. There's a family across town planning a funeral this morning."

Jess patted his arm. "You look done in. Why don't you grab a nap, and I'll take the girls where they need to be?"

He shook his head. "You've done enough already. Besides, I'm sure you've got plenty to do on Myrtle's place."

"You trying to get rid of me?"

"No!" His head shot up. "Gosh, no. I like having you back home." He raked his hand through his hair. "In fact, I was wondering if you'd like to come with me and the girls to the Magnolia Festival tomorrow. That is, if you don't mind spending more time with my hellions."

"They weren't that bad." The smile she shot him said otherwise. "It's just that I have a lot to do over at the house."

Something inside him couldn't let her retreat. "I tell you what, let me get the girls situated, and then I'll come over and help."

"I can't let you do that. You need to sleep."

"Surely there's something you need another pair of hands for."

"All right." She eyed him like she still wanted to change her mind. "But under one condition."

Excitement rose as it hadn't in months, years perhaps. "Name it."

"Get some shut-eye before you come over. Believe me, you're going to need it later this evening when the girls get back home."

"And you'll go with us to the festival?"

She rolled her eyes. "Yes, I'll let you drag me to the darn Magnolia Festival, but don't even think of asking me to ride the Ferris wheel."

"Two tours in Afghanistan and you're afraid of a carnival ride." He chuckled.

The corners of her mouth turned up. "Exactly. That should tell you something."

Jessica brought levity to his life that had been lacking for longer than he cared to recall. Even with all she'd been through, she could still see things in a positive light. "It's a deal and a date. I can't wait."

Chapter Three

Jess let out a breath and gauged the distance between her and the next kiddie ride. "You guys, go on ahead. I'll catch up." She tried ignoring the shooting pain running down her left side. "No more lifting huge boxes of books," she muttered. Lack of sleep added to her lethargy. Every time she closed her eyes, Sam and that lopsided grin of his invaded her dreams.

"You're limping." He slowed his pace to walk alongside her. "Do you need to rest?" Wrapping an arm around her, he urged her to a nearby bench. "Girls, let's take a breather for a second." They gathered around as their dad handed out water bottles.

"Might be a good idea." Jess resisted the urge to lean on his shoulder as she slumped to the bench. Falling for Sam wasn't in the plan. She had an appointment with a realtor to list Aunt Myrtle's house, and the military contractor from Alabama called to schedule a second interview for next week. If the job prospect didn't work out, she had friends in Colorado who'd invited her to visit. Either way, her days in Millsboro were numbered. As she took in the sights and sounds of the town's fair, the pull of the road wasn't as strong. Could the man and his four daughters have something to do with her lack of wanderlust?

Sam slung his arm around her shoulders, sending her pulse soaring. "You're working too hard. You've got to let me help you more with the heavy stuff." He combed his fingers through her hair.

"I don't know. You've got enough on your plate." Jess stretched her sore muscles, buying time while she weighed her options. Having his assistance meant Aunt Myrtle's house went on the market sooner. However, accepting his help also increased her exposure to his charm, something she'd never been able to resist.

"It's the least I can do for you watching the girls." He winked. "Not only are they all in one piece, they seemed to have had a good time with you yesterday."

"Fine. You can help, but only with the bulky things. I can handle the rest."

"Does it hurt?" Penny eyed the prosthetic leg showing below her shorts.

Sam stiffened beside her. "Don't be rude."

Glad for the distraction, Jess waved away his concern. "No, that's okay. I told them the other day how I got injured and showed them my prosthetic." She brushed a stray curl from the girl's face. "Right now, Penny, it hurts a little. But since we've had a moment to rest, I'm good to go."

She grinned. "Oh, goody." She pointed up ahead to the tents where people sold crafts and homemade food products. "Let's go down there, Daddy. I want another dress for my Prairie Girl doll."

Sam pressed his lips together. "Ahhh, I don't know…"

She clasped her hands in supplication. "Please. I won't ask for anything else today."

"Okay, my shiny Penny." He shot her a smile that didn't reach his eyes.

Jessica walked into foreign territory nearly as unfamiliar as Afghanistan had once been. The bright colors of the quilts and shiny mason jars filled with garden-fresh vegetables spoke of warm, inviting homes filled with love. Sam and the girls plowed along the dirt paths as if they'd done this many times. Jess recalled the paintings on the kitchen walls and the bistro table. Perhaps Lindsay had been fond of shopping from craft fairs. The wares in the next stall caught her attention. "Sam, look at these." She ran her hand over the oak table's smooth surface.

"It's nice." He nodded. "Very solid. You're not thinking of buying it, are you?"

"No, silly. For you. This is exactly what you need in the kitchen. That little thing you've got now is entirely too little for you and the girls." She rapped her knuckles against the top. "And you won't be scrubbing food out of the grooves of this table."

Alice folded her arms across her chest. "My mom made that table."

"Oh." Her gaze shot to the stricken eyes of Sam and his girls. Even Chloe seemed to clue into Jessica's terrible faux pas. "I didn't know. It's a beautiful table and all. I just thought…"

"It was the last thing Lindsay made before she got sick. It's been a reminder…" Sam's jaw ticked. "Anyway, you had no way of knowing." He drew in a breath. "What ya say we head back home for some ice cream sundaes?"

The girls reacted to their dad's suggestion with cheers. But on the way home, Jess couldn't shake the sense she'd put a damper on their day out. Alice's death-stare confirmed the notion. After they climbed out of Sam's SUV, Jess waved to his crew. "It was fun." She headed toward Myrtle's back door. "Thanks for including me."

Sam thumbed over his shoulder. "You're passing up ice cream?" The spark had gone out of his eyes, deepening her regret.

"Yeah." She rubbed her leg. "I'm more tired than I thought." Her leg ached but not as much as the center of her chest. Why hadn't she picked up on the significance of the tiny table? See, this was why she had no business getting tangled up with Sam. "I need an ice pack more than ice cream."

He narrowed his eyebrows. "Text if you need anything. I'll see you after my next shift."

"You bet." She raised her hand to the girls. "See you tomorrow afternoon."

Jessica made her way through Aunt Myrtle's cleaned-out kitchen and into the living room where she was currently repainting the tobacco-stained walls. She slumped onto the plaid sofa. Chairs, bookcases, end tables, and other furnishings took up the center of the room. Every piece had been a part of her childhood, and it would all go into the dumpster or be donated without her giving it a second thought. In fact, Jess held no emotional attachment to her own possessions, not even the service medals she'd earned.

She trailed her hand along the scratchy fabric of the sofa. She and her brothers had watched countless hours of TV here. A memory of Sam's expression came to mind. Was something inside her broken that she couldn't seem to form attachments? Would she feel the loss of Sam and his girls when she left Millsboro? Given the day's disaster, it certainly seemed they'd be better off without her.

****

Two weeks later.

"Happy Father's Day!"

Sam stumbled into the kitchen, scrubbing sleep from his eyes. "Hey, what's all this?" He'd heard noises from below and hoped he wouldn't meet a small disaster when he stopped pretending to sleep and came downstairs.

Ella pointed to the fully laden table. "We made you breakfast."

"I made you a present at daycare this week." Penny thrust the construction paper tie toward him. "See, we dyed the macaroni first, then glued it on."

"Wow. That's fabulous." He hung it around his neck as he took his seat. "I'll wear it all day."

Alice slid a plate of pancakes in front of him. "There's powdered sugar and jam on the table."

He took a hesitant bite. Delicate flavors of vanilla and cinnamon bloomed in his mouth. "Man, this is good." He chewed and swallowed. "Where'd you learn to make this?"

"Sergeant Martin."

He frowned. "She makes you call her that?"

The corner of his daughter's mouth turned up. "No, she lets us call her Jessica."

Ella lowered her fork and wiped her mouth with a napkin. "Miss Jessica has been teaching Alice to cook. She's also been reading with me and helping Penny with her multiplication tables."

That sounded more like the Jess he knew. She'd sacrificed her own college scholarship, staying in town to ensure her brothers finished school. "I hope you tell her 'thank you.'"

Guilt shone on their faces. "I see how it is." He shook his finger. "You girls, be nice to her. She's doing me a big favor."

Ella climbed in his lap and planted a syrupy kiss on his cheek. "We will. I promise."

They chatted while eating the delicious breakfast Alice had made. When they'd consumed the last piece of bacon, she asked, "What shall we do today?" His oldest stood and began collecting everyone's plates.

"Hey, hold up." He caught her hand. "I'm very proud of you. This was fantastic."

She beamed. "I'm glad you like it. Happy Father's Day."

"Since it's my special day, I say we turn on the sprinkler this afternoon."

"Can we grill out hot dogs for supper?" Chloe asked.

Sam scooped his youngest into his arms. "I think that's a brilliant idea, and I know just who we should invite—"

"Miss Jessica!"

The chorus of small voices pleased him. Spending time with the lovely woman next door would make a great day even better. Sam glanced at his oldest, who was studiously loading the dishwasher. Three out of the four wasn't too bad. "What do you say?"

She shrugged. "Like you said, it's your day."

"I'll go over later and see if she wants to join us." He took a skillet from her hands. "I also think the dishes can wait. It's been a while since I've beat you at rummy. You up for a hand?"

She flashed a rare grin. "You're on."

As his girls squealed and danced around the kitchen, Sam's thoughts traveled next door. Since the fair, he and Jess had exchanged no more than a few words. He grabbed a soapy dish towel and began wiping down the table. Jessica's suggestion he replace Lindsay's table with something more practical had made complete sense. Shame burned in his chest at the way he'd reacted. He scrubbed over the bits of china his wife had painstakingly arranged.

Lindsay would always be part of his life—a vital part. Jess, on the other hand, represented both past and present. He tossed the cloth in the sink and joined his girls in the living room. Time would tell if the beautiful woman next door would be in his future as well. As he shuffled the playing cards, he had a sense he'd learn the answer when he walked next door later.

****

Knock, knock.

Jessica jolted at the sound she'd been dreading since Sam's girls spilled out his back door. For a moment, she considered ignoring the firm rap. She'd been avoiding those brown eyes of his and the apology she owed him for her callous suggestion at the fair. Instead, she laid down the trowel she'd been using to tile the bathroom, wiped her hands on a nearby rag, and faced the task ahead.

Jerking the door open, she drew in a breath. "I'm sorry for being so insensitive the other day. I should have known there was a significant reason you had the table. Please forgive me for not having a better sense about what you and the girls are going through."

Sam took a step back. "You're still worried about that?"

She nodded. With the apology came the flood of shame she'd experienced in the moment.

"Jess." He tilted her chin to gaze into her eyes. "Like I said before, you had no way of knowing, but if it makes you feel better, apology accepted."

The weight of guilt rolled from her shoulders. Aunt Myrtle was right about one thing. Confession was good for the soul.

"The girls and I want to know if you'd like to come over. We're grilling hot dogs for supper."

A rejection poised on her lips. Why would they want an outsider to intrude on their Father's Day celebration?

"That is, if you aren't tired of us." He cocked an eyebrow. "I know how much you love listening to squabbling children."

His lopsided grin did her in. Always had. "Sure. Let me get cleaned up, and I'll be over."

Following a shower and a mad dash around the kitchen to throw together a salad, Jess crossed the narrow strip of grass separating the two houses. As she neared Sam, his attention turned from the grill to her. An expression quickly crossed his face, one she couldn't interpret, but it made the blood rush to her cheeks nonetheless.

"I don't think I've ever seen you in a dress before, Jess."

She'd long since gotten over folks getting a gander at her prosthetic leg, but the halter top dress showed more of her arms and shoulders than her typical wardrobe of t-shirts. "Yeah, well, I'm behind on laundry, and I thought since it's Father's Day and all…"

"You look—" He swallowed hard. "You look very nice, Jessica."

Jessica? When did he start calling her that?

"Anyway, I made watermelon salad." She thrust the bowl at him. "I hope you and the girls like it."

He peered into the plastic-wrap covered bowl. "Jeez, Jess. It looks healthy. Why'd you go and bring a thing like that?"

She chuckled, relieved to have returned to typical Sam-and-Jess territory. "Because neither of us is getting any younger." She poked his side. "The girls tell me you made chief a few months back. Riding a desk instead of an engine, you've got to watch your girlish figure." The jest held no weight. As her hand made contact with Sam's stomach, Jess felt the ridges of muscles beneath his shirt.

"Well, if it's anything like the other dishes you've been teaching Alice, healthy or not, it'll be delicious. I've been meaning to tell you how much I appreciate all you're doing for my girls. They haven't been this happy since before—" He turned his attention to the grill.

"It's been my pleasure. They're great fun, and I'm having a blast with them." At least, most of the time. Alice still kept her at arm's length when they weren't in the kitchen together.

The girls chose that moment to show that beneath a thin veneer of girlish play lay four warrior women in the making. Penny turned the garden hose on the sandcastle Ella and Chloe were creating. Ella bolted from the sandbox and began pounding her younger sister while Chloe erupted into loud cries. Alice, who'd been reading under a shade tree, joined the melee by grabbing the hose and spraying her brawling sisters.

Jessica stalked over to the girls. "Cut it out. All of you." She took the hose from Alice and flung it aside. "Girls, what happened? One minute you're playing and the next you're trying to kill each other."

"Alice sprayed the hose in my face."

"Penny ruined my sandcastle."

Jessica stabbed a finger in their direction. "Apologize, both of you. And to your dad. This is ridiculous. You're sisters, family. No one else in the world is going to have your back the way family does. Besides it's your dad's day to relax. He shouldn't have to be dealing with you two going at it tooth and nail."

Ella and Penny hung their heads. "Sorry, Daddy."

"Sorry, Dad." Alice scooped up Chloe and wiped water from the still-whimpering toddler.

Sam shook his head. "Thank you, girls. Please set the table. Supper's ready." Frustration laced his words. When the girls moved over to the patio set to comply with his instructions, he dropped to a plastic seat and let out a breath. His jaw ticked.

Her pulse raced. God, not a repeat of the fair, please. "I don't know what came over me. I'm sorry if I was out of line."

He glanced up at her with eyes that once again held a small spark. "Are you kidding? I've been playing zone defense for the past year. It's nice to have someone to tag-team with."

Not since the army had she been part of something larger than herself. The sense of inclusion wound its tendrils around her heart. "I'm glad I can help."

Supper progressed without so much as a ketchup incident. After a quick cleanup, the girls played tag with the dog until twilight when their game turned to catching lightning bugs. With the leftovers stowed in the kitchen, Jess joined Sam on a wooden glider at the back of the yard. He reached for her hand, lacing his fingers with hers. A jolt of electricity shot up her arm, made stronger when she looked down at their intertwined fingers. "Blue nail polish?"

His deep chuckle resonated inside her. "Ella's idea. She wanted to give me a mani-pedi for Father's Day."

Her laugh started in her belly and spilled out her lips. "Oh my goodness, your girls are a hoot. I'm so glad I've had the opportunity to know them."

He tightened his grip. "I'm happy you're back, Jessie."

"Me, too." She shuttered her eyes.

He turned to face her. "Really?"

"Yeah. I can't believe I'm saying this, but coming back to Millsboro is the best thing I've done in years."

"I can't tell you how thrilled I am to hear you say that."

Her heart pounded against her chest as his gaze continued to penetrate hers. "It's true. It's given me the closure I've needed for all these years."

"It's done the opposite for me." He brushed his hand along her hair. "Seeing you again has opened up all these feelings I bottled up when you left. I loved my wife, and we built a beautiful life together with our girls. That doesn't mean I stopped loving you."

Her breath caught. "Oh." He loved her all this time? Jessica's words tangled on the way to her lips.

He leaned back but continued to play with her hair. "You don't have to say it back. I just wanted you to know how I feel."

"Miss Jessica, come play," Penny called.

She glanced at Sam's girls who were dancing around the dark backyard with glow sticks like little fairies. "Be there in a minute." Of course, she loved Sam. Time and distance hadn't changed that. Now his daughters held a special place in her heart as well. She had to take a job, and once she settled Aunt Myrtle's estate, there'd be no place for her to live. A sharp ache set up shop in her chest. Leaving this time would rival the pain of driving over that IED.

Chapter Four

"I'd never have guessed Myrtle's house would sell in less than a day." Sitting across the concrete table from Jessica, Sam continued recapping the whirlwind events of the past few weeks. "Full asking price, waived the inspection, closed in less time than it takes to say, 'Jack Robinson.'"

The July sun was just beginning to bear down on the first patrons at the hot dog stand where Jessica and Sam had worked during high school. She took a sip of limeade and stared at the footlong in front of her. "Certainly not what I expected." Completing her mission should have come with a little more job satisfaction. Aunt Myrtle's bills would be covered, per her Last Will and Testament. There'd even be a nice family moving in next to Sam and the girls. None of that seemed to alleviate the weight pressing on her chest.

Sam reached across to snag one of her tater tots. "What? Dairy Delight not to your taste anymore?"

"No, it's fine."

"I should have taken you someplace better to celebrate closing on the house."

"Really. It's okay. When would you have had the time anyway? You've got to pick up the girls at noon. Alice has that orthodontist appointment later today." Besides, she wasn't in the partying mood.

Having finished his meal—and part of hers—Sam crumpled up their food wrappers and then stretched. "We spent many summer nights here, didn't we?"

She glanced at the serving window and the teenage girl leaning through the opening. "It's infinitely more enjoyable on this side."

"Remember the time Ole Buddy let us off early and we went down to Fuller's Lake?"

"Yeah." The memory of that night bloomed to life. Sam had kissed her for the first time. Not long after that night, he'd told her he loved her, wanted them to be together. Back then, the pain of her growing up had proven too great for her to remain. Now staying wasn't an option for other reasons. "Speaking of jobs." She willed the words from her lips. "I got offered that position in Alabama I was telling you about."

"Oh." He knitted his brows. "When do you start?"

So not the question she wanted him to ask. "I thought since I have to be out of the house on Friday, I'd drive up then."

"That's the day after tomorrow." He let out a breath. "Okay, then, the girls and I will just have to make the most of you while you're still here."

"I figured since you found a housekeeper, you'd be good to go, but if she can't start by your next shift, I can leave Saturday or Sunday."

"That's not what I meant." Sam took off his ball cap and ran his fingers through his hair. "I knew all along you were here only temporarily. We—" His gaze shot to hers. "I've enjoyed having you back. It just felt like old times, that's all."

"I've loved being back. Much more than I thought I would." She spent far too many hours imagining what her life would have been like if she'd stayed. "You've raised four wonderful little women. You should be proud of that."

"That means a lot coming from you." The corner of his mouth turned up. "I guess you've already done your child-rearing, with your brothers."

A tiny laugh bubbled up. "It's not exactly the same, but I do feel some measure of pride in getting Ryan and Matt to adulthood in one piece. They've turned out to be good family men."

"All thanks to you, I'm sure." He cocked his head, his gaze again boring into hers. "Have you ever wanted babies?"

"I've thought of it." Especially since she'd taken on caring for his girls. Goodness, she was going to miss them. Tears pricked the backs of her eyes.

Ask me to stay!

Fear of rejection kept her from voicing her desire. Her own parents hadn't wanted her and her brothers. The primal abandonment she'd suffered had always gotten in the way of her forming attachments to people—or so said a therapist she'd once seen. Despite Sam expressing his love for her back on Father's Day, there was a big difference between loving someone and finding a place for her in his future.

"Maybe that will happen for you someday…once you've settled in Huntsville."

Pain lanced through her heart. "Who knows?"

Sam's phone buzzed. He pulled it from his pocket and looked at the screen. "It's Mrs. Dupree."

"She's the mom who's having Chloe over for a playdate, right?" Penny and Ella were at First Baptist's Vacation Bible School, and, as usual, Alice was home reading.

He nodded as he slid his finger across the phone's screen. "How are the girls doing?" He rubbed his forehead, listening to a neighbor down the street. "I'll be right there." After ending the call, he stood and quickly gathered their trash.

"What's wrong?" Her pulse thrummed in her ears.

"Chloe's running a fever. It's high. Mrs. Dupree took her temperature, and it's one hundred three."

"Let's go." Jess bolted for Sam's SUV. "I'll drop you two off at the house and then pick up Penny and Ella from VBS."

He climbed in behind the wheel and put the truck in gear the second she clicked her seatbelt. "I've got plenty of Children's Motrin, but I'm out of Gatorade."

"I'm on it." She'd pitch a tent in Sam's backyard, and the job could wait. Jess wasn't leaving until Chloe's fever was gone.

****

Sam eased down the hallway, peeking in on the older girls as they slept. At the bottom of the stairs, he stopped cold at the sight of Jess cradling Chloe in her arms. He drew nearer, his gaze falling on his daughter's steady breathing before turning to Jessica. In sleep, her expression had relaxed, in contrast to the past thirty-six hours. Who knew something as common as strep throat could make a child so sick? He longed to stroke the loose strands of Jessica's hair or caress the curve of her cheek. He dared not—she'd earned her rest—and doing so would only make letting her go more painful.

She stirred from her place in the recliner. "What time is it?"

"A little before five." He lowered to the edge of the coffee table, so they could talk without waking Chloe. "Why don't you stretch out for a bit? I've had a couple hours shut-eye, so I'm good for a while." Later that day, Jessica had a good six hours on the road to Alabama, and he didn't want her sleep-deprived while doing it.

"If you're sure." She lowered the footrest.

Chloe stirred, clinging to Jess's shirt with a whimper.

Jess patted her back and resettled in the recliner. "Better not risk moving her. She's only been sleeping about an hour."

He brushed the three-year-old's head, relieved to feel her cool skin. "When did her fever finally break?" Despite several doses of antibiotics and fever reducers, Chloe's high temp continued through the previous day and into the night.

"About forty-five minutes after the last round of meds. I think she's finally turning the corner."

"I certainly hope so." He let out a breath. This was the first time any of them had been sick since his wife died. "If she is on the mend, don't be surprised if she's running circles around us by noon."

"I can—" Jess tried to suppress a yawn and failed miserably. "I can totally believe that. Kids are resilient." She rubbed her eyes.

Sam leaned down and drew his sleeping child into his arms. "You need a nap."

"Fine, you win." She stood, stretched, and then tumbled onto the sofa. "I can pack the car after breakfast. That'll give me plenty of time to get to Huntsville before dark."

He took Jessica's spot, tucking Chloe's head in the crook of his neck. As Jess tugged a quilt over her shoulder and closed her eyes, he longed to ask her to stay. A nice, long speech formed in his head, a far more eloquent one than was likely to actually come out of his mouth. He'd tell her how much he loved her and how he wanted to build a life with her.

It wasn't a lack of conviction, or courage, that kept the words locked up tight. His Jessica had already spent a lifetime putting others' needs before her own, first with her brothers and then in service to her country. He had four very boisterous daughters to raise, and as the last few hours had proven, doing right by them meant sacrifice. As much as it pained him to let her go, he couldn't ask her to take on the task of caring for his girls. Jessica deserved to focus solely on herself.

Dawn began filtering through the windows, leaving him with only a handful of hours to spend with the woman he loved. He watched her breathe and memorized every contour of her silhouette as she rested.

"I love you, Jessie. Always have, always will." He whispered the words into the still morning air. "That's why I have to let you go—again."

****

No one had loaded a car more slowly than Jess did later that morning. Nor had anyone had quite so much help. "Here you go, Miss Jessica." Alice handed over the oversized cooler with both hands. "I packed you some snacks for the road."

Jess peeked inside, her eyes widening at the number of sandwiches and drinks. "Wow. That's fabulous. Thanks." She could do a cross-country haul on those groceries.

"There're brownies and chips in here." Ella passed her the grocery bag.

Tears threatened. What was she going to do without these girls in her life? "Looks like you've thought of everything."

Sam stepped out into the yard with Chloe in his arms and Penny close behind. Jess offered to put off her departure until the girl was completely well, but Sam had politely and firmly refused the offer. "All set?"

She had to swallow twice to get the lump out of her throat. "I'm as ready as I'll ever be." Everything she owned fit inside the backseat and trunk of the sedan. There was even sufficient room for the giant picnic. "I'll be singing 'Sweet Home Alabama' before you know it."

"That's funny." Sam's smile didn't reach his eyes. "Call when you get there, will ya?" He closed the distance to stand within arm's reach. His aftershave filled her senses.

Jess clenched her fist to keep from reaching for him. "Sure thing." She turned to the girls who'd gathered around the side of her car. "You all can come for a visit once I get a place rented. I can take you to the Space Center."

Sam tousled Chloe's hair. "You'd like that, wouldn't you?"

She buried her face in her dad's chest and refused to answer.

"She's still not feeling well," Sam said. "I know we'd all like to come for a visit sometime."

Jess turned to Ella. "Let me know when you've finished reading Chronicles of Narnia. If you like it, I'll send you the rest of the books."

Her bottom lip quivered. "Okay, I will." She latched onto Jess's waist, squeezing her hard.

Next, she turned to Penny. "Be sure to wear your helmet every time you ride your bike." She tilted the girl's chin. "If I get a good report from your dad, I'll send you some glitter nail polish."

The tears that streamed down the girl's face were nearly Jess's undoing. How did soldiers with families face back-to-back deployments? She turned to Alice. "You, my dear—"

The teen stiffened as Jess went in for a hug. Jess quickly recovered, extending her hand instead. "You've become quite the gourmet chef. I can't wait to hear what you've cooked up next."

Rather than wait for a reply, she moved on to the last and hardest goodbye—Sam. First, she pressed a kiss to Chloe's cheek. "Feel better soon, princess." While she was still caressing the toddler, Sam's arms encased her.

"It's just not going to be the same around here without you." His voice came out deep and gravelly like the time he'd worked the house fire and had inhaled some smoke.

She'd never be the same after her experience with Sam and his girls either. "For me, too," she managed through a throat clogged with tears. Breaking free from his embrace was one of the hardest things she'd ever done. "Well, I better get going." Arranging her lips into a smile, she waved to the family who were huddled in a group.

Jessica climbed behind the wheel and inserted the key. The dashboard lit up with the usual signals. *Funny, I don't* remember having this much fuel in the tank. She shrugged and recalculated her first pit stop. "Call you tonight."

She turned the ignition, and the engine gave a couple of coughs and sputters before dying. She tried again. This time the engine made even less promising groans and grinds. "What in the world?" Her car was as reliable as Detroit made them.

After sending Sam and the girls back inside—no sense in having an audience—she unlatched the car's hood. An hour's worth of tinkering later, Jess resigned herself to calling a tow truck.

Sam stood next to her as her sedan disappeared around the corner. "How soon did Wally say he could look at it?"

"I lucked out. They're completely dead over there, so they can start working on it right away." Something inside her screamed luck had nothing to do with her car's untimely breakdown

Ella and Alice bounded out the back door. "We have a great idea," they said in unison.

Alice took the cooler from Jess's hand. "Since Miss Jessica can't leave just yet, let's take her lunch to the park."

Sam eyed his daughter. "I don't know."

"Chloe's perfectly fine," Ella chimed in. "I just caught her coloring on her bedroom wall."

Sam turned to Jess. "It's up to you."

She studied the two older girls. While she might not have given birth, she'd been around enough kids—and scheming recruits—to know something was afoot. For the moment, though, she'd relish a few more moments with Sam and the girls. "I think I remember seeing an old blanket in the upstairs linen closet. Grab it, and we'll load up your dad's SUV."

The girls shot each other a knowing look before racing back inside.

Sam's eyes narrowed. "Do you get the feeling?"

"Yeah." Could it be the girls had been praying for her departure to be delayed, and that angels were in the business of granting those wishes?

Later that afternoon, Jess took a call from Wally's Garage. "You've got to be kidding." So it hadn't been angels at work after all. What was she going to tell Sam?

Chapter Five

Following the picnic, they returned to his house. While the girls played in the backyard, Sam walked Jess back to her place. "Did you find out what's wrong with your car?" He held the screen door for her.

"Yeah." Jess studied the old lock like working it required an engineering degree.

He turned to get a better look at her face. "If money's the issue—"

Her head jerked up. "No, no. I've got that covered, and the garage said they'll have it fixed by tomorrow at the latest. The new owners even agreed to push back their move-in until Sunday." She opened the back door but stayed on the porch.

"Well, what's wrong?" Could she be having second thoughts about leaving? His heart sped up.

"It seems…someone put water in my fuel tank."

"They did what?" His voice matched his temper. "Of all the shenanigans those girls have pulled."

She raised her hands. "I didn't say it was one of yours, Sam. It could have been anyone."

He released the screen door, letting it slam with a bang. "You seriously expect me to believe that?"

"I was hoping." She folded her arms across her chest. "I didn't even want to mention it to you, except I didn't want whoever did it to try that on the new housekeeper."

"Don't worry about that." He glared at his house, as if his anger could penetrate through walls. "My little prankster will rue the day she learned that trick." Although if his suspicion was correct, the culprit wasn't so little anymore.

"Rue, huh?" Her lips twitched.

"Yes." He growled his frustration. "The weeks until school starts are going to be pretty miserable for one young lady."

She touched his arm, sending his pulse thrumming for a completely different reason. "Don't be too hard on her, okay?"

Sam took a step toward his own back porch, "Yeah, sure. I'll send the guilty party or parties over in a while with an apology."

Once inside the kitchen, he found Alice sitting at the table by herself. She lifted her head from her hands as he drew closer.

"It seemed like a good idea when I watched the YouTube video," she said, answering his unspoken question. "I wanted to give you another chance to ask Jess to stay or for her to change her mind."

He drew up a seat next to her. Nothing about his daughter's behavior indicated she liked Jessica much less wanted her to be a permanent part of their family. "But you went about it the wrong way."

"I know, but I didn't want her to go." Her voice rose an octave before she succumbed to tears.

"Me either, sweetheart." He patted her head. "I told her how I feel about her, but she decided to go anyway."

Alice looked up, her mouth twisted in a tight bow. "But did you show her, Dad? I mean, really let her know you wanted her to stay?"

He turned his hands up. "I wanted it to be her decision."

"Men!" Alice rolled her eyes. "You're always telling me actions speak louder than words..." She leaned in, meeting his gaze. "Well?"

Holy cow! His thirteen-year-old daughter had better relationship sense than he did. Given Jess's childhood, it was unlikely she'd be willing to risk rejection, especially after the incident at the craft fair. "I have an idea that might show her how much I want her to be part of our family." He wagged a finger in Alice's direction. "One that won't result in car damage." Or heart damage, he hoped.

She raised her hands in surrender. "I know. I owe Miss Jessica an apology, I have to repay the cost of the repairs, and I'm grounded for life."

What more could he add? "I'm glad we could have this little conversation." He rose, making way for her to scoot past him. "When you get back, I need you to watch your sisters for an hour or so. I have an errand to run."

Alice cocked her eyebrow.

"What?" He smiled. "Your old man's smart enough to listen to good advice when he hears it. Let's just hope I'm not too late."

****

Jessica eased the screen door closed and stepped off Aunt Myrtle's porch for the last time. Her gaze traveled the narrow space to Sam's house, Alice's apology still echoing in her ears. The teen expressed contrition for her actions readily enough, but afterward, it seemed other thoughts weighed on her mind. Jess poked and prodded around possible topics to no avail. In the end, she repeated the offer to have the family up for a visit—a promise she'd keep despite breaking the one to wake the family before setting off for Alabama. She cringed when her car door groaned as she opened it.

"Were you just going to leave without saying goodbye?" Sam slipped from the shadows of his porch, activating the security light as he stepped across the yard to her car.

Her stomach twisted at the taut lines around his mouth and eyes. "That was the plan." Heaven knew she couldn't endure another scene like the day before. "I know it's not very brave of me…"

"Then it's a good thing I was up early." Sam took her hand, cupping it between his. "It's been brought to my attention that I've failed to adequately express how much you mean to me." He pulled her in for a kiss. "I love you, Jessica Martin."

Tears spilled down her cheeks. Why was he telling her this now? "I love you, too, Sam. I'm sorry I didn't say that before." One of the many regrets she'd take with her.

"I made a purchase yesterday evening I'd like you to see, if you have a moment." He tugged her back to his house. "I'm hoping it'll do a better job showing you how I feel than I am at telling you."

Jess stumbled along with him, her brain too numb to process what was going on. He led her into the kitchen, flipping on the overhead light. The tidy space looked the same as it had hours before.

"See." He gestured to the breakfast nook.

An oval table and six oak chairs replaced the bistro set his late wife had made. "Okay?" So he'd finally decided she was right about the mosaic top collecting food. Why did that require the early morning show?

"There's room for all of us now." He wrapped an arm around her waist.

Jess recounted the chairs, her brain finally playing catch-up. "Does this mean...?" She needed to hear the words.

"The girls want you to stay. I do, too." He pointed to the table. "There's room for you, not only in my home, but in my heart." Thumbing away the tears from her cheeks, he added, "Please, tell me you feel the same."

She brushed her hand over the wooden surface, imagining a future with her, Sam, and the girls gathered around it. It would be messy and loud. Alice wouldn't always be as open as she had been last night. The alternative was simply unthinkable. "I do, Sam. There's room for all of you." Jess took a seat. "What will we tell the girls?"

Sam joined her, taking her hand. "What say after breakfast we take them to look for wedding venues?"

Joy filled her soul, spreading her lips into a giant grin. "Fantastic idea. Afterward, Alice and I can look up recipes for layer cakes. I want us to bake the best wedding cake ever."

The End

Melissa's Chicken Squares

Ingredients

1 rotisserie chicken
1 8-ounce package of cream cheese
2 cans of crescent rolls
Salt and pepper to taste

Directions

Allow rotisserie chicken to cool to the touch.

Bring cream cheese to room temperature.

Preheat oven to 350 degrees.

Open crescent rolls onto baking sheet. Then make 8 rectangles by pinching together triangles.

Once chicken has cooled, debone the meat and shred into bite-size pieces.

In a large bowl, mix chicken and cream cheese together. Salt and pepper to taste.

Spoon mixture into the center of the crescent roll rectangles.

Bring the points of the rectangle to the center and pinch together. Some of the chicken/cream cheese mixture will show through.

Bake for 12-14 minutes until the crescent roll is brown.

These can be enjoyed hot or cold.

Melissa Klein

Melissa Klein writes contemporary romance about everyday heroes fighting extraordinary battles. Whether facing the demands of caring for a child with special needs or the struggles of a soldier returning home, her characters take on the challenges life throws at them with perseverance, courage, and humor. She won Georgia Romance Writers Unpublished Maggie award in 2013 and Rose City Romance Writers Golden Rose award in 2012. When she's not writing, she enjoys gardening, travel, and spending time with her family. She lives with her incredibly supportive husband outside of Atlanta.

You can find Melissa
at www.MelissaKleinRomance.com

Turning The Table On Love

Ciara Knight

Acknowledgments

Thank you to Linda Joyce for her invitation to join this special project and for all her hard work to make it happen.

Ciara Knight

Turning The Table On Love

Chapter One

Fairy lights glistened inside mason jars on the front table, casting muted light on the donation box. Avery Morgan only hoped she'd impressed the guests enough to dig deep into their pockets to support Hope Angel House, a place she'd once called home.

"Ms. Morgan, I must say." An older woman, with overly teased white hair and massive jewelry draped around her neck, squeezed Avery's hand so hard her knuckles ached. If she was correct, this woman was Dalilah Shoebomber, one of the deepest pockets in town. "The next time I need an event coordinator, I'll be calling you." She leaned over, and Avery feared the slight woman would face-plant from the weight of her accessories.

Before Avery could reply, three bright flashes blinded her. The press photographer lowered her camera and greeted them. "Yes, I must agree. Your staff did an amazing job. I don't know how you and your staff pulled this off. I mean, this room—it looks like a photo shoot for a top architectural magazine."

Avery wanted to laugh. *Staff? What staff?* She glanced around the room. It had taken her days to tie all that tulle into large bows and glue lace and burlap to mason jars to create the shabby chic centerpieces. At least, her efforts hadn't been for nothing. She looked at the press photographer and smiled. "Thank you."

Mrs. Shoebomber released Avery's hand and touched her necklace as if to readjust the weight. "When I heard the benefit would be held at the Hope Angel House, I thought it was a huge mistake. I mean, these kinds of events should be upscale and lavish. Who knew you could pull off this kind of barnyard-meets-modern-elegance?"

Barnyard? Avery took a long breath and thought about her words before she spoke. "Thank you. I appreciate your praise." It had taken months, but she'd finally perfected the technique of only saying what was absolutely necessary, instead of spewing the first thought that popped into her head. "Since we're raising money for the new community kitchen, I thought it would be best to have the fundraiser in the recreation hall. That way, donors can tour the old kitchen and see how much we need a new one."

Ms. Shoebomber moved her hand to her mouth to cover an exaggerated gasp. "Yes, well, I couldn't agree with you more. I admit I only managed to peek into the kitchen, but I was too frightened to actually enter. They should probably tear it down instead of waiting until the new one is built. I mean, don't each of the small apartments have kitchens?"

Avery had prepared for this question, planning to say what donors wanted to hear, but for some reason her heart took over. "Many residents are unable to cook for themselves, so they have to get their meals from the community kitchen. Without it, there's no way to feed that many people. We also teach

LOVE AROUND THE TABLE

cooking classes, which would have to be cancelled if the old kitchen was torn down. It's where I learned how to cook, so I could prepare meals when my brother was released since we didn't have parents anymore after the accident." The weight of her words hung heavier than all the jewelry in the room, and she realized she had to lighten the mood quickly. Donors like charity, not tragedy. "It's also where everyone comes together to laugh and socialize during times of hardship."

Mrs. Shoebomber nodded absently, as though only half-listening. "Socializing is so important, even for these people," she said in a wistful tone.

Avery ignored the snobbish comment and turned to pose for one more picture with *the* Dalilah Shoebomber, heiress of a major shoe enterprise. Avery always wondered if the woman's last name was a coincidence or if the Shoebombers had changed their name to fit the industry. What came first? The name or the business?

One of the servers tapped her on the shoulder. "Ms. Morgan, we need more Parmesan cheese."

Avery plastered on her best social smile. "Please excuse me. I need to tend to a few matters." Skirting guests and tables, she headed to the kitchen and snagged more grated cheese from the back-up stash she always toted with her, then refilled the glass serving dishes at each of the tables.

"Never thought I'd see these old biddies eating family style," said a male voice with the familiar tone of a classic Ford Mustang's revving motor. Not just any Mustang, but a restored 1967 Mustang with aftermarket exhaust that sounded like its owner—Mason Gregory, the high-school crush-turned-pro-baseball-player.

Avery clutched the edge of the large banquet table and turned slowly. Her memory served her well, too well. He had the same slight dimples, perfect eyebrows, perfect hair, and perfect face. She hadn't seen Mason since before the accident. Before the truck hit their tour bus, causing her life to crash and burn. Before her parents died and her brother was hospitalized. Before she'd entered Hope Angel House.

"Um, did I say something wrong?" Mason leaned back, his eyebrows rising toward his hairline, another thing she remembered about him.

"No. I, uh, I mean, I was just surprised to see you. That's all," Avery stammered, struggling to spit out a single sentence.

He stared at her a moment. "Have we met before?"

With those four words, Avery wanted to crawl under the white tablecloth and hide like she had when she was a little girl. "I, uh, we knew each other as children." If you called the one guy she'd spent every waking moment in grade school hanging out with and every night dreaming about—and when that special day came when she was supposed to go on a date with him, but she couldn't go because her parents died—knowing him as a child. Yeah, sure.

"That's right. High school. You moved away, right?" He leaned past her, taking up what little oxygen she managed to inhale in the overcrowded room. She scooted to the left, then turned to find him snagging some calamari. She worried it had turned cold and chewy by now.

"Yes, I couldn't finish high school... Not at the time, anyway."

He twirled the Lazy Susan with too much gusto, and it spun like a tilt-a-whirl at a county fair. Red marinara sauce sloshed out of its bowl and splattered the front of Avery's white dress. She gasped and stumbled back, momentarily frozen as her mind raced with what to do. She was less concerned about the bright red splotches as she was about what the donors would think if they saw her. She really didn't need any more reasons for Mrs. Shoebomber to think Hope Angel House was a barnyard.

Mason grabbed a hand towel from one of the servers and started wiping the spots into long streams of red.

Before she could react, another bright flash blinded her. "Oh, what a shot," the press photographer said, lifting the camera again. "Smile." After several more flashes, the woman lowered the camera to her chest and lifted one hand in the air. "I can see the headline now. Avery Morgan coordinates a food faux pas to land rich and famous Mason Gregory."

"Funny, Margaret. Now run along if you still want that exclusive." With a sigh, Mason dropped the towel onto the table and straightened his suit jacket. Avery had to commend his tailor. The jacket fit to perfection, highlighting his slim waist, broad shoulders, and firm backside.

Margaret quirked her lips to one side as she glanced across the room. "Fine, but I don't think your date likes what she's seeing right now." Margaret pointed her camera lens toward a gaggle of women near the champagne fountain. As if on cue, one of them, blessed by the goddess of gorgeous legs, sauntered toward them.

Margaret pointed her camera lens at Avery and Mason again. "One more for good measure."

Like a magnet, all eyes followed the woman as she made her way across the room to Avery and Mason. Panic bubbled up from the pit of Avery's stomach. Her career, her reputation, her future business opportunities were all on the line. And she needed those business opportunities if she was ever going to be able to pay her brother's tuition without having to return to answering phones at a law firm with a handsy lawyer.

Clicks of high heels drew closer. Avery still didn't know what to do, so she smiled. She smiled through the photos, through the apologies and repeated offers to pay her drycleaning bill, and through Mason Gregory strutting out of the building with an irritated and beautiful woman on his arm. She smiled as the donors averted their gazes. She smiled through Mrs. Shoebomber's comments on the state of her appearance. The important thing was she didn't show her true emotions about Mason and his grand reappearance. The one that got away. She just kept smiling

Chapter Two

Mrs. Duncan, one of the regular volunteers at Hope Angel House, stood at Avery's side and eyed the press release on her cell phone while the kids ate breakfast. "It's not that bad." Mrs. D. wasn't just any volunteer. She was the one who had helped Avery get through her darkest time. She was Avery's very own angel.

Despite being in her late sixties, the woman was still beautiful. She had the same bright eyes, same bright smile, and same bright soul as when Avery first arrived at Hope Angel House.

Avery placed her cell phone on the counter in the corner of the kitchen. "Not bad? It looks like I got attacked by a mutant tomato from that cheesy horror movie you made me watch with you."

"Oh, come now. It's not that bad. If you squint, it's like one of those Rorschach tests."

Despite her irritation at being headline news over some spilled marinara, Avery chuckled.

Mrs. D. crossed her arms over her chest and leaned against the orange Formica kitchen counter. "So, what's really got you so stressed?"

Avery quirked a brow at her. "Why do you say I'm stressed?"

"Because you're using the same coping mechanism you did when you first arrived here at the age of seventeen." Mrs. D. removed apple muffins from their pan and placed them on a cooling rack. "Not to mention, I'm pretty sure that boy in the picture next to you is the same one you had a crush on back then."

Avery picked up the muffin pan and put it in soapy water in the sink. "You remember the guy I talked about from high school?" Avery knew Mrs. D. paid attention to each child at the facility, but it always surprised Avery how much the older woman really knew about them.

"Of course, I remember. You grew up with him, and he finally asked you out, but you never got to go on your date because of the accident. Months later, when you sent him a message, he never responded. I remember everything you've told me, hon." She offered a warm smile as she took dirty dishes from two little boys and sent them on their way. "Did you ask him why?" Mrs. D. rinsed the dishes then washed the muffin pan while Avery scrubbed the stove, careful not to knock off the loose knobs.

"No. He didn't even remember me."

One little girl with pigtails set her plate down on the kitchen island. "Done," she announced with all the pomp and circumstance of a red-carpet event.

Mrs. D. bent over. "Good girl. You ate your fruit this morning."

"Nah, Susie ate it for me. Can I still have my muffin, though?"

Mrs. D. sighed. "Yes, go ahead."

The little girl snagged one from the rack and skipped away.

"Oh, I'm sure he remembers you. You two grew up together. And I bet he was so dazzled by your beauty and success that he accidently spun that Lazy Susan too fast."

Avery gaped at her. "How did you know about the Lazy Susan? It didn't say anything about that in the article." She chuckled. "That's right. Mrs. D. knows everything."

Mrs. D. put her hands together and bowed like a wise man.

"Yes, well, I doubt I dazzled anything. He left with a model on his arm, with plenty of others seething with envy in their wake. I mean, he's a professional baseball player who looks like a GQ model with a shot of extra gorgeous. Why would he be dazzled by me?"

Ignoring her question, Mrs. D. said, "I wonder if Mr. Gorgeous was your benefactor when Austin was released from rehab."

Avery shook her head at such a ridiculous thought. "No way. He didn't have that kind of money back then. And even if he did, he left for college right after that and never bothered to think of me again."

"So, you think he doesn't even remember you and never gave you a second thought after leaving last night?"

"Nope, not a one." Avery rinsed out the dishrag and placed it in a pile for the wash. More kids brought their plates and set them on the counter, then scurried off with giggles. It always surprised Avery how happy the small children were in spite of their lives being turned upside down from some catastrophic event.

Mrs. D. waved for her to follow, leading Avery into the recreation room. She knelt behind the supply cabinets, and Avery stood on her toes to see what she was doing. A moment later, Mrs. D. popped back up and handed Avery a large white box tied with a bright red ribbon.

"What's this? It's not my birthday."

Mrs. D. shrugged. "I don't know. It's not from me."

Avery analyzed the box as if it were a strange animal. "Who's it from then?"

Mrs. D. removed a small envelope from the bow and handed it to Avery. "Read the card."

Avery rolled her head to one side and gave her a look. "I don't have to. You already did."

Mrs. D. hip-bumped her. "It's from Mason. Open it."

Avery's hands shook, and her thoughts raced as she untied the bow and opened the box. Inside was a beautiful white dress, elegant enough for a bride. White lace, white chiffon, and white beading. "Whoa," she breathed. "This had to have cost a fortune. It's…it's—"

"Something you'll like, I hope," Mason's voice echoed from across the recreation hall.

Mrs. D. winked then disappearing faster than the kids at chore time. Avery swallowed and turned slowly. Slow enough to allow her time to think before opening her mouth. "Returning to the crime scene to finish me off?"

He leaned against the doorframe and scanned Avery from head to toe. "I don't think I'm cut out to be a criminal, so I better keep my day job." He pushed from the doorway and crossed the room. "So, do you like it?"

She eyed the beautiful dress, one she could never afford with the meager salary she earned from her struggling business. "Mason, this is too much. You didn't have to do this."

"I ruined your other dress, right?"

"Yes, but somehow I doubt you bought this on clearance." She ran her fingers across the ultrasoft material.

Mason stopped by her side and eyed the dress himself. "No, I didn't. One of my sisters told me where to shop."

"They always did have excellent taste. How are your sisters?"

"Good. One's in college now. The other one's married with a baby on the way."

"Wow. It has been a long time." Avery caught a whiff of his cologne. The scent had changed from what he'd worn in high school. It smelled more grown-up, deeper, more mysterious with a hint of playboy. She forced her attention back to the dress. "This is way too extravagant and expensive. Besides, it was an accident." She pushed the box toward him.

He shook his head and pushed it back. "I have a confession to make. It wasn't entirely accidental. I was upset, and that's why I spun that Lazy Susan too hard. It was a shock to see you after so long."

Avery fought back a smile, but it won. "You *did* remember me."

"How could I forget? We had been dancing around the topic of dating for years, and then you finally said *yes*, only to disappear without a word. "

The room fell silent, except for the distant sound of children playing on the lawn out back and the slow tick of the clock on the wall. "I sent you a message," she said, her voice small.

"When? Where?"

She rubbed her forehead as if to recover the memory. "I texted you, but you never replied."

His lips curved on one side, and he harrumphed. "I never got it."

"You didn't?"

"Why didn't you call me?"

Avery dropped her head, fighting the emotion welling up inside of her. Had he really not gotten the message? "I couldn't... At the time, I couldn't even..." It had taken weeks for her to say the words aloud. *My parents are dead.* "Didn't you hear what happened? It was all over the news a few days later...once they found the other driver."

Mason touched her elbow in a gesture of comfort, the way she'd dreamed he would for months after her parents were killed, and she was left to care for her little brother alone. "No. I went by your house, but you weren't there. I asked my sisters, and they told me you'd left. After all, it was summer break. I thought you'd ditched me, so I left for college early to get over you." Slack lips, eyes filled with grief, confirmed the truth of his words.

"All this time, I thought...I thought—"

"That I abandoned you?" Mason moved closer, touching his knuckles to her cheek. The way she'd imagined he would on their date. A date she'd wanted to go on for years but had concluded it would never happen. She fought the lump rising from her chest and the burning threat of tears. "If I'd known, I would've never abandoned you. I would've been by your side."

Chapter Three

Cool air filtered through the open window of Avery's office. The scent of fall and the sound of crunching leaves always warmed her heart. It was her favorite time of year. Fall meant the end of summer with its bad memories and the beginning of the Christmas season. Christmas bazaars and holiday parties kept her busy, but there was still one question that plagued her.

Would Austin make it home for Christmas this year?

She shook off the loneliness and willed herself to let her brother have a real life beyond Silver Creek, Tennessee. A life beyond the sadness. Mrs. D. was right. Avery needed to move on and find someone to start her own family with. Who had time to date? What man wanted to hang out at a community center with children who are recovering from horrible accidents?

Her cell rang, drawing her back to reality. "Avery Morgan Event Planning."

"Hello. I am calling about an event I need planned. According to Mrs. Shoebomber, you're the person in town to plan a major event. Do you think you'd be able to handle an upscale engagement party for two major celebrities?"

Avery blinked as if to see through the scam. Was this real? Something of this significance could pay Austin's college tuition for the rest of the year and possibly the next.

"Hello?" the woman on the phone said.

"Yes, I'm the person to plan an event of that scale in Silver Creek."

"Great," the woman replied. "We will be there on Monday at two o'clock. As I said, we're going for classy with a finding-home theme. Be ready to present at least two concepts, and they better be exceptional. Do you understand?"

Avery didn't need to check her calendar. Business had been slow and wouldn't pick up until December. "Yes, I understand. I'll see you on Monday at two o'clock."

Without another word, the woman hung up.

Avery stared at the phone for a moment, confused by the woman's blatant rudeness. Then she set the phone down on her desk and clutched the arms of her desk chair. A flood of possibilities and fear washed over her. Could she pull off such an event? What would it be like to work with celebrities? Who were the celebrities? If she had thought to ask, she could do a bit of research on them and come up with appropriate concepts.

She'd done plenty of weddings, but they were small-town weddings. She'd done large fundraisers but nothing as large and extravagant as a celebrity engagement party. Not in Silver Creek. The benefit for the center had been her largest event to date.

The center.

She glanced at the clock. Even if she did have the opportunity to land the contract of her career, some things were more important than business. Besides, she still had all weekend and most of Monday to prepare for her initial meeting. She shut the window and headed out the door, locking it behind her. If she hurried, she'd make it to movie night with the kids.

A sports car pulled up in front of her office, and she stopped in her tracks, seeing Mason at the wheel. The sight of him gave her that squirrels-hunting-for-food sensation in her belly. She smiled and headed to his car. "What are you doing here?"

"A wise woman told me I might find you here, and that I should race over while I still had a chance to take you to dinner."

Avery didn't need to ask who the wise woman was. The nudge had Mrs. D. written all over it. Maybe the woman had been right, and Mason really had been the benefactor who helped pay for Austin's rehab after the accident.

Avery placed a hand on her hip and tilted her chin to the side in a playful way. "I'm afraid I have other plans this evening."

"Oh." Mason, the most handsome and sweetest man she'd ever known, looked disappointed by her answer, and she couldn't help but smile.

Was this her chance?

Mrs. D. was the person she trusted most in her life, a surrogate parent for the ones she'd lost. If she sent Mason here, maybe Avery should give him a chance after all. She still found it hard to understand how he couldn't have known about the accident that tore her family apart, but perhaps he had a good reason for that. "Would you like to join me?"

He stepped back and held open his leather jacket to show off his hunter green button-up and khaki pants. "Am I dressed for the occasion?"

"You'll fit in perfectly. Promise." Avery winked.

"Okay, let's go then." He scanned the parking lot. "Where are we headed?"

"I'll direct you." She tilted her head toward his car, and he raced over to open the door for her like the perfect gentlemen he'd always been. "Do you like movies?" she asked as she slid into the passenger seat.

"Yes, except they don't allow for much conversation." He closed the door, rounded the car, and hopped behind the wheel.

"Don't worry. Talking's allowed in this theater." She put on her seatbelt and watched him press the ignition button. The car rumbled to life. "I see you still like loud cars."

"Loud? She sings like an angel." Mason maneuvered the car out of the parking lot and waited for instructions.

Avery pointed down Main Street. "That way."

He waited for the light to change at the edge of the parking lot, then turned the way she had directed him. "Did my sisters know?"

"Know what?"

He shot her a sideways glance. "About what happened to you and your family? You said it was in the news. My family had to know then, right?"

"I would think so." Avery watched the buildings pass as they drove down the street, and for the first time since her little brother left for college, she allowed herself to remember the small town the way it once was. The way it had been when she still had family around her. The corner ice cream parlor where they'd go on Friday nights after dinner. The church they had attended every Sunday. The nail salon where she'd gone for her first mani-pedi with her mother.

Mason covered her hand with his. The warmth, the loving touch was foreign to her. She'd hugged her brother and Mrs. D. on occasion, but that was it. She'd spent the last seven years raising her brother, getting him off to school every morning, and working long hours to pay the bills. There had been no time for any real romance, not while trying to build a career without a college degree. Not with the job of being both mom and dad to a young boy who had to go through a year of physical therapy just to be able to walk again.

"It had to have been so difficult. I wish I would've known." He pulled off to the side of the road, put the car in park, and faced her with the most intense expression she'd ever seen. "If I had known, I would've returned. I would've stayed. Stayed for you, Avery."

She fought the flood of emotions bubbling to the surface. Hope, love, fear, and anxiety all swirling together. "I know. I clung to that hope for several weeks after the accident. I even called your sister at one point and asked about you. She said you were away at college and wouldn't be back for a while."

His expression shifted, his soft eyes hardening, and his lips thinned. "I promise you I'll find out why." He let go of her and turned back to the steering wheel, gripping it tight. After a moment, he closed his eyes and let out a long breath. As he pulled back onto the road, he reached for her again. This time, she squeezed his hand to thank him for his words. The boy she'd grown up with would've done anything for those who needed him.

Discussing the accident that killed her parents and injured her brother always left her with the urge to lighten the mood. "Do you remember when we were fourteen and my brother went missing?"

"Do I ever." He nodded and let out a whistle. "I thought he'd be grounded for life when your parents finally found him."

Avery directed him to turn then said, "I thought you'd never speak to me again after riding our bikes for hours looking for him, only to return home to find him hiding in the closet."

"Are you kidding? It was the best day of my life up to that point. I got to spend several hours alone with the girl I had a crush on. The one who was like no other girl at school."

"Me? I never knew. You always dated cheerleaders, and then, there was the class president."

He sighed and rolled to a stop at the next light. "They were easy to get dates with, but you weren't. You were special, focused on school, a talented dancer, an amazing people person. I mean, everyone loved you. It took me so long to work up the courage to ask you out. When my sister told me you'd left Silver Creek, I assumed you decided you didn't want to go out with me after all, but didn't want to tell me face-to-face."

"What brings you back now?" Avery asked, still trying to wrap her head around the fact he was here in Silver Creek, in this car with her, holding her hand.

The light changed, and he drove on. "It's complicated, but business brought me here. Kind of a back-home publicity stunt to launch me into a new career. I'm afraid my baseball career is over. Bad shoulder. So it's time for me to find the next big adventure life has for me." He rolled to a stop once more. "Where to now?"

"Oh, turn left."

He nodded. "Toward the Hope Angel House? I heard you spend all your free time there now that your little brother's left for college. I wasn't surprised. It's one of the things I always admired about you. While the other kids were off drinking and partying, you were volunteering at homeless shelters, serving meals and chatting with the residents."

She shrugged. "I enjoy being there. I want to help other kids get through what I went through, the way Mrs. D. helped me." She traced the scar on his hand, the one he'd gotten from helping her work on her car when they were seventeen. She still felt guilty for enjoying the act of doctoring his hand. It meant she got to be close to him. That was the day he'd asked her out. "I'm sorry about your shoulder. I know how much you love to play. I never missed one of your games in high school." If she was honest with herself, she also followed his pro career.

They sat silently for a moment. Questions continued to plague her all the way to Hope Angel House when they pulled into the parking lot. "Why do you think your sisters told you I'd left? If they knew about the accident, then they would've known the truth, I was still here." She glanced out the window at the old building that had once been her home. "I thought we were all friends."

"I don't know, but I've already put a call into them, and my parents. It's obvious they kept me away on purpose, though. I thought it was strange when they wanted to go skiing every year for Christmas instead of celebrating at home, but I can't think why." He opened his door and raced around to open hers, then offered his hand. "Let's get to that movie."

She took his hand, and they made their way to the rec center. "I know this isn't exactly what you had in mind when you asked me to dinner. If you don't want to be here…"

He kissed her knuckles. "I like it here. Mrs. D. gave me a tour this morning, and I signed up for story time while I'm in town."

Her stomach knotted with hope at his words, yet she slipped her hand away, feeling the need to protect her heart. It was easier to face the truth now, instead of tomorrow or a week from now. Mason had already disappeared on her once. What was left in Silver Creek to keep him from disappearing again?

Chapter Four

Avery leaned back in her chair and yawned, exhausted after staying up until two in the morning working on the proposals for the celebrity engagement party event. The distraction of Mason returning to Silver Creek hadn't helped her focus at all either. They'd had a fun evening. Of course, it wasn't a real date, what with the kids and other volunteers around, but it had been nice to spend time with him.

The doorbell rang, so Avery shuffled to the door to find Mrs. D. standing on the front porch holding two cups of coffee. "I thought you'd need this."

"Thanks. I do. Come on in." Avery opened the door wide, and Mrs. D. stepped into the small entry of her modest home.

"You really did it this time." Mrs. D. said as she handed one cup to Avery and then scooted past her into the living room.

Avery wiped the sleep from her eyes and took a long draw of rich, eye-opening goodness. "What are you talking about?"

Mrs. D. sat in the recliner and gave her that disapproving look Avery had always hated, where her lip tightened as if she were sucking on a sour lollipop. "Do you like Mason or not?"

Avery plopped down onto the pale-blue couch. "I did." The silence that ensued warned Avery Mrs. D. didn't like that answer, so she took a long inhale and thought for a moment. "Yes, I do."

"Then why'd you blow it?" Mrs. D. huffed.

Avery leaned back into the cushions and closed her eyes, trying to deal with her affection for a man who had left her once and would very likely leave her again. He was a successful baseball player women fought over. He dated models and drove sports cars. Why would he want to stay in Silver Creek and date her? "He's just going to leave again."

"Maybe. Maybe not. You said yourself he never knew what happened to you and your family. That he would've returned from college to be by your side, but his family kept the news from him." Mrs. D. set her coffee cup on the table and shifted closer, placing a hand on Avery's knees. "Dear, you need to start living for yourself again."

"I know. And I'm trying, but I don't have time to think about romance right now. I have my business and the center." At Mrs. D.'s stern look, Avery sighed. "Besides, I'm not going to fall for a guy that might be gone tomorrow or the day after."

"Not going to fall for him?" Mrs. D. brushed hair from Avery's eyes like her mother used to. "Honey, you fell for him when you were in elementary school. He's been the only one you've ever loved. This is your chance. At least, if you try, you'll know if he lives up to the myth or not. And if not, well, then you can move on with your life."

"What if I find out I love him even more than I thought I did, and he disappears again?" Avery took in a stuttered breath at the thought of her heart breaking the way it had seven years ago. It had never healed. She foolishly thought it had, but after just a few hours with him, she could feel the fissures widening at the thought of losing him again.

"Is this coward in front of me the same girl who single-handedly raised her little brother and left a stable job to start her own business? Just as there's a possibility he might leave, there's an equal possibility he'll stay. Are you going to miss the chance to find happiness because you're afraid of what might never happen?" Mrs. D. leaned away and swiped tears from her eyes. "I know I'm not your mother, but if she was here, I'm sure she'd tell you to take the chance. To try and see what happens, instead of clinging to what could have been, regretting the fact you never took the chance."

Avery took another stuttered breath, fighting her own tears. Not just from the fear of her heart breaking, but for the love she felt for Mrs. D. "You might not be my biological mom, but you're a mother to me just the same."

Mrs. D.'s face lit up at her words. "Then take your mother's advice and go find him. Give this a shot. He thinks you pulled away the other night because you don't feel for him what he feels for you. That he'd come on too strong."

Avery shook her head. "That's not—"

"I know that, but he doesn't," Mrs. D. said gently. "So, go tell him."

"I don't even know where to find him." Part of her hoped that would buy her time to think and sort through everything, but she wasn't surprised when Mrs. D. had a countermeasure.

"He's at the center this morning reading to the children. He's a good man, Avery. Not good enough for my little angel, but no man every will be." Mrs. D. stood and grabbed Avery's arm, pulling her from the couch and into her arms. Mrs. D. only hugged her for a moment before releasing her. "Now, go shower. It's time for you to go on a real date. The date you never had a chance to go on before." She moved toward the front door, then paused. "You deserve happiness, hon. All you need to do is accept it."

Arguing with Mrs. D. never worked, but Avery couldn't help stalling in the shower and taking a few extra few minutes to blow-dry her hair. What if the date went terribly? What if he left tomorrow?

But, what if he didn't?

Chapter Five

Avery entered the rec center and spotted Mason perched on a small chair that looked like it would break underneath him at any moment. In front of him, a half-circle of children sat cross-legged. His knees were nearly at his chest, and she'd never seen a more adorable sight.

He glanced up at her and paused for a second.

"Hey, mister. What happens to the rabbit?" a little boy with bright blond hair asked.

Mason lifted the book back up to read. "Right. Sorry, little man. I'm shirking my reading duties here."

The little boy who was new to the center giggled, covering his mouth and pointing at Mason. "He said *duty*."

Mason's face turned all sorts of red, and he cleared his throat.

One little girl raised her hand. "What's *shirking*?"

"Who cares? I want to know what happens to the rabbit," the little boy scolded.

Mason leaned over, resting his elbows on his knees. "It means when someone avoids or neglects their du…responsibilities."

Avery joined them and sat next to the little boy. His eyes grew saucer-big, no doubt fearing he was in trouble, but she only patted his back and sat crisscross applesauce at his side, listening to the rest of Mason's story. "Let's find out about that rabbit."

Nodding mutely, the little boy sat rod-straight with his hands in his lap. After a couple minutes of listening to the story, the little boy leaned into her and whispered from the side of his mouth, "Can I still have ice cream?"

Avery tucked him into her side. "Are you going to be polite?"

He nodded, and his attention remained fixed on every word Mason spoke until he closed the book and said, "The end."

All the kids clapped and hopped up. The little girl pulled her elbows to her hips with her fists tight and screamed, "Ice cream!"

They all flooded into the kitchen where Mrs. D. waited with their treat.

Mason pushed from the tiny chair and offered his hand to help her off the floor. "How did I do?"

"You're a natural. I think you might have found your new calling."

Mason wrapped his arm around her shoulders and led her toward the kitchen. "Does that mean I earned ice cream?"

"I would say so." Avery liked the way the weight of his arm pressed against her shoulders, and the way his stride matched her pace despite his long legs, and the way he looked down at her with warm eyes. "I'm glad you came. I was worried I'd scared you off."

"Me, scared? Never." They reached the kitchen, snagged their individual serving cup of ice cream, and Mrs. D. ushered them out back to the garden. It was peaceful and quiet outside, with the rambunctious kids still causing chaos inside the kitchen.

Gold and red leaves floated down from the large oak tree and covered the ground, summer's flowers long gone. Mason led her to the bench under the tree and sat down, turning to face her at his side. "I see why you love it here. These kids are amazing. This place is incredible." He opened the ice cream and removed the little wooden spoon from the bottom. "I always knew you were something special, but you're even more than I thought."

Heat spread over her skin, and she fought not to turn away. "I think you win the amazing card. You are a famous baseball player, after all."

Mason set the small cup of ice cream on the arm of the bench and took her hand in his. "But you survived. Not just that, but you thrived. When you lost your parents, you took care of your brother. A boy who couldn't walk for a long time. You carried on, even though you thought I'd abandoned you. My sisters grew up with you, yet they didn't even come to visit. Even without the support of family or friends, you still thrived. You're the most amazing person I know."

She glanced back at the kitchen. "I wouldn't say I was completely without support."

His head dropped as if shame weighed it down. "I spoke to my sisters. I'm not sure I can ever forgive my family, but I found out what happened."

Avery set her own ice cream down on the ground and placed her hand on top of his. "And?"

Mason took a long breath, and his hands shook. "I don't remember the last time I've been this angry, if ever. They knew, Avery. They knew what happened to you and your family, but they didn't tell me." His lips formed a tight line of anger.

"Why?"

Mason looked at her with a pleading headshake. "They said they did it to protect me. They didn't want me giving up college to take care of you and your brother."

Avery thought for a moment. "Then they were right to not tell you."

Mason leaned back and narrowed his gaze. "What?"

"Trust me, they did it out of love. So don't be too upset with them. They only wanted what they thought was best for you. Listen, I was angry for a long time. I was furious at the driver who hit the bus and caused the accident. I was mad at the tour company, you, the world, and God. Then the first time my brother walked again, all my anger faded away. In that moment, my hope was alive once more. He worked so hard and succeeded despite the loss he'd suffered. It was through my brother I realized what forgiveness really meant, and what hope was." She squeezed Mason's hands. "You have a family who loves you. Don't waste a minute being mad at them."

Mason moved his thumb back and forth on her fingers, and her hand warmed. "As I said, you're amazing."

Chapter Six

Sunday and Monday morning flew by as she threw herself into creating the best presentation possible for the celebrity engagement party. It was difficult to focus with Mason being in town, but she needed this contract if her business was ever going to take off. It was all she had after Austin left for college, and she couldn't let one more thing slip away.

The old clock from her father's home office ticked away on her wall. She loved the *tick-tock* as if her father watched over her every second of the day. Yet, as the hands ticked past two o'clock, then two-ten and two-twenty, Avery's nerves gnawed at her.

A half-hour after the appointed time, the door flew open. In walked a short woman with tall heels, two phones, a bag, an oversized notebook, and a stress-filled gaze. Avery stood and rounded her desk, offering her hand, but the woman looked down her nose at Avery. "First, before you meet your potential new clients, I need you to sign a nondisclosure agreement." The woman dropped her stuff onto a chair, opened the oversized binder, and tossed a wordy document onto Avery's desk.

Avery leaned against the corner of her desk. The clock ticked away for a few seconds while she read over the paper in front of her.

The woman shoved a pen in her face. "Hurry up. Sign it, or we'll go somewhere else."

Avery ignored the offered pen and rounded the desk, sitting to review the two-page document.

"It's a standard nondisclosure." The woman *tsked* and tossed the pen on the desk. "We don't have much time for this meeting. Our schedule is full today."

Avery remembered her father's words from when she used to help him at work as a teenager. *Never sign a legal document without reading the fine print.* "Yes, well, I had two o'clock as the meeting time on my books, and I waited. Certainly, I can have a minute to review a document before signing it."

The woman huffed but cleared the seat of her stuff and plopped down into the chair.

Avery read through the document, then looked over at the woman. "This says, if I speak of this to anyone, including the bride and groom, without Cindy Delacorux being present, then you can sue me for everything I have."

"Yes, I'm Cindy Delacorux." She shrugged. "So, don't tell anyone. It only needs to remain a secret for a few days. After we make the big announcement, that clause is null and void. Of course, you can never share specifics of the event, as stated on page two."

"Yes, I understand that." Avery took a long breath, arguing with the little voice in her head that told her not to sign. But if she let this contract go, she could lose her business in a matter of months. Still, signing a nondisclosure didn't guarantee she would even get the contract. They had to like the proposals she'd worked up.

Reluctantly, she lifted the pen and scribbled her name on the document.

"Great. Now that we are done, my client will be joining us in a few minutes, but go ahead and start." Ms. Delacorux leaned back in the chair and texted someone on her phone. Avery waited, but the woman never glanced up.

Fine. She'd dealt with divas before. She'd treat this woman the same way she'd treated Trixie Donovan, head cheerleader, diva, and all-around snob when Avery had planned her shotgun wedding. She spun the computer screen and joined the woman on the other side of the desk. "I have two concepts for you. The first was inspired by your words of *returning home*. It's a modern chic small-town theme with country elements."

"Stop. Am I wasting my time here? I mean, seriously? Country? You obviously don't know your client."

"No, I don't." Avery fought the urge to tell the woman to lose the attitude and listen, but that wasn't the way to run a business. "However, I do have another concept to share that might be more to your client's liking." She flipped to the other presentation. "Here, I have Cinderella meets old Hollywood glamour."

Ms. Delacorux sat forward and lowered her glasses down her nose to eye the picture of the elaborate setting. "I believe you have something here." She pointed to a picture of hurricane lamps with gold sparkle flameless candles. "Can those things there be changed out? They're hideous."

"Yes, we can change them to something else. Perhaps tall vases with long-stemmed flowers or feathers."

The woman nodded, offering her hand. "This I can work with. I'll text my client to join us. Excellent work. I have to admit I'm shocked. You definitely have a talent for this. What are you doing here in small town USA?"

"It's my home," Avery answered, but she'd already lost Cindy's attention to her phone. Her thumbs moved quicker than a bumblebee after pollen.

"She'll be in here in a second." Cindy closed her oversized notebook and moved the rest of her belongings out of the way. She then opened a bottle of water, put some colored drops in it, shook it, and put it on the desk.

The door opened, and in stepped not just any attractive woman—but the gorgeous blonde who'd been Mason's date at the banquet.

Avery forced herself to stand on wobbly legs and offer her hand. "Hello. I'm Avery Morgan. I believe we met briefly at the benefit the other night. I didn't realize you were getting married."

The blonde ignored the greeting and sat in the chair as if she were afraid to touch anything. She took a sip from the bottle of water Cindy had prepared. "Of course, you didn't. We wanted to keep it a secret until the big press release." She turned to Ms. Delacorux. "Didn't you already explain this to her?" she snarled. A pang of sympathy washed over Avery.

"Yes. Of course, I did."

Avery settled the laptop in front of her. "Will the groom be joining us today as well?"

The woman fluttered her hand next to her ear as if the question were beyond stupid. "He'll do whatever I tell him to do. Don't worry about that. What does a baseball player know about weddings anyway?"

Avery lowered to the chair next to the model before her legs gave out. It couldn't be Mason. He would've told her if he was getting married. Wouldn't he? He wouldn't have held her hand or gone to see her at the center if he was engaged. Mrs. D. wouldn't have encouraged him if she knew. No, it had to be one of his friends.

Forcing the thoughts away, she cleared her throat. "If you settle on my design, I'll need the full spelling of both the bride's and groom's names as you'd like to see them appear on any invitations or event décor." Avery lifted a pen to a piece of paper on her desk.

Please don't be Mason. Please don't be Mason.

"You already know my name. Everyone knows me."

Avery swallowed, not wanting to admit she had no clue. The only magazine she ever bought was for travel and leisure. "I want to make sure I have the spelling correct, that's all."

The woman took another sip. "Larissa Love. L-a-r-i-s-s-a. And I hope you can spell *Love*."

"Yes, of course. And the groom?"

Please don't be Mason. Please don't be Mason.

"Mason Gregory."

Chapter Seven

Sitting at the kitchen island sipping hot tea, Avery rubbed her eyes. Unfortunately, the tired, puffy feeling remained. She hadn't been able to sleep a wink, suffering from the same heaviness in her heart she'd had the day she saw her brother in the hospital with all the tubes and machines connected to him.

Mrs. D. poured herself a cup and sat by Avery's side. "Are you sure? I mean, I didn't see him as a player, or someone who would do something like this."

"Yes, I'm sure." She half-chuckled. "I had always dreamed of planning a wedding with him. I just didn't know it would be to someone else." She swiveled in her chair and eyed Mrs. D. "Did you know I used to practice writing my name with his last name on my notebooks?"

"I remember. I found you once or twice in the early months doodling Avery Gregory, but then you stopped."

Avery sighed. "What could I do? There was no way I could chase after the man of my dreams when my brother needed me. Besides, I figured if he wanted me like he said he did, he'd come see me here. My fantasies about it kept me going. He'd get down on one knee and beg for my forgiveness for abandoning me. He'd bring me flowers and tell me how sorry he was for what I was going through, and tell me how he'd never leave me again."

"Go talk to him. Find out what's going on."

Avery couldn't bring herself to face the man. Even knowing he had lied to her, still her pulse raced and her heart fluttered whenever he got near her.

Avery took a sip of her soothing chamomile tea, but it only soothed her throat, not her soul. "I can't. I signed a nondisclosure agreement. I shouldn't have even told you, Mrs. D. I say something to Mason and he goes back to her, I could be sued."

Mrs. D. traced the rim of her cup. "That's troublesome, but it can't be in effect forever."

"Only for a few days. Apparently, there'll be a big announcement. After that, the nondisclosure is null and void."

The room fell silent for a moment. Mrs. D. inched to the edge of her chair. "Then you'll know in a couple of days. Can you handle it for that long?"

"It's a job. I'll deal with the bride. And if Mason does show up at a meeting, then I'll have my answer. As much as it hurts, I need this work. It could put me on the map, and I could finally afford to pay Austin's tuition without worrying every semester."

Mrs. D. rubbed Avery's shoulder. "You're a good girl. The best sister, and your parents would have been so proud of you, but it's time for you to start taking care of yourself and stop worrying about everyone else."

Avery shrugged. "Once Austin can support himself, then I'll stop worrying about him and start thinking about my future. For now, I need this contract." She stood and emptied the remains of her teacup into the sink. Needing a distraction, she started pulling ingredients out of cupboards for her chocolate chip cookies. The kids always loved her cookies, and seeing their smiles was the highlight of her day because, just like her, snack time gave them a sense of home and family. She only hoped the oven worked long enough to bake them.

Mrs. D. rinsed out her own cup and then left for work, heading over to the apartments to greet the new parents arriving.

Avery hummed and mixed ingredients, attempting to keep her thoughts light. When she put three trays of dough into the oven, a familiar voice called from down the hall.

"Excuse me. Am I interrupting?" Mason said.

She forced herself to lift her chin and act as if nothing were wrong. If she confronted him, she'd be in breach of that blasted contract.

She plastered on a smile as she turned to face him. "Hello. How are you today?"

As he moved toward her, she grabbed the container of sugar and bent down to put it away. When she stood, he was in her personal space.

"Hey, I missed you." Mason touched her hair, but it might as well have been her soul, considering the reaction her body had. She fought the fluttering in her chest, the rapid pulse beating in her neck.

She ducked around him and scrubbed the island free of sugar and flour and anything else she could pretend to see.

"What's wrong?" Mason leaned against the kitchen sink and crossed his arms over his chest. "Did I do something?"

Did he do something? You mean besides forgetting to tell me you were engaged? She scrubbed the counter harder.

"I came to tell you I might have to leave at the end of the week to settle some business back in Houston," Mason said, his voice low and dark.

Avery turned and rinsed out the sponge, standing next to him at the sink. "I hope you have a safe trip," she said in her happiest tone.

"That's all you want to say?" Mason turned and reached for her, but she bolted out of the kitchen and into the recreation hall.

She couldn't be so close to him, not now. She had to keep her mouth sealed. She wanted to punch him for not telling her about the engagement, and in the next, she wanted to believe it wasn't true.

She set up several tables and unfolded chairs from a stack leaning against the back wall. A few minutes later, she noticed Mason standing in the doorway to the kitchen watching her.

He pushed from the doorway and crossed the recreation hall. He pulled something from his jacket pocket. "I want to give this to the center to help with the new kitchen." He held a check out to her, and reluctantly she took it, but he grabbed her shaking hand. "Talk to me, Avery. I know there's something wrong."

Avery stiffened and tried to pull away, but he had a tight grip on her hand. "Don't do this."

Before she could respond, she noticed smoke drifting out of the kitchen and into the recreation hall. "Oh no!" Avery yanked her hand free and ran to the kitchen. Smoke billowed from the oven. "No. No. No!"

She turned off the oven and yanked the door open. More smoke rushed out, causing her to cough and wave her arms in front of her. Mason grabbed an oven mitt and pulled the cookies out, setting them on the stovetop. They were gooey, bubbling piles with charred edges.

"The kids. They'll be so disappointed." She collapsed into one of the counter stools and set the check down. Only then did she notice all of the zeros.

"I hope that will help buy a new oven," Mason said softly.

She wanted to throw her arms around him and thank him, but she didn't. Instead, she stood and offered her hand. "Thank you, Mr. Gregory. This will help the center greatly."

Chapter Eight

Rain clinked against the window of the recreation hall. Avery sat at one of the tables staring at the image on her phone, punishing herself for believing in a happily-ever-after.

"How long are you going to torture yourself? That picture isn't going to change. Neither is the headline," Mrs. D. said. "Now, put it down and go talk to Mason, or I will."

Avery turned off her phone and rested her head in her hands. "There's no reason to talk to him now. That headline says it all. *Supermodel and pro baseball player to make power couple history.*"

"I don't care what that says. There's something not right here. Talk to Mason now." Mrs. D. took both of their cups and headed to the kitchen. "This is your chance."

Avery looked up and followed Mrs. D.'s gaze to the door where Mason stood with a box in his hand.

"I brought some cookies for the kids in case your oven was still broken," Mason said before slowly stepping farther into the room as if a wild animal might charge if he moved too quickly. "I'm leaving tomorrow morning, so I had hoped we could talk. I came straight over when I woke up this morning."

Avery didn't say a word. Her chest ached at the sight of this amazing man. Mrs. D. was right. Something didn't add up. How could a man who thought about children at a center, who sat through a movie with cartoon characters, and donated an exorbitant amount of money to rebuild a community center kitchen, be a philanderer?

He set down the box in front of her. "I made these last night. My sister came and helped. We talked for a long time. Even though I'm still angry at my family, I took your advice, and we're working through it. She feels horrible about how she treated you. She said she used to come here and drop off makeup and magazines, but told the staff not to tell you who they came from. My parents apparently helped with some of the medical bills for your brother's rehab. Guilt money, I guess."

Avery sucked in a quick breath. "That was them? I thought you'd all abandoned me."

Mason slid into the chair beside her. "I'd never abandon you."

Avery stood, needing to escape the strong pull of Mason Gregory and the possibility of something that could never happen. "The kids will be here any minute. I need to finish setting up for breakfast."

"I can help." He followed her to the kitchen. "That will give us a chance to talk before I leave tomorrow."

"What do we have to talk about?" An edge crept into her voice. She fought the anger, resentment, and love she felt for him.

"Everything." Mason snagged her arm and turned her to face him. "Please. I know something's wrong. I can't fix it if you won't tell me what it is. Do you hate me because of what my family did? If so, I don't blame you, but I never chose to leave you. I could never choose to leave you." His voice cracked.

"I thought you were leaving tomorrow." Avery pulled her arm free and grabbed the dishes from the kitchen counter, glancing at Mrs. D. briefly before rushing out to set them on the tables.

He grabbed another stack and followed at her heels. "Yes, but only for a week or so. You could come with me. I'd love to introduce you to some of my friends. I'll be back, not just for the photo ops and publicity my agent set up here in town, but to spend time with you, too."

She spun around, wanting to pummel his chest or slap him, but she didn't. "Publicity stunt? Is that all it is to you? You're going to marry some girl for publicity?"

"Marry? Some girl?" Mason ran a hand through his hair and scanned the room as if looking for answers. "What are you talking about?"

Hope knocked at her heart, but fear bolted the door before it had a chance to open. She snagged her phone from the table, turned it on, and shoved it in his face. "I'm the event planner for your wedding to Larissa Love. How ironic is that? I actually believed you wanted to date me, yet, all this time you're here to marry another woman. I guess that makes me a fool."

Mason moved the phone closer as if he needed reading glasses and then clutched her upper arms. "Don't ever say that. You are not a fool. You could never be that. I'm the fool." He tugged her closer, forcing her to meet his gaze. "I had no idea the publicity stunt was a marriage proposal. I did not, and never will, propose to Larissa Love. I don't blame you if you don't trust me, but I promise I'll prove it to you." He released her and headed for the door. "I'll be back, and when I return, you'll know just how much I have and always will love you."

****

Breakfast with the kids went by slower than usual. The rain had faded into a mid-morning drizzle, but a storm still raged inside of Avery. Mrs. D cleaned up the breakfast dishes in the kitchen while Avery wiped down the tables in the recreation hall. It was time for her to head to her own job and her uncertain future.

Mrs. D. placed the last clean dish on top of a stack. "You doing okay?"

Avery retrieved her purse from the cabinet. "Yes, but I don't know what to do. If Mason's telling the truth, then I lose this amazing opportunity for my business that will pay Austin's tuition. But if he is engaged, that means he lied to me. Either way, I lose."

Mrs. D. pulled her into a motherly embrace. "You've been through worse. You are the strongest person I know. Just understand no matter what, Austin will be okay. There's always college loans, and you have friends to help, too."

Avery hugged the woman back. "I know. You've been there for me since day one. I've been so lucky to have you in my life. I'm not sure how I would've made it through those first few months without you."

Mrs. D. released her and took a step back, putting a hand on each of her cheeks. "You've always been such a blessing in my life. The daughter I could never have. Trust me when I say, you gave as much as you got."

The sound of heels clicked in the recreation hall, drawing them both to the doorway. Larissa marched across the room and put both hands on her hips when she reached them. "Do you know why I've been summoned here? No one summons me, not even my fiancé."

Avery bit her tongue, knowing attitude would cost her the job if Mason and Larissa really were getting married. No matter how much it would hurt to plan their wedding, she had to do it for her brother.

"Because you have thirty seconds to make a decision that will affect your career enormously." Mason entered with a large bouquet of flowers in his hand. "First, you're going to tell Avery the truth about how you manipulated my agent, and then admit I never had any knowledge of this fake engagement."

She huffed and spun on her heels. "Please. I'll do no such thing."

Mason towered over her with an expression Avery had never seen on his face before. Disdain. Anger. "Secondly, you're going to tell the media when they arrive in five minutes that the posts were a mistake. Some overeager reporter jumped the gun." Larissa opened her mouth, but Mason leaned closer. "And that you are actually engaged to your longtime boyfriend, talent agent, Jeff Crater."

Larissa straightened, her posture ramrod straight. "And if I don't?"

He stepped back and held a hand to his chest. "Then I'll inform the media how heartbroken I am after discovering your torrid affair with Jeff. And I have photos to prove it."

"You wouldn't." She narrowed her gaze and tilted her head down like a bull ready to charge.

"Does Barry Bonds hold the home-run record?"

Several people entered the recreation room, and before Avery had a chance to catch up or escape the insanity, Mason stood between them and held her hand just tight enough that she couldn't slip away.

"Okay, we're here." The press photographer from the benefit entered, followed by two other people. Margaret eyed the three of them. "What's the big news?"

Mason glanced at Larissa, then back at Margaret. "I thought you'd want the scoop on the biggest socialite news around."

Margaret rolled her eyes. "The story of you two already broke. It's all over the Internet."

"Yes, but it's wrong," Mason said in a smooth tone as if it were just another day.

"Are you saying you two aren't really getting married?" Margaret asked.

Mason looked down at Larissa while still holding Avery's hand.

Larissa straightened her dress and lifted her chin. "No, we're not."

Margaret shook her head, but she lifted her camera and took pictures anyway. "I don't understand. Then why was she at Avery Morgan's event business planning a wedding? Why did her publicist make the announcement?"

"She was there planning a wedding, but I'm guessing some online news reporter wannabe decided to juice up the story. You see, Ms. Love is marrying talent agent, Jeff Crater. That's why she was meeting with Ms. Morgan. They were trying to plan a secret, intimate wedding here in Silver Creek, but her PR rep decided to go public."

"Is this true?" Margaret asked.

Larissa nodded. "Yes. But of course now that everyone knows, we'll be—"

Mason held up a hand to stop her. "Making it a large, lavish event, which Avery Morgan will be coordinating. Also, this amazing woman decided that since she has everything in her life, including true love, she and Mr. Crater ask donations be made to the Hope Angel House in lieu of engagement and wedding gifts."

"Wow! That's so generous of you." Margaret and her entourage swarmed around Larissa, snapping pictures and firing questions at her.

Mason tucked Avery into his side and headed to the corner of the rec room where they'd first been reunited. He set the flowers down on the Lazy Susan, then positioned Avery in the chair, and got down on one knee. "I'm not sure I want more time in the public eye. I think I want to retire and find something to do that fills my heart more than my pockets. I have enough saved that I can live here and never work again if I wanted."

Avery's hands shook. Her lip trembled and tears stung her eyes. "Do you want to?"

"That depends." He spun the Lazy Susan until the flowers came within arm's reach. He retrieved them and held them out to her. "Do you want me to stay? Do you care for me the way I care for you? The way I've always cared for you?"

Avery fought the lump in her throat and thought about everything that had happened. All the years she'd been alone, the craziness of the past few days, the hope of having Mason in her life again. Then she remembered Mrs. D.'s words. *You deserve happiness. All you need to do is accept it.*

"Avery, I'm telling you I have and always will be in love with you. If you'll have me, I'd like to take you on a real date, one that lasts the rest of our lives."

She closed her eyes, taking it all in and trying to process it. Mason Gregory was, and always would be, the only man who had ever made her feel safe, special, and loved. "Yes, I'll go on that date with you."

He leaned forward, placing one hand on her cheek, and kissed her.

In that moment, she realized her life had not ended the day of her family's accident. It had been put on hold, paused for the last seven years. Now, that Mason had just pressed *play*, life could begin again. A new life with the man she loved.

The End

Ciara's Slow Cooker Pot Roast

Ingredients

4-5 pound lean chuck roast

1 bag baby carrots

3-4 russet potatoes, quartered

1 envelope Onion Soup Mix

2 cups red wine or beef broth

1 yellow onion chopped

½ teaspoon pepper

½ cup flour

1 14.5-ounce can tomatoes, diced

3 tablespoons oil

Directions

Combine pepper and flour. Dredge roast in flour mixture and brown on all sides. Transfer to Crock pot. Add the remaining ingredients. Cover and cook on low for 6 hours.

Ciara Knight

Ciara Knight is a *USA Today* and Amazon Bestselling author who 'Fights for Love One Book at a Time' that spans the heat scales. Her popular sweet romance stories take readers into small-town romance full of family trials, friendly competition, and community love.

For more about Ciara, please visit her website at www.ciaraknight.com

Keeping Families Close™

Ronald McDonald House Charities® Atlanta

Keeping families close™

Thank you for purchasing this paperback book.

100% of royalties of the eBook support Atlanta Ronald McDonald House Charities. Community support is vital to the organization and to achieve their mission, ARMHC depends on the generous support of individuals like you. If you would like to make an additional donation directly to Atlanta Ronald McDonald House Charities, please go to https://armhc.org/
We are grateful for your support!

The Authors

From left to right: Rachel Jones, Constance Gillam, Ciara Knight, Melissa Klein, Linda Joyce, and Marilyn Baron.